SAWYER

A CAROLINA REAPERS NOVEL

SAMANTHA WHISKEY

By Samantha Whiskey

ALSO BY SAMANTHA WHISKEY

Nixon

Roman

Hendrix

The Onyx Assassins Series:

Crimson Covenant

Crimson Highlander

Crimson Warrior

Crimson Truth

Crimson Kiss

Crimson Hunter

A Modern-Day Fairytale Romance:

The Crown

The Throne

NOW AVAILABLE IN AUDIOBOOK!

CAROLINA REAPERS SERIES
Spicy southern nights meets the chill of the ice in this hot
hockey romance series!
Axel
Sawyer
Connell
Logan
Cannon

SEATTLE SHARKS SERIES
Let the Sharks spice up your commute!
Grinder
Enforcer
Winger
Rookie

ROYAL ROMANCE SERIES
These twin princes are sure to help you escape!
The Crown
The Throne

To those who have lost but still cling to hope

1

SAWYER

"**C**an I get a Coors Light?" a guy in a red tie shouted above the crowd as he leaned across the bar.

"No problem," I answered. I poured his beer by muscle memory and moved on to the next customer. The bar was busy, but that was typical of a Saturday afternoon during hockey season. The Sharks weren't playing until later, so we had the Reapers' game on, which was in the third period in Tampa.

I listened to what commentary I could hear between filling orders but didn't glance up much.

Had to admit, it hurt like a bitch to watch. The only thing harder than not reaching your dream? Tasting it for twenty-eight seconds.

"Hey, McCoy, weren't you the emergency goalie for the Reapers a few months ago?" Charlie, one of our regulars, asked like he could read my fucking mind.

"Sure was," I answered while I poured another beer.

"He was a goalie down at U-Dub, remember?" another regular chimed in.

"That's right," Charlie replied, leaning forward. "Everyone around here figured you'd go pro."

So had I. That's what I wanted to say.

"Oh, yeah?" I answered instead because that was the easiest thing to say.

I had been a damned good college goalie. I just hadn't made the cut for the NHL. Not that I hadn't gotten my shot. Luck had made Faith Gentry—now Vestergaard—my roommate, and since Faith's brother Eric turned out to be the goalie for the Sharks, he'd gotten me a tryout.

I just hadn't been fast enough to make the roster.

"Vestergaard scores!" the announcer called out, and this time my gaze jumped to the screen.

A small smile lifted my lips. Faith's new husband was a great guy. It just sucked that he'd moved her all the way to South Carolina. But that was how I'd ended up in a one-day contract as the emergency goalie for the Carolina Reapers when their backup had gone down.

Now I had a Reaper jersey with my name on it that hung on my closet door, and a twenty-eight-second memory of exhilarated perfection that nothing else could top.

It was something I'd hold on to because it turned out that majoring in exercise science meant I was qualified to be a trainer at the local gym and hold down a few shifts at Rusty's, the local sports bar in my Seattle neighborhood. I busied myself with more orders, sliding down the bar, away from the regulars. There was only so much prodding a wound could take, and I was feeling raw tonight.

"Hey, Sawyer! How's your mom?" another regular asked as he slid into the empty seat.

Fuck me, there was no escape tonight.

"Good as can be expected," I replied, forcing a smile to my face. Mom was the reason I stayed in Seattle. She'd stuck by my side as long as she was physically able, and I would do the same for her.

"You're a good kid," the older man said, just as the bar erupted into a series of groans, gasps, and mutters. "Damn, would you look at that?"

I followed his line of sight and turned to face the giant screen at the end of the bar. My stomach flopped. Fields, the backup goalie for the Reapers, was down and grabbing for his knee—the same one he'd injured months ago.

The game went to commercial, and I knew it had to be bad. I took care of waiting customers, poured a few shots for the group that had just walked in and held my breath until the game came back on.

"Hey, McCoy, think they'll call you to be their emergency goalie again if Fields is hurt?" Charlie asked.

"Nope," I answered with a wry grin. "It's not like they're due to play Seattle again any time soon." Not until playoffs, and since both the Reapers and the Sharks were leading their respective conferences, there was a good chance they'd see each other in May.

"Still, that's gotta be something," Charlie said with a shake of his head. "Being out there with them."

"It was," I replied. But I wasn't foolish enough to think that lightning would strike twice.

The game continued with Thurston in the net, but he was slow glove-side and had been since last season. Guy was getting older and it showed, not just in his glove, but the sluggish skating and mediocre reaction time. He was a legend, but even legends aged. The network showed clips taken during the commercial break of Fields being carried out on a stretcher, and I cursed under my breath.

No one wanted to go out like that.

The Reapers won five to two, but those last two goals had been scored on Thurston, glove-side of course.

Two hours later, I walked out after my shift as the clock hit five. I still had time to hit the gym and get a good workout in. Tomorrow was Sunday, meaning no training sessions. I could sleep in, then pick up some of Mom's favorite bagels and head up to her place before the pick-up game I had scheduled.

My phone rang. The caller ID listed it as *unknown*, but I never took chances. I answered the call with a swipe of my thumb, sending up a quick prayer that it wasn't about Mom.

"McCoy," I said, keys in hand.

"Sawyer. Thank God you answered," a gruff voice answered.

Holy shit. No way. There's no fucking way.

"Can I help you?" I asked softly, scared to even *think* that it was who I thought it might be.

"This is Coach McPherson with the Carolina Reapers."

My keys hit the asphalt. It really *was* him. Gage McPherson. Former star player for the Seattle Sharks and coach of the brand-new Carolina Reapers. The man who'd put me in for the last twenty-eight seconds of my first and only NHL game, simply because they were up four to zero, and that was the kind of man he was.

"Sawyer?" Coach asked. "You there?"

"Yes, sir," I answered quickly, clearing my throat. "You just caught me off guard."

"I can imagine. Look, it's been a shit night, so I'm going to keep this quick. Remember that tryout clause in your one-day contract?"

I leaned against my truck to stay standing. "Yes, sir. Vaguely." Faith had prodded the Reapers to add it at the last minute. It stated that if I played in the game, even for a second, I was automatically invited to try out for the Reapers next year if they held open tryouts. But since Thurston was mostly on board to bring Fields up, I knew there wouldn't be an open slot, hence no tryout. I wasn't naive enough to get my hopes up.

"Fields is out. Tore the ACL."

I hissed in sympathy.

"That means you're up, son. We're hosting a limited tryout tomorrow in Charleston, and you've got an invite."

I swallowed past the lump that had somehow grown in my throat. "Sir?" I questioned once my voice was capable.

"Won't be many of you. We've got a call going out for about a dozen goalies. But I have to warn you, those boys have all been playing in the minors. I'm rooting for you, but you have to bring the goods tomorrow, McCoy."

"Tomorrow," I repeated. How the fuck was I going to afford a last-minute ticket?

"Tomorrow," Coach McPherson confirmed. "We've got four days off, and the new guy has to be ready before we play Chicago."

Before I could reply, I heard a feminine voice I recognized in the background.

"I've got this," Coach reassured her. "Damn, it, Langley!"

There was a slight rustling, then the sound of a door closing and a quick intake of breath.

"Sawyer?" Langley Pierce-Nyström, the head of the Reapers' PR team came on the line. She was good friends with Faith and had run the Sharks' PR for years before leaving Seattle.

"Hey, Langley."

"I stole the phone so Gage couldn't listen in. Look, I'm texting you the information, but I have a jet ready to leave when you are, courtesy of Lukas since we can't be seen showing favoritism. And by *when you are*, I mean, you'll have your ass on that flight by seven p.m., do you understand me?"

Her fierce tone finally cut through my shock. "Langley, I don't play in the minors. I play pick-up games on the week-

5

end. I can't compete. Hell, if I couldn't do it right out of college, there's zero fucking chance now," I admitted quietly.

"You're still training?"

"Yeah. I'm in great shape, just…" I sighed. Last time I'd come so close, and the pain that followed my failure had been debilitating.

"Sawyer McCoy. You get home, get your gear, and get to the airport. Do you understand me?" she hissed in a whisper.

I was ripped in two—the part of me who recognized that this chance would never come again, and the self-preservationist who begged me to be happy with what my life was now. And with my mother here and in need of constant care, what business did I have getting on a plane in the middle of the night to chase pipe dreams?

"I will send Axel if you don't agree right this minute."

"Damn, Langley, you're married to the scariest motherfucker in the NHL," I muttered.

"No, that award goes to Cannon, but I'm sure you'll get along just fine. Now I'm serious. I know your personal life is complicated, but if you make the roster, I'll personally help you get everything and everyone situated. Get on the damned plane. I'll meet you in Charleston with the keys to my place. We're all rooting for you." She hung up without letting me respond.

I didn't slow down long enough to let myself think. I grabbed my gear, some clothes, my practice jerseys, and called Mom. Then I grabbed my Reaper jersey at the last second and walked out the door.

I got on the damned plane.

* * *

A HALF-HOUR after dropping my stuff at Langley's old apartment, which was conveniently within walking distance of Reapers' Arena, I strolled past the doorman with a nod and headed into the night.

It was one-thirty in the morning in Charleston, but only ten-thirty my time, and though I should have been exhausted, I was hyped up enough to run a fucking marathon.

The air was thick with humidity as I made my way across the street to Scythe, the bar Faith and Harper had taken me to the last time I was in Charleston. I stuck to the crosswalk at the corner of the busy intersection. The last thing I needed was to go to jail for jaywalking and miss my tryout. Though the thought did hold some level of appeal.

I glanced toward where the street ended at Reapers' Arena. Shit, I could read the sign from here, that's how close I was. No bank-named arena, or sponsors needed for that team. The whole thing was financed by billionaire Asher Silas. He built the state-of-the-art facilities, hired the best team, and when the best gear wasn't up to his standard, he hired a development team—headed by his genius sister, Harper—to invent it. He was a tech tycoon with a passion for hockey, and while I'd never met the guy, Harper loved him, which was enough for me.

Harper had been my other roommate, and once Faith had started dating Lukas, it wasn't long before Harper had fallen head over heels for Nathan Noble, a defenseman who was now with the Reapers. Funny thing was that she'd never mentioned her brother was on the cover of Forbes Magazine in all the years we'd lived together. The same as she hadn't advertised that she lived with me while we went to the University of Washington. She was too loyal for that shit.

I opened the door to the bar and was greeted by Def Leppard blaring from the jukebox. A bachelorette party sang along at the top of their lungs, and the bride was up on the

7

corner table, both hands in the air while a waitress shook her head.

Bypassing a few empty tables and a few crowded ones, I grabbed a seat at the empty side of the bar.

"Sorry, but last call was a few minutes ago," a waitress told me with a wince as she approached another crowded table.

"That's okay. I'll take this one."

The sound of her voice had me turning back toward the bar, and a corner of my mouth lifted into something that was almost a smirk as she came into view, walking toward me from the swinging door that led to the kitchen.

Echo Hayes stopped in front of me, and then stared me down with an arched eyebrow. "Aren't you a little far from home?" she questioned with a slow southern drawl, staring pointedly at my Pearl Jam shirt.

I took in her black Ramones T-shirt that had been cut so it draped off one shoulder, and let my eyes trail down her cut-off shorts that barely covered her ass, fishnet stockings, and black moto boots. Fuck, this woman had curves for miles, and desperately needed a giant warning sign that read *danger* all over her. By the time I reached her pixie-shaped face, diamond stud nose ring, turquoise eyes, and purple hair that fell in various shades down her back, I was smiling, and she was glaring.

She was incredibly beautiful and so fucking sexy that I was going to have to shift my jeans if I stared too long.

"You have no idea," I replied to her snarky question. There was zero chance in the world she remembered me. Maybe if I'd been with Harper and Faith—

"Bourbon?" she asked.

My jaw slacked momentarily in surprise. "You remember?"

"You're not exactly easy to forget, even if you're not with

8

the Queens of Reaper Village." Her eyes took their turn with me, and I felt her gaze on my skin as if it was her hand, stroking over the muscles of my biceps, caressing the pecs that stretched the material of my T-shirt, down to the waist she couldn't quite see with the bar in her way, then back up, lingering on my neck until she reached my eyes. Then she blinked, her gaze softening. "You look like you need a drink."

Without another word, she reached for the same bottle I'd had last time and poured it neat. She really did remember.

She slid the drink across the bar and then leaned on the counter so only the expanse of black granite separated us. "Start talking, West Coast."

I took a sip of the bourbon and savored the burn as it slid down my throat.

"Fields is out," I said quietly, unsure of what information the Reapers had released.

"Yeah, I saw it." She tilted her head, exposing the pale, smooth skin along her jawline. "Is that why you're here?"

"I had a tryout clause in my contract."

Her eyebrows rose.

"That's because I was an emergency—"

"Goalie," she finished, pouring herself a glass of water. "You played in the last minute of the third period during the Sharks' game." She took a drink and then grinned. "What, you honestly thought I didn't know who you were the first time you walked into this bar?"

"Damn, are you that good with all hockey players?" I asked, then took another smooth sip of bourbon. It settled in my stomach with a warm glow.

"Just the Reapers," she answered with a shrug. "So you're here to try out for Fields' spot?"

I nodded slowly, fixing my stare on the amber liquid swirling between my palms as I spun the tumbler through my hands.

"Hate to tell you how to prep, but most guys on the verge of making the NHL try to get some sleep the night before. They don't head to the bar right after walking off the plane...assuming you were in Seattle tonight."

"I was," I confirmed. "It's hard to explain."

"Try," she ordered in a tone that didn't leave any room for argument. "Your tender little feelings are safe with me, West Coast. I won't spill your secrets to your girlfriends."

"You and I both know they're not my girlfriends." I shot her a look, and she laughed. The sound was low and husky, and it sent a shot of lust straight to my dick. She had the kind of mouth built for smiling, and smirking, and teasing. Just the thought of those perfectly shaped lips wrapped around my cock was enough to make me shift on the barstool.

"Yeah, I do," she agreed. "But you're way too much fun to fuck with."

Our eyes met, and I felt that same crackle of energy I had when I was here last time. Chemistry was something you had, or you didn't, and we clearly did. "I'm a lot of fun to *fuck with*," I agreed, and nearly smiled when I saw a light blush rise in her cheeks. "But yeah, Harper and Faith were my college roommates."

"And now their guys will be your teammates. Sounds like one happy reunion over at Reaper Village, so why are you sitting in my bar?"

"Your bar?" I teased.

Her eyes narrowed. "You know what I mean. Don't make me get the scythe down. It would be a shame to have to clean blood off the floor."

"Calm yourself, East Coast," I said with a wink.

"Stop stalling," she challenged, those turquoise eyes seeing deeper than I wanted her to.

"Fuck, your eyes are incredible," I said before I could stop myself. I'd never seen that color of Caribbean blue before her, or since.

"Yes, I know. Now talk."

I would have rolled my eyes at her vanity if I hadn't seen that blush deepen a little. Nice to know I had an effect on the woman who clearly liked to be the one with the upperhand.

"I didn't make the Sharks when I tried out last year," I admitted. "It..." I shook my head and took a deeper drink, letting the fire reach my stomach before I continued. "It destroyed me. I didn't enter the draft, so having that chance, and coming so close only to realize I really wasn't good enough? Fuck, that was brutal."

Echo didn't respond. She simply watched me with waiting eyes, listening—which was what made me keep talking.

"Noble told me to go to the minors, but my family life is complicated."

"How?" she asked, ignoring her name being called down the bar.

"My mom has Parkinson's. Stage four." The words came easily, considering I almost never said them. Those who needed to know already knew, and it was nobody else's damned business what was going on with my mom. But there was something about the way Echo was looking at me that ripped the words free as effortlessly as if I were talking about what I'd had for breakfast.

"I'm sorry," she said softly, but without the pity in her eyes I'd become accustomed to seeing when people found out. "That must be incredibly hard on you both."

"Thank you. It is. She's in an assisted living center. She has been since I left for college." I shook my head after taking another sip, finishing my bourbon. "I stayed in Seattle, of course. I wasn't going to leave her. But she demanded I get what she called a 'normal college experience' and told me that I couldn't do that if I was living at home with her. So she moved herself into the assisted living center, and I moved Faith and Harper in as my roommates to help cover the costs so Mom wouldn't lose her house."

"Damn." Echo shook her head.

"What?"

Another customer called her name down the bar, and she held up one finger in his direction. "Nothing. I was just hoping you were an Abercrombie-model-douchebag."

"You were?" I asked slowly.

"Sure was. Would have been a whole lot easier, trust me." She nodded with pursed lips and glanced toward her customer before sliding a freshly poured glass of water into my hands. "Wait here. I have to go tell Earl that I'm not serving him any more tonight, and I don't care how miserable his wife is to go home to."

She walked away, and I shamelessly watched her ass swing as she went. Okay, that was a douchebag move, but that ass was made to be watched.

"Hi there." An intoxicated blonde wearing a tiara and veil leaned heavily on the counter beside me, pressing her breasts together above her low-cut tank top. Ah yes, the bride who had been table dancing a few songs ago. "You're pretty hot."

"Thanks," I answered with a practiced smile. "I...like your tiara."

She drunkenly wiped the back of her hand across her lips. "So, I never do this, but I have this bucket list I'm supposed to finish tonight," she whispered loudly. "You know, part of the party." She pointed to her chest, where her status as the bride was emblazoned in glitter.

"Okay?" My eyes flickered to the bridesmaids who were gathered a discreet distance behind her, watching us without said discretion.

"So, do you want to be number eleven?" She grinned as

she blatantly undressed me with her eyes, lingering on the bulge in my jeans that wasn't there for her.

Fuck no, I didn't.

"Is number eleven, take a shot with a stranger?" I offered as her bridesmaids giggled drunkenly.

"No. But if you take me somewhere quiet, I'll show you," she offered, letting her fingers trail down her chest to her neckline.

"Sorry, I have to pass. I have an early morning." I turned my body to face toward the bar in hopes that she'd get the point.

If she didn't, Echo blatantly wrinkling her nose at her got the point across loud and clear. "You ladies need me to call you a cab?"

"We have a limo," the bride snapped, then turned and walked out, her bridesmaids following her like little obedient ducklings.

"You missed a sure thing right there, West Coast. And if you'd mentioned that a Reaper tryout was the reason you were getting up early, I bet a few of her friends would have joined in." Echo watched me with blatant curiosity. "Not a one-night stand kind of guy?"

"I don't mind one-night stands," I said with a shrug. "But I don't fuck women who belong to other men, let alone ones who are marrying them."

"Not a cheater," she said, raising her glass of water. "Noted."

"I'd rather cut my dick off than cheat, or be with someone who does. When you give your word, you keep it. It's as simple as that. What the fuck does marriage even mean to someone who does shit like that?" I nodded toward the door.

"What does marriage mean in general?" Echo challenged. "It's stupid to promise yourself to someone for the rest of your life like you have any control or say in what's going to

13

happen. People fuck up. They leave. They cheat. They die. I don't know why we don't contract marriage for terms. Shit, it worked out well for Langley, right?"

I chuckled. "It did." I chugged the rest of my water and set the glass on the counter. It was good to know that Echo was trustworthy. There were very few people who knew how Langley and Axel started out.

"Look, unfortunately for me, I like having you here," Echo drawled with a roll of her eyes. Before I could ask her exactly what she meant, she continued. "But you need to get some sleep. Forget about everything that's holding you back and give it what you have."

"And if I make it?" I asked her. "Then what? I move my mother out here? I'm gone three to four days a week? She's alone in a facility she doesn't know? I can't just walk out on her. I fucking refuse." The last words came out harsher than I intended, but Echo didn't flinch.

She looked around the bar, her eyes lingering on the soft leather of the booths, the high-end stone of the bar, and what looked to be hand-carved built-ins that housed the expensive liquor supply. "You know, my dad and I always dreamed of owning a bar together. We'd talk about what brands we'd keep in stock, and what music we'd allow on the jukebox. I told him I drew the line at Waylon Jennings, but he always preached that it wasn't a bar without him." A smile lifted her lips, and I knew without her saying another word that she'd lost her father. "He'll never get to see our dream because he's gone. I'll have to build my dream without him." Her eyes met mine, and my heart clenched at the emotion she fought to keep at bay. "I bet your mother would give everything to experience your dream with you, so don't use her as an excuse."

"I just don't know what good making the team will do if I

can't leave her in Seattle and it's really unfair to move her here, away from everyone she knows."

"I just don't know why you think you make the choices for a grown woman," she countered, then sighed. "Look. The first step is to make the team. That's what earns you the right to make the decision about taking the contract. That's what gives you the chance to *offer* the move to your mother. It's not all on your shoulders, you know."

"Yeah, you're right on that," I agreed. "I have to make the team first."

The rest? I wasn't sure she understood what it meant to be the caregiver at twenty-three years old. Hell, I'd been doing it since I was fifteen, and it was unfair to expect anyone to really understand.

I stood, then took my wallet from my back pocket.

"Absolutely not," she told me, waving her hand at me.

"I'm not going to short your drawer," I argued.

She snorted. "I'll make you a deal, West Coast. You make the team, you can pay me for the drink."

"And if I don't?" I asked.

"My guess is that you'll run up another tab getting shit-faced, so I win either way." She shrugged with a little smirk that made me want to haul her across the bar and kiss her.

"That's a deal. You are something else, Echo."

Her eyes widened. "You know my name."

"You're not exactly easy to forget." I grinned, throwing her words back at her as I walked out of the bar.

* * *

MY HEART POUNDED as I stood in the locker room, my gear snapped, and my skates tied.

The eleven other contenders headed out silently. It had been a full half-hour of blatant appraisal as we dressed in the locker room. There were some players I recognized from the minors, and three I'd played against in college.

They were all on the ice more frequently than I was, that was true.

But I was better than they were. And I hadn't been licking my wounds for the past six months. I'd been at the gym every day. On the ice a few times a week. Running six miles every morning. My body was a machine, and it was ready for whatever my heart wanted.

And it wanted that Reaper jersey.

I followed the line out of the locker room and down the hall toward the ice, then stopped when I came to the line of players who waited at the glass.

"We're not waiting for you, dumbass, move along," Cannon Price snapped at the guy in front of me, and the goalie rushed past. The notorious hothead out of Detroit was the fastest skater I'd ever seen, but I wasn't sure even he could keep up with his mouth.

"Jesus, Cannon, we might have to play with these guys," Lukas reminded him, rubbing the bridge of his nose. Faith's husband had gone from being a rookie on the Sharks to the experienced player on the Reapers in the time I'd known him.

Cannon transferred his helmet to his other hand and shook his head. "It's going to be McCoy. Just don't fuck up out there."

"What he means," Porter growled at him, stepping forward with a shake of his head. "Is that we support you. We want the best goalie for the team, and we know it's you." Porter was another player out of Seattle, who'd used his free agency to move his career and his family to South Carolina.

"Thanks, guys," I said as they all pounded on me in friendship, their gloves softening the blows.

"You already have a Reaper jersey with your name on it,"

Axel said in heavily accented English, towering above me by a good four inches. "Now let's get you a nametag in that locker room. Get out there, kid." He thumped my back as I moved forward.

God, the arena was fucking huge. But the ice? That was the equalizer. It didn't matter how many fans you had watching—that net stayed the same size.

"Look at me," Nathan Noble said quietly as I paused just before the ice.

I turned my head to look at Harper's fiancé, who'd worked his way up through the minors with sheer grit and determination.

"You've got this. What's the difference between a guy whose career ends in college and the one-in-a-million shot?" he asked me, just like he had last year after I'd failed to make the Sharks.

This time I knew the answer because he'd given it to me.

"Talent and drive." My chest expanded, knowing I had what it took. Knowing this was my dream. Hockey was my passion, my reason.

"Damn right. Get out there and prove you've got both." He slapped me on the back, and I took to the ice like I owned it.

Because that net was my home and that fucking jersey? It was *mine*.

2

ECHO

J wiped down the black granite bar for the umpteenth time that day, ensuring the custom stone gleamed between rushes. We were finally slowing down for the night and since there wasn't a Reapers game— or a bachelorette party—I'd likely already seen all the action I was going to get.

A soft smile shaped my lips as I tossed the towel in the bin I kept handy behind the bar. I loved this place, loved every single thing about it, from the amber lighting and the smells of cedar and whiskey to the sounds of rambunctious men shouting at the top of their lungs about hockey.

Home.

This bar was home to me, and about the last thing on this planet I actually loved.

Hope you like it, Dad.

Every now and then, in the quieter moments, thoughts of my father would slip past my barriers. Not that I needed to keep memories of him locked away, but damn did they *sting*. It never got easier, missing people you lost, but the pain...morphed. Sometimes into something more manageable. Other times it twisted into emotions sharp enough to cut.

I'd lost enough people to know that, to have a fucking master's degree in it. Losing people was my curse in life, and no amount of spells or wishes or prayers would ever change that for me.

People died.

People left.

But my life? Kept on going.

The entrance door swung open and I straightened, thankful to be jerked back to the present. I plastered the bartender mask I'd perfected years ago on my face—the look that screamed *I'm inviting but I could also kick your ass.* Bartending 101: you must look both friendly and terrifying, or the inebriated patrons will never respect you or your space.

"What'll it be?" I asked as I scanned my stock of mixes, fixes, and glasses beneath the bar.

"Do you have anything on this menu that isn't deep-fried?"

I froze. My inventory forgotten with the sound of that deep, slightly tortured voice, and my smile turned into a full-on smirk.

I slowly trailed my eyes up, finally settling on the man sitting before me.

Broad shoulders, cut chest, neatly trimmed beard decorating that strong jaw, and eyes that were storm-cloud gray.

I held his gaze, slowly twirling my finger to indicate the entire area. "It's a *bar*, West Coast."

He set the tiny plastic menu facedown. "Bars can have fish."

"Yeah, when it's beer-battered and deep-fried."

His laugh was short, too quick. "Some bars have grilled fish."

19

"Scythe isn't one of those hipster breweries with glazed brussels sprouts as an appetizer. We've got cheese smothered burgers, salted fries sizzling out of the deep-fryer, and our fish is beer-battered."

He nodded, a flicker of amusement in his eyes. After he'd taken a few too many seconds to respond, I broke the silence.

"Twice in two days," I said. "You must've taken a liking to me."

"Maybe," he said, that amusement doubling. "Or maybe the bar you work at happens to be right across the street from the apartment I'm now occupying."

"So I guess that means you survived the first cut?" I asked.

"Six goalies down, five to go."

I grabbed a glass and filled it to the brim with ice, then water, and slid it in front of him.

"This isn't bourbon," he said, taking the glass and drinking from it.

"Nope. And we both know whiskey isn't going to solve your problems. Especially not when you stomped in here looking for health food."

He chuckled, setting the drink down. "I didn't *stomp*."

I arched a brow at him. "*Please*. I could practically feel you all Jurassic Park style before you reached the door."

His grin flared before he glanced down, surveying himself. "Now you're making me feel self-conscious," he teased.

I leaned my elbows on the bar, drawing as close to him as I dared. Close enough to know he smelled like cinnamon and rain. "You know you're a perfect specimen, Sawyer McCoy."

"But?" he challenged, never breaking our gaze.

"But," I said, leaning back to my normal position behind the bar. "I can feel the nerves vibrating off of you."

His shoulders sank a fraction.

"Relax, West Coast," I said and set a small bowl of celery—

the stalks I usually adorned my bloody Marys with—in front of him. "Chew on that for a sec." I spun around, heading toward the kitchen in the back.

"While you what?" he called after me, but I was already through the kitchen doors, cell in hand.

Ten minutes later, I'd called one of my co-workers to cover the rest of my shift, and texted the Reaper crew. Making fast friends with Langley Pierce, Harper Thompson, and Faith Vestergaard had been one of the best developments in my life, and it also gave me access to the rest of the team when necessary.

Tonight absolutely called for it.

"All right," I said as I came through the doors and around the bar instead of behind it. Sawyer spun on his stool to face me, his head slightly tilted.

"All right, what?"

"Let's go," I said, motioning for him to follow me as I headed toward the exit.

"Where are you taking me?" he asked, but followed as I left the bar. "Don't you need to work?"

"I called someone to cover my shift. She'll be here in a few minutes, and we're slow right now so the waitress inside can handle things until then. No worries, West Coast."

"Won't your boss be pissed that you left?"

I smirked. "Yeah, she can be a real bitch, but I know how to handle her."

I led him around the building to the back where I parked my car. Early evening had turned the sky a wicked mixture of indigos and grays and coated everything in a light shadow. The outcropping of trees hugging the back lot did nothing to help the somber setting, and from the worried look in Sawyer's eyes, he felt it.

"Relax," I said, holding open the passenger door for him and waving him in.

He eyed my fingers on the door, my nails a polished midnight. "Is this where I get initiated into your cult or something?"

I snort-laughed. "What, you don't trust me?"

He took a few steps closer, towering over me as he held my gaze. "I don't really know that much about you," he said the words with an edge of hunger like he wanted to remedy that fact as quickly as possible.

My pulse spiked, his scent and warmth covering me despite him being inches away.

"Your friends know me," I said, my voice softer than it was moments before.

Sawyer held my stare a few more seconds before nodding and sliding into the car.

I shut the door a little harder than necessary, cursing the desire churning through my veins. It'd been too long since I'd had anyone in my bed—so long that I wanted the boy next-freaking-door. Not my usual type, not by a long shot.

"You want to tell me where you're taking me, Echo?" Sawyer asked once I was behind the wheel.

"To get something healthy to eat, of course," I said, pulling onto the street.

A low sigh left his lips, one that almost sounded like disappointment.

I navigated the streets with ease. I'd lived here my whole life and could drive the route in my sleep if I had to, but I never grew tired of the trip into historic downtown Charleston. I loved the unique mish-mash of old buildings and new, and the amount of history seeped into the foundation supporting them.

"Wow," Sawyer said as we parked in front of my favorite seafood restaurant. He stuck close to me as I led him toward the white and blue building with floor-to-ceiling glass windows boarding the entire structure. A wooden patio wrapped around the place and hovered over the water hugging the edge of land the restaurant sat atop.

I flashed a grin at the girl behind the bar as I beelined it toward the back patio.

"Your friends are already here," she called.

"Thank you, Kylie!" I hollered over my shoulder.

"What friends?" Sawyer asked.

"Ours," I said, reaching back to grab his hand and hurry his pace. "You don't mind, do you?" I asked when he'd stopped dead in front of the glass doors that showed the entire back patio had been taken over by the Reapers and their girlfriends or wives.

"I…" he shook his head. "Echo, I—"

"You're nervous," I said. "I get it. Trust me. It's a huge epic life-changing thing you're doing. But," I said, glancing at the tables outside. "I think being around your future team will help."

"Future team," he said, cocking a brow at me. "You know I can't afford to think like that."

"Well, *I* can." I winked at him. "Besides," I continued, pulling him through the door and sighing slightly when he actually came with me. "You said you wanted fish. This is the best place within fifty miles."

"Better than Scythe?"

"Better *fish* than Scythe," I said. "I've still got the best drinks in town."

"That she does!" Langley walked up to me, followed by Harper and Faith, and squished me in a group hug. It'd only been a week since I'd seen them last, but it felt long overdue. What could I say? We all worked too damn much.

"How is my favorite bartender?" Faith asked as I settled into a chair across from her, Sawyer electing to sit next to me. Lukas, Axel, and Noble completed our table, with Connell MacDhuibh, Cannon Price, Hudson Porter, and

Logan Ward dominating the round-top next to us. Outdoor heaters were scattered across the wooden patio, chasing away the crisp bite in the air so customers could enjoy the view of the glistening water lapping at the patio's base.

"You know me," I answered.

"I do," Faith said, eyeing me. "Which is why I'm shocked you cut your shift early to dine with us." She glanced at Sawyer, who'd fallen into an easy conversation with Noble.

I shrugged, leaning closer to my girls. "He needed to get out of his head for a bit."

Harper smirked, and Langley raised her brows at me. "Is *dinner* the only way you'll be distracting him?"

Faith playfully smacked Langley's arm, and I rolled my eyes.

"Absolutely," I said, holding my hand over my heart. "Scouts' honor. I have no intention of corrupting this one," I jerked a thumb toward the clean-cut Sawyer, who just so happened to be eavesdropping on our conversation, just like the other three hockey stars at the table. They were as bad as high school chicks.

Sawyer flashed me a challenging look. "Corrupt *me*?"

I patted his shoulder. "Don't worry, West Coast," I said. "Your innocence is safe with me."

"Why does everyone always assume Sawyer is the innocent one?" Lukas asked, eyeing the girls.

"Yeah," Noble said. "You four didn't see him in Vegas last year with those two blonds—"

"And the saying *what happens in Vegas?*" Sawyer cut him off.

Noble laughed, raising his hands. "Right. My bad."

I surveyed Sawyer, searching for the wildness Lukas and Noble hinted at, but I couldn't see past the perfect manners, the perfectly trimmed beard and the clean skin with no visible signs of ink. This man was good to his core. Though, I supposed he could still be a devil in the sack.

I handed him a menu from the table. "The grilled snapper is legit. Add some brussels sprouts on the side and I guarantee not one puck will slip past you tomorrow."

He grinned. "You guarantee it, huh?"

I nodded as the waitress came over to take our orders, and my smile doubled as Sawyer ordered exactly what I'd recommended.

He leaned closer to my cheek as the waitress hurried off to put in our orders. "Guess I do trust you," he whispered in my ear, and warm chills raced across my skin. The breath caught in my throat when he smirked and pulled away, returning to his conversation with the guys.

After an hour spent eating, bantering, and joking with the Reapers, I was relieved to see Sawyer's nerves had ebbed. He seemed damn near at home among the family of pro-hockey players and some of that weight he normally carried had lifted over the course of the night. And when he laughed? It stole my breath.

I did my best not to gape at him, not to stare.

Because surely it wasn't *his* fault that heat pooled between my thighs and a craving wrenched deep in my core.

Surely it wasn't the *literal* boy next door making my stomach flip.

Because I didn't believe in love or relationships anymore, and men like Sawyer McCoy?

They either broke your heart or tied you down. Planted roots, punched out kids, and lived happily ever after.

And I wasn't that kind of princess.

Not anymore.

3

SAWYER

I tipped back my helmet and drained my water bottle over my face. I was hot, sweaty, exhausted, and loving every fucking second of it.

There were only two of us left now that it was Tuesday afternoon, and I stared down the ice at my competition, who was using his break to do the same exact thing. The kid was good, no doubt. Fast reflexes, great skating, lethal glove. But Zimmerman had a shit attitude and struggled with reading the skater coming at him at times. Plus the fact that he was willing to walk out on his college team mid-season didn't sit well with me.

But I wasn't the one calling the shots.

Coach McPherson stood at the bench, talking to Coach Hartman, the goalie coach, comparing notes and looking my way every time they looked down the ice at Zimmerman.

"You're doing great," Connell MacDhuibh said with a grin as he peeled off his helmet and stopped to rest at my goal. God help everyone if the Reapers ever made this guy captain because the refs would never understand that thick Scottish burr through his helmet.

"Great enough?" I asked quietly between bursts of water from my squeeze bottle.

"In my opinion? Yes. In theirs?" He looked back toward the coaches and shook his head. "Who the fuck knows what they think."

"Comforting."

"Look, they already threw Nyström, Porter, Noble, and Vestergaard out after the whiner-baby down there complained that they were tossing you easier shots. I can be honest, or I can powder your arse." He shrugged.

"Good point." They hadn't been going easier on me. I was simply better than the twenty-year-old kid. Not that twenty-three was much older, but I had two full seasons of experience on this guy.

The coaches started nodding, and I knew my break was about to end.

"Switch sides," Coach McPherson ordered the skaters. "We're going to give this another fifteen-minute scrimmage and see what happens."

Connell dropped his fist on my shoulder twice, gave me a supportive smile, and left, taking his helmet with him.

I put my helmet back on and settled into the goal.

The Reapers, absent four of their best thanks to our personal connection, traded sides, and met for the faceoff.

There was a stillness I loved about the faceoff. The way the ice went quiet in anticipation of the action to come. Then all hell broke loose.

I'd definitely had the better defense last shift, so this was about to get interesting. I tracked the puck with single-minded focus, keeping the defensemen in my peripherals until they charged forward.

Cannon-fucking-Price. Of course he was the one flying at me like a bat out of hell. I'd never seen a faster skater, let alone faced one. Price outmaneuvered the defenseman, and a second later he had a clear path. He came down the ice so quickly that I barely had time to skate out and adjust my stance before he was on me.

I let go of everything I knew about this guy's stats and watched his movements. Holy shit, his puck-handling was incredible. He came closer, deked right, but then his weight shifted, and I saw it, the tiny balance adjustment that had me reaching with my glove.

The puck hit with lethal force, and I savored the slight sting because it meant I had it. I fucking *had* it.

Coach Hartman blew the whistle and skated over.

"How the hell did you see that?" he asked, taking the puck from my glove.

"He shifted his weight," I answered.

Coach stared at me with lowered brows, his eyes searching for something that I couldn't name, and therefore couldn't produce. Then he nodded slowly and a slight smile lifted the corner of his mouth. "Okay, then."

He skated off to the bench, and Coach McPherson blew the whistle to start again.

A half hour later, I was dead on my feet, but I'd saved all but one shot.

Zimmerman had the same record.

I sat in the locker room, ignoring the noise of the other players around me, let the sweat drip from my hair, and summoned the energy to move. I'd never played that hard for that long, let alone gone three days in a row at the same pace.

My cell phone buzzed from the locker behind me, and I reached for it out of sheer muscle memory.

Unknown: Did you know that wombats make cube-shaped poop?

What the actual fuck?

I looked up and scanned the room around me, wondering if I had become the next target on Connell's ever-growing prank list. Guy couldn't take anything seriously except hockey. When no one so much as looked my way, I fired off a reply.

Sawyer: Who is this?

Unknown: Come on, West Coast, you think I'm going to make it that easy for you?

My smile was instant. I quickly saved her in my contacts, already feeling a little lighter.

Sawyer: You just did. How did you get my number?

Echo: I have friends in cold, icy places.

This time I grinned. She'd asked about me enough to track down one of my friends and get my number.

Echo: I'm guessing you're still alive?

Sawyer: Just finished. I'll probably know by tonight.

Echo: Did you know that bananas share fifty percent of their DNA with humans?

I laughed outright, which earned me a few sideways glances from the guys.

Sawyer: You are so random.

Echo: Bet it made you laugh.

Sawyer: It did. Thank you. I'd better hit the showers before you can smell me from down the street.

Echo: Is that you? I wondered what that heinous odor was.

I shook my head, but before I could put my phone away, another text came through.

Echo: Forty-two percent of people admit to peeing in the shower...so be careful in there.

Sawyer: Goodbye, Echo.

Echo: Watch where you step.

Her trick worked. By the time I walked into the shower to rinse off the workout, I was shaking my head at her antics instead of hanging it with worry.

I'd done my best. Worked my ass off and left everything

out there on the ice. Now it was out of my hands and in the coaches'.

* * *

THREE HOURS LATER, I sat in an empty conference room at Reaper Arena, staring at the long expanse of mahogany that served as a conference table. I knew Silas had spared no expense when he'd built the arena. Everything from the practice ice to the training room was state of the art. But seeing it up close and personal was awe-inspiring.

I looked at the clock. It had been five minutes since I'd been shown into the room with no explanation from Mr. Silas's personal assistant. Zimmerman wasn't here, so I had to assume that he'd had a separate conference room, or his meeting was yet to come.

Either way, I was here for one of two reasons: to be offered a contract, or be sent home to Seattle.

The door opened with a click, and I rose to my feet. My mother would have killed me if I'd stayed sitting while the coaches and Asher Silas himself walked into the room. The coaches both wore their Reaper jackets, while Silas had on a suit that cost more than I'd made all year.

"Sawyer," Coach McPherson greeted me with a nod that gave nothing away. Guy had to be a kickass poker player.

"Sir," I answered, reaching across the table to shake his hand, then Coach Hartman's, and finally Asher Silas's. It was surprisingly rough for someone who spent all his time making billions in the tech industry.

"It's nice to finally meet you," Silas said with a slight smile. "My sister speaks very highly of you."

"Harper is one of a kind," I replied with an easy grin.

"She is," he agreed, releasing my hand and relaxing his stance before they took their seats in front of me.

I sat slowly, concentrating on keeping steady and not shaking like a leaf in a windstorm. NHL goalies didn't shake. They were steadfast, dependable, the backbones of their teams.

"Eric Gentry told me I'd be an idiot if I didn't pick you up," Coach McPherson said, leaning back in his chair.

"Gentry is a phenomenal goalie and a great guy," I answered, ignoring the invitation to tout my awesomeness. I was good, but I wasn't Gentry good.

"He is," Coach agreed. "He also said that you're a family-oriented man with a lot on his shoulders."

Asher Silas leaned forward in his seat, while Coach Hartman kept that soul-stare on me, picking me apart without having to say a word.

"My mother," I said easily. "She has stage four Parkinson's. That's why I chose Seattle for college, so I could be close to her. Well, that and the full ride to U-Dub didn't hurt."

That earned me a chuckle from the three men who would decide my future.

"I do put her first, Coach, because she put me first. It's been the two of us since I was fifteen. That doesn't mean I can't devote myself to my team—"

"Stop," Coach ordered softly, putting his hand up slightly, palm out. "I'm a family-first man. I believe the Reapers are only as strong as the men on the ice and the families who stand beside them, which means we don't ask you to choose. We ask how we can support."

"Sir?" At least my voice didn't crack.

"We have several assisted living facilities here in Charleston that provide first-class care," Silas said. "Or if you'd prefer, we can find excellent at-home care to make sure your mother is cared for." A corner of his mouth lifted.

"Though from what I've been told, she quite likes the company of other adults."

"You've been told?" I repeated like a fucking parrot.

"By your mother, herself," he confirmed with a nod.

Holy fucking shit. Asher Silas called my mother?

Did that mean…

"We'd like to offer you a contract, Sawyer," Coach McPherson said with a grin.

My stomach flopped, and something I was terrified to call happiness welled up in me so fast that I almost jumped out of my seat.

"A contract?" I repeated, and this time my voice lifted at the end.

"You're our guy if you want to be," he confirmed with a nod.

I glanced at Coach Hartman, who nodded.

"You're slow in the footwork, but that's probably due to not playing in the last few months," he noted. "But your instincts are unlike anything I've seen."

"Thank you," I replied, knowing I'd be dealing with a coach who didn't pamper or coddle. "I'm not afraid of hard work."

"Oh, I know," he answered with a grin that spoke of my upcoming shape-up at his hands.

"What do you say, Mr. McCoy?" Silas asked with a slight tilt to his head. "Would you like to be a Reaper?"

I quelled my immediate instinct to shout in the affirmative. "Yes, sir. I would love nothing more, but there's someone I need to talk to, first."

"Go ahead and call her," he said through his smile. "In the meantime, I've heard you don't have an agent, so Axel sent his down. Does that work for you? You'll want someone to go over this contract."

I nodded mutely. Of course I didn't have an agent. I never thought I'd actually need one.

"Excellent. We'll bring her in immediately."

With that, I walked to the corner of the conference room and whipped out my phone. None of this was real until she agreed.

She answered on the first ring.

"Sawyer?"

I leaned my head against the cool glass of the window and grinned. "Mom. They want me. I made it."

"Oh, honey!" Her voice broke, and I would have given anything to be with her in that moment. All the time and cost. All the equipment and the tears. All of the times she'd hauled me to practice...it had all paid off. "Sawyer, I'm so proud of you!"

I laughed softly through misty eyes. "Mom, I won't do it if you want to stay in Seattle. I'm not going to leave you, but I won't make you give up everything you know, either."

She sighed. "You cannot live your life for me, Sawyer McCoy."

"I'm not," I promised, looking out over the street and seeing Scythe just a few blocks away. "I'm living it *with* you."

"Honey, why don't I just go up to Virginia and be with my sisters?" she offered softly. "I won't hold you back."

My heart twisted. "Mom, you're not holding me back. And if you live here...if *we* live here, then either we can do at-home care, or we can find another place that you like even better. But if you don't want to come, then I'll turn them down. I'm not going to walk off and leave you for money." I fucking refused to turn into what *he* had been. We might share the same blood, but I didn't carry his selfish or weak nature. "This is a decision we make together. As a family. Because that's what family does."

She quieted for a moment. The only sound coming

through the phone was her steady, soft breathing. Mom had always been that way, strong, steady, reliable. Everything about her spirit was unbreakable and formidable. It was her body that refused to keep up with her.

"I'll come," she answered. "But at the first sign that I'm even remotely a burden on you—"

"You could never be a burden, Mom." My heart jumped, and my body flooded with a restless energy. "Are you sure?"

"One condition."

My hand gripped the phone tightly. "Anything."

"I want a jersey that says Mama McCoy, just like when you were in college." Her voice cracked again, and I just about lost it. This woman had given up everything for me and was ready to do it again.

"You got it." I blinked away the light sheen of tears that blurred my vision and stared out at the Charleston skyline. "God, I wish I could come over and celebrate with you, but my first game is the day after tomorrow. I don't even know when I can get up there…" I trailed off, realizing how hard it was going to be to find the time to get my mother moved. We only had three days off from games most weeks, and my guess would be I had ice every day.

"Don't you worry about that. This lovely Asher boy called me and told me he'd send his own plane! Can you imagine that, Sawyer? He owns a *plane*."

"Yeah, he does, Mom. He owns the Reapers." I laughed, and let myself feel it for the first time—the complete, all-consuming joy of having my lifelong dream turn into a reality.

"Oh, well, that's nice," she said simply, and I wondered if she had the slightest clue who Silas really was in the scheme of the US—hell, the global—economy. "Well, he said he'd send a team out to get me packed and bring me right to you when I was ready."

I stood and looked back at the team of men, and now a woman I had to guess was Eden Jones, who represented both Hudson Porter and Axel Nyström. It was hard to believe a guy who was as cutthroat in business as Silas had taken the time to reach out to my mother.

"You just let me know, Mom," I said.

"Well, I think I'd like to see you play your first game," she answered as if that wasn't the day after tomorrow. "And Sawyer, you'd better call up those friends of yours and go celebrate. You understand?"

"Yes, Mom." This time my gaze drifted back to Scythe. "I love you."

"Not nearly as much as I love you. Good thing I look really good in Reaper blue."

She hung up while I was still laughing, and I made my way back to the group. "My mother said you'd send a plane for her when she's ready," I said to Silas.

He arched an eyebrow over Harper-like hazel eyes and nodded once.

"She's ready now. She'd like to be here for my first game," I answered.

"Does this mean you're taking us up on the offer?" Silas asked.

"Don't you answer that!" Eden snapped, pointing a finger my direction. The twenty-something was short in stature, but not in attitude, that was for sure. Then again, her dad was a hockey legend, so it wasn't hard to see where that bravado came from. "Not until we go over this contract. And Silas, he's not paying for that plane ride. You offered it. You pay for it. And I expect a healthy relocation allowance for his mother's trouble."

"Yes, ma'am," Silas answered with a smirk. "We'll leave you two to discuss the contract. When you love it, and you *will*, let me know. We have the press coming in for an announcement in three hours."

Well, that was a way to put me on deadline. Not that I could blame the man. They were short a goalie and due back on the ice in forty-eight hours for a game.

"Yes, sir."

"Anyone who's held my sister's hair back over a toilet gets to call me Asher or Silas," he countered but shook my hand.

"Does that mean—" Hartman started.

"You're not on that list," he said before walking toward the door. "You've got three hours, Sawyer."

They filed out of the room, leaving me with the woman who was now my agent.

"Well," she said, sticking her hand out. "I'm Eden Jones. Axel and Porter have told me a lot, but Langley won't shut up about you, so I feel like I already know you."

"Sawyer McCoy." I shook her hand. "If they trust you, then I do. Thank you for taking me on."

"You're welcome. Now let's make sure you don't get screwed over."

Three hours later, the contract was signed, and a Reapers' jersey covered my torso.

"You ready?" Eden asked, nodding toward the room where the press waited.

"One second."

I finished firing off a text.

Sawyer: I'm coming by the bar in a little bit. Looks like I need to pay my tab.

I waited with held breath as the dots cycled, showing she was typing out a reply.

Echo: That's amazing. I can't wait to see you.

My eyes flared wide.

Echo: Don't let that go to your head.

I laughed. God, this woman was keeping me on my toes.

Sawyer: I'll try not to. And if you want to see me sooner, just put on ESPN.

Echo: I wish you could see me roll my eyes. Go do your thing, big shot.

Sawyer: Be there in a few.

I put my phone away with a wide grin and faced the petite, beautiful woman who'd just negotiated my contract like a pit bull. When she raised her eyebrows, I nodded.

"Now, I'm ready."

4

ECHO

"To Sawyer," Axel said, holding up a shot of whiskey. Every other Reaper in the bar had the same shot raised, myself included. "Not a new friend or a new team member, but an addition to this family. To the newest Reaper who will take us all the way to the Cup!" He threw the shot back, and we all followed suit before cheering the man of the hour.

Sawyer Fucking McCoy.

He would be the newest addition to my Reaper-filled bar.

I should *be* so lucky to stare at all the gloriousness that were the Reapers. But...there was something about Sawyer that I hadn't been able to work out of my system on my own —and believe me, I'd tried.

Several times.

Didn't matter, I couldn't get his scent out of my nose or his voice out of my ears. Every time I stopped thinking about him he texted or walked through my doors. Not that I minded his company, because I didn't. I got a kick out of distracting him with random facts or keeping him humble with my more than down-to-earth jabs. And he was as funny as he was polite, but the way my body kept reacting to his presence made complicated emotions tangle in my stomach. Emotions I had no intention of addressing.

"You drinking on the job, Echo?" The man in question strolled up the bar, setting down his empty shot glass.

I took it, sliding it into the bin of used glasses behind the bar. "Just the one," I said.

The Reapers had been celebrating Sawyer's new position on the team for a little over two hours now, and I'd only taken the shot because Axel was making the toast. When the captain of the Reapers opened his mouth, people tended to listen, including me.

"I'm never going to get to have a drink with you, am I?" he said, elbows on the bar.

"What makes you think that?"

"You're always working," he said.

I raised a brow at him. "And soon you will be too."

A seriousness covered his slightly hazed eyes for a few moments as he nodded. That familiar weight of responsibility settled over his previously carefree demeanor, and it punched me right in the chest.

"Hey," I said, leaning over the bar so he could hear me over the roar of the Reapers. "You find a way to buy out my usual profit tonight, and I'll shut this place down to everyone except the Reapers. *And* I'll have that drink with you."

His eyes shuttered. "Give me the number."

I rattled off half of what I usually made on nights like this, and Sawyer quickly wove through his crowd of teammates. Within minutes, I had cash in the till, and was locking up Scythe for a private party.

I climbed onto the bar, hollering to get the rooms attention. "All right, Reapers," I said. "You've just bought yourself a night at Scythe. I'll still make you drinks but feel free to help yourself if I'm occupied!" I flashed a smirk down to Sawyer.

"And, just for fun, let's get the newest Reaper as drunk as possible. Who's with me?"

A deafening round of cheers erupted in response, and I swore Sawyer flinched.

I hopped off the bar, my boots hitting the ground right next to him. I craned my head back to meet his eyes. "You asked for it, West Coast." I took the whiskey from his hand and threw back the rest of the contents.

Sawyer's gray eyes widened as I slammed the empty glass on the bar.

"What do you want to do now that you have my full attention?" I asked, the sweet burn of bourbon warming my insides.

Sawyer parted his lips, his eyes flaring, but Connell MacDhuibh wrapped an arm around his shoulders, stopping whatever he'd been about to say.

"Drinkin' games," Connell said, his accent rolling over the words. "Porter's already got a Kings game going over there," he pointed to the table across the room where Hudson Porter sipped from a club soda before he shuffled a deck of cards. "Now let's get a Truth or Dare game started over here." He pointed toward the other side of the room.

"Truth or Dare?" Sawyer asked, but let Connell tug him across the room. "I haven't played that since middle school."

"No shite?" Connell asked, plopping down at one of the low-tops. "It's even better with liquor."

"You think everything is better with liquor," Axel said, taking a seat with Langley in tow. Faith and Lukas followed, as did Harper and Noble. Logan Ward was the last to complete our group, leaving Cannon Price and a few other players to play cards with Hudson and his wife.

"Not everything," Connell said as I took the final seat at the table.

"Really?" Axel challenged.

Connell poured himself another finger from the scotch bottle he'd gotten from behind the bar. "Well," he said. "I sure as shite ain't skating with a drink in hand, eh, Cap?"

Axel laughed.

"The ice," Connell continued. "Is the only thing in existence better than a drink," he said, taking a drink for emphasis. "Better than food. Better than sex," he pointed to the women at the table, eliciting territorial growls from the husbands at their sides, and he raised his hands up in defense.

"What about a good prank?" Langley challenged, and Connell's eyes lit up.

"Aye', a solidly executed prank is a close second to the ice."

"A prank is above sex?" I blurted.

He laughed.

"Depends on the woman," he said, shrugging and taking another pull of his scotch.

"That's cold," Noble said.

"A well-executed prank takes time, planning, calculation. It cannot be random. You have to *know* the person you're going after. Have to understand what makes them laugh. Or understand what the others in the room will laugh *at*. It's not as easy as seducing a woman."

We all laughed at that.

"Clearly," Lukas said as the laughter died down. "You haven't seduced the right woman." He tugged Faith in closer, kissing her forehead.

A twist stung my stomach. I was used to seeing the affection between my girlfriends and their husbands, but some days were harder than others. Not that I was a relationship girl, but I used to be. Used to think I was in love. Used to think I was capable of being cherished and desired on more levels than just physical.

I'd been an idiot. A stupid girl desperate for love, for connection, for someone who *stayed*.

My ex, Chad, had been the well-mannered, respectful stockbroker before he'd crushed my heart with the white lines he loved more than me. Before he decided that nothing else mattered, not even our years together.

I'd never be that stupid again. Because it didn't matter whether someone left or if someone died. Love hurt more than it was worth.

"Who starts?" Lukas asked, breaking through the haunted memories of my past.

I hurried over to the bar and grabbed the bourbon bottle and some glasses before returning to the table. I needed another drink if Chad had somehow slipped past the mental cage I kept our history in. It didn't matter that we'd been cordial the last time we'd spoken. I hated myself when I looked into my past, and therefore it was locked in a box and buried in the bottom of my soul.

"Connell, this was your grand scheme. You start," Sawyer said.

"With pleasure," he answered, downing the rest of his scotch and pouring himself another. He pointed with the glass in his hand at Logan Ward. "All right, pretty boy, truth or dare?"

Logan fiddled with the longneck resting on his knee. "Truth."

"Gah," Connell groaned. "All right then. Why is it that you have the face of an Adonis and bunnies literally fall at your feet, but we never see you take one home?"

Logan slowly brought the bottle to his lips, taking a good long pull before he responded. "Sex isn't a sport to me. Not a race. And not everyone is good at it. The right partner, the person who can match you stroke for stroke? That is worth waiting for."

A consecutive *aww* tumbled from all the girls' lips, including mine. That was such an unexpected answer, even the men at the table were floored for a few seconds before booing. I knew it was all in good fun, seeing as how more than half the men at the table were happy, moon-eyed, and married.

"Not bad, Ward," Connell said, taking another drink. "Not what I expected, but not bad." He sighed. "You're up."

Logan scanned the faces around the table, and I was surprised by the anticipation filling my body. God, I may as well have been fourteen again.

"Faith," Logan said, glancing at Faith with a smirk. Lukas cocked a brow at him, a silent warning to keep it cool with whatever was about to come out of his mouth. Logan noticed, pressed his lips together, and shook his head. "Truth or dare?"

"Dare," Faith said proudly and elbowed Lukas in the ribs.

Logan hissed as she handed him to the wolves.

Lukas chuckled, his intense stare not leaving Logan's. I almost felt sorry for him.

"I dare you to…" Logan's brow furrowed. "To kiss Lukas." His words released on a disappointed breath, and we all booed—except for Lukas.

"That's not fair," Connell whined. "If you lot aren't going to make it interesting then what's the point?"

Faith proceeded to give Lukas a super-fast yet somehow super-sexy kiss.

"It may be a little hard to keep it interesting," I joked with Connell. "Seeing as how half this group is married and the other half…" I gestured to Sawyer and Logan. "Is straight-laced."

Faith snorted while Sawyer scoffed at me.

"Hold up," Faith said after taking a fast drink. "You think *Sawyer* is straight-laced?"

43

I smiled. "I didn't say it was a bad thing."

"No, no, I get that," Faith said. "But seriously, *Sawyer*? Speaking as someone who lived with him for three years? I've heard things *no* one should have to hear."

"I can attest to that as well," Harper added. "There was an entire week in March he ruined because the girl wouldn't stop screaming for hours every night. Sounded like he—"

"*Sawyer* is sitting right here," he interrupted her, rolling his eyes as he sipped his whiskey.

I eyed Faith, still unbelieving.

"Fine, here I'll prove it. Sawyer pick truth."

He laughed. "I don't know why I let you women boss me around."

"I do," Connell said.

Sawyer sighed. "Truth."

"Where is the craziest place you've had sex?" Faith smirked.

"Oh, now we're getting somewhere." Connell rubbed his palms together as he glanced at Vestergaard. "Your wife is a spitfire."

"You have no idea," Lukas muttered, tucking her in close to his side.

Sawyer raked his fingers through his hair, his eyes calculating.

I chewed my bottom lip, preparing myself for the cute boy-next-door answer like *in the back of my pick-up truck by the lake* or *in my long-term girlfriend's beach house at sunset.*

"There are a few runners up," he finally said, elbows on his knees as he hooked the crowd's attention. "Like the time against the window in Club Thirty-Five's VIP lounge," he said, and Faith and Harper's mouths dropped. "Or the restroom at the Blue Lagoon during a Hozier concert."

My heart rate kicked up at the thought of Sawyer getting off in a public place—the thought was so *not* the stand-up guy who would kiss your cheek at the end of the night like he portrayed himself to be.

"But the real winner was with Amber Hodgekins, senior year, back of the bus."

"What?" Faith laughed, and I echoed her question.

"Those other two were runners up to a *bus*?" I tsked him.

"It wasn't about the bus," he said. "Or the fact that there were fifteen other students on it. It wasn't about being in public. It came down to one, primal need. I *wanted* her. So badly I couldn't wait until we got back to my house. And she wanted me too. So it was a quick, shove-the-panties-to-the-side,   thank-God-you're-wearing-a-skirt   kind   of moment."

Our group of friends was silent save for a whistle from the Scotsman.

Sawyer turned toward me, noting my parted lips and my eyes that likely gave away my shock at his answer.

"What?" he asked, tinkling the ice in his whiskey glass. "Haven't you ever been that consumed with need? Hasn't anyone ever made you feel like that?"

I shut my mouth and swallowed hard.

I loved sex, but I'd never needed it so bad that I couldn't *wait*.

But that low, pulsing ache in my core now? It was pushing me to that damn edge. The one that screamed if I didn't at least have a taste of Sawyer McCoy soon, I'd combust.

Just a taste. That's all I'd need.

Then I could drop him back to the customer-only category.

Because neither of us had time for the other, and maybe that was why I wanted him so badly.

That, and the fact that he smelled like dessert and looked like the best kind of wet dream. Those long, lucid slow-burn dreams where you can feel every single sensation down to your toes.

"Connell, truth or dare," Sawyer asked.

"Dare, naturally."

Sawyer glanced to me, then headed toward the bar. He came back with an empty shot glass and a box of matches with the Scythe logo on it. He poured a shot of scotch into the glass, then struck the match, lighting the shot on fire. He leaned close to me. "I'm guessing you'd stop me if this wasn't allowed," he whispered.

I waved him on.

"I dare you to take this shot." Sawyer gently pushed the flaming shot near the Scotsman, the rest of the group leaning away from the fire.

Connell smirked. "That's a Tuesday night back home, rookie." He scooped up the shot and tossed it back, the flame extinguished with the fast movement. He slammed the empty glass upside-down on the table. "Lemme' show you what a *real* dare is," he said, pointing his finger at Sawyer.

He rolled his eyes. "Fine. Dare."

"I dare ye to kiss Echo Hayes."

Oh hell fucking yes. I'd wanted to know what those lips felt like since he walked into the bar for the first time, and with no-strings attached? Major bonus.

"What are we, five?" Sawyer chuckled, taking another sip of his whiskey.

Don't freeze up, West Coast.

"Six, actually," Connell said. "Now I'm talking a real kiss. Not that married ish we got from the Vestergaards."

"I resent that!" Faith teased and kissed Lukas again, simply because she could.

"I swallowed fire, little Sawyer McCoy," Connell taunted. "Think ye can find your balls and kiss a pretty lass like Echo?"

46

5

SAWYER

*T*he sweet burn of bourbon slid down my throat as I cocked an eyebrow at Connell. "You're serious." What kind of junior high shit was this?

"You can always cry chicken," he answered, waggling his eyebrows.

"I'm not in the habit of kissing women who don't want to be kissed," I countered, leaning back in my chair. Not that I didn't want to kiss Echo. Shit, I had to consciously stop myself from reaching for her.

It wasn't just because she was beautiful—which she was. I'd fucked more beautiful women than I cared to think about. It wasn't just that she had the fuck-off attitude that I'd never been able to resist. It wasn't even the funny text messages or the way she'd shut down the bar for all of us.

Any one of those would have hardened my dick, but combining them all...now that was a fucking aphrodisiac.

I wanted to kiss Echo because there was an undeniable part of me that demanded to know how she tasted. To know if she poured that same passion into a kiss that she gave to everything else in her life. I wanted to know...her.

"She doesn't exactly look unwilling, now does she?" Connell challenged, nodding to my right.

I glanced over to Echo, who stared at me with her head slightly cocked to the side, waiting to see what I would do. A single eyebrow rose in challenge.

"Pick something else," I ordered Connell without looking away. The first time I kissed Echo—because at this point it was an inevitability—I wanted it to be because we were both so hot for each other that we couldn't contain ourselves, not because we'd been caught in a dare.

A slight smile tilted Echo's lips, which immediately drew my attention. Damn, her lips looked so soft. Not colored with a heavy lipstick, just a light gloss that made me want to pull her lower lip between my teeth.

"Och, that would be breaking the rules," Connell argued.

"It's just a kiss," Echo said softly with a shrug, pushing back from the table and standing in one smooth motion.

My chair groaned in protest as it slid across the hardwood. The tension between us was so taut that my body followed hers, standing just to keep near.

"You're okay with this?" I asked her just as softly, my brows lowering as I turned to face her. The two feet that separated us had felt like plenty of distance a few minutes ago, but now she might as well have been in my lap or a million miles away. It all hinged on her answer.

She stepped forward, closing that distance, and my stomach tightened. Then she raised her hands to rest on the thick cotton of my button-down shirt and looked up at me.

"Do your worst, West Coast," she whispered as her gaze flickered to my lips. "It's just a dare."

"Just a dare," I repeated, my arm wrapping around her so my hand could rest between her shoulder blades.

"Doesn't mean anything," she assured me.

"Not a thing," I agreed.

I lowered my mouth to hers and brushed a kiss over her lips. That was all it would have been—the dare fulfilled. But she sighed softly and pressed her lips more firmly against mine, and I didn't draw back like I'd planned.

I kissed her again, drawing that plump lower lip between mine and tasting the light cherry flavor of her gloss. My tongue swept over that lip and her breath caught, her hands gripping my shirt. She opened under me, and I forgot where we were, who was watching, and why the hell this was even happening.

My only thought was getting closer to her.

My tongue sank into the welcoming heat of her mouth. Fuck, that sweet cherry taste mixed with the bourbon she'd been drinking, and I was instantly addicted. My tongue swirled around hers, and she whimpered softly, pressing her body fully against mine.

I sent my hand up her back to fist in the soft purple hair at the nape of her neck. With a gentle tug, she gave into the wordless demand, tilting her head back so I could take her deeper. Her body softened against mine, and I grabbed her waist to keep her steady as I learned the sweet hollows and curves of her mouth. Her tongue against mine was the sweetest fire, burning me with every stroke she gave back.

"Damn."

The mutter from behind us brought back enough of my common sense to remember where we were. When I moved to lift my head, Echo's hand rose to my neck and kept me right where I was—kissing her.

I groaned as my cock hardened, more than agreeing with her request.

My hands dropped to her ass, and I easily lifted her slight weight. Her legs wrapped around my waist as her arms did the same around my neck. Without breaking the kiss, I walked us back toward the bar, then pivoted so my back hit the swinging door, sending it sailing into the kitchen as we crossed the threshold.

I lifted my head just long enough to see the open expanse of stainless steel that occupied the center of the kitchen. Three steps later, I had Echo on the counter while I stroked the curve of her waist.

Our eyes met in a clash of need and desire. I'd never wanted anyone like this before in my life, never wanted to drown in a pair of eyes like I did Echo's. "Fuck, you're beautiful."

Those turquoise eyes flared, and she pulled my mouth back to hers, her nails biting little marks into my neck that somehow sharpened the pleasure of kissing her. Our tongues tangled, stroked, and demanded as we gave in to the pull between us. Her hips rocked forward, meeting the hard length of my cock, and she gasped, but still didn't pull away.

Instead, one of her hands dropped to my belt loop, and she tugged me closer.

Fuck me, any closer and I'd be peeling off her jeans and finding out if she tasted just as sweet everywhere else. The thought alone made me groan.

I tore my lips from hers, then set my mouth to her neck.

She arched harder against me and exhaled on a hiss. "Good God."

"Sawyer," I corrected her before biting the little section of skin where her neck met her shoulders.

She moaned, pressing her breasts against my chest. Her nipples were so hard I felt them through the velvet of her tank top and my shirt. My mouth slid back to hers in a long, drugging kiss as my hand slipped to her breast, rubbing her nipple against my palm before gently cupping her.

Fuck, she filled my hand perfectly.

She fit me perfectly.

Her taste, her light vanilla scent, her quick little breaths, they were all...perfect.

She matched me kiss for kiss, leaving me with no doubt that we weren't just compatible, we were combustible.

Her hand at my belt slid under my shirt, and her fingertips traced the line of my abs, following the outer indent from the bottom of my rib cage down to where it deepened and disappeared into my pants. Then I was the one hissing, my cock straining against the tight confines of my jeans.

Her hand moved to the front of my jeans and she cupped my dick, squeezing me lightly. Pleasure shot through me like lightning, branching out to affect every limb, every cell in my body. "Echo," I groaned, leaning into her touch.

"Damn," she whispered, her hand measuring me from base to tip through the denim.

I grinned with pure masculine pride at her appreciation. Then my hand slid under the stretchy velvet fabric of her tank top and then her bra. Her bare nipple rubbed against my palm, and I squeezed her lightly once. "Damn," I repeated.

Echo laughed, and my heart tripped over itself as she pulled me back to her mouth. Fuck that was sexy. I'd tested my limits in college with all the cliché shit star athletes did. I'd taken plenty of girls to bed and even had a few monogamous relationships. But I'd never been with someone I could laugh with in the middle of making out and not have it ruin the mood.

Fuck, I wasn't sure even a bucket of ice would break the thrall she had me in. Most likely I'd pick up a cube and drag it down her body until she was begging me to replace it with my mouth.

She nipped lightly at my lower lip, and I gave into the playful nature of the kiss, lightly feathering her nipple with my fingers over and over, teasing but not giving her what she so obviously needed.

51

"Sawyer," she whimpered against my lips, arching to press her breast into my hand.

"I could kiss you forever," I admitted as I took her nipple between my thumb and forefinger and gently rolled the bud, then pinched.

She cried out and squeezed my cock in her hand. Then her body started rolling against mine, and I knew how easy it would be to get her off. Her body was practically humming with sweet tension, and her breaths only came faster as I gave the same treatment to her other breast.

"Fuck, I want to touch you," I growled as my thumb toyed with the button on her jeans.

"Yeah?" she asked, her eyes hazy with need, the color burning even brighter. Her nails raked down my back, bringing every nerve ending to life, and she didn't need to flex the other one to remind me where it was—my dick was well aware. "And what would you do with me?" she dared.

My lips twisted in a wry smile. This woman thought she had me figured out. What had she called me? Straight-laced.

I always did love a challenge.

My hand dropped between her thighs—over her jeans, and I cupped her heat, nearly coming undone at the warmth radiating against my skin. "If I had you naked?" I started, running my lips over the piercings that ran down her ear. "I'd lay you back on this table, spread your sweet little thighs, and drape them over my shoulders." I pressed in with my middle finger, pushing the seam of her jeans against her clit.

She cried out again, her thighs tightening around my hips.

My cock throbbed, but I ignored its demand and concentrated on Echo, moving my lips to her jaw.

"Then, I'd lick and suck at you until you were shaking under me, begging me to come." I rubbed against her clit, and she whimpered. When she tried to rock forward on her own, I lightened the pressure, keeping her from taking control. Then I pulled back just far enough so I could look in her eyes, so she'd know I meant every word. "Once you were delirious with need, bucking against my mouth, I'd fuck you with my tongue so I could taste you when you came."

My own game got to me because now that was all I wanted to do.

Her lips parted, her eyes flaring with surprise and something so primal that I almost went for her zipper.

"So, we said a kiss, not seven minutes in heaven!" Connell's Scottish bur was muffled slightly by the kitchen door.

My gaze shot to the door, and the window in it, but he wasn't looking in. Good, now I didn't have to actually kill him.

"Holy shit," Echo whispered, letting her forehead fall against my shoulder.

I eased my hand from between her thighs and tucked her breast back into her clothing before wrapping my arms around her. "Yeah," I agreed. Holy shit was about right.

"I guess we should go back out there," she grumbled.

"Right." My chest heaved as I tried to calm my breathing. "Just as soon as you let go of my dick." If she squeezed me one more time we were going to be here way longer than seven minutes.

She gave a little squeak of surprise and then laughed as she released me. "Sorry," she said with zero apology in her tone or expression.

"I'm not," I told her. Sorry was the furthest word from my thoughts. Hard, aching, pulsing...those were way closer.

I gripped her waist and lowered her to the tile floor. Her eyes locked with mine, and that tension snapped back into place, hot enough to burn us both to the ground. I quickly put a few feet between us, knowing I'd have her back on that counter in a millisecond if I didn't get some distance.

Her eyes dropped to my erection, and she tugged her bottom lip between her teeth. Then she quickly shook her head and swallowed. "Okay, um, follow me."

"I might need a minute," I countered, my voice sounding like I'd just raked it over shards of broken glass.

She marched ahead of me, her distressed jeans cupping her ass so well that I groaned.

"Come on," she urged, offering me a shaky smile as she looked over her shoulder. "I've got you covered. Trust me."

Well, either she had me covered, or I was about to open myself up to locker room torture for the next five years. I followed her out, and when I cleared the door, she tugged me forward three steps...right against the bar where I was hidden from the waist down.

"Ten! I give it a ten!" Langley called out.

"Eleven!" Harper offered.

"Did you see the way he picked her up? So fucking hot. That's definitely a twelve!" Faith added from Lukas' lap.

"Yeah, yeah," Echo waved them off. If I hadn't seen the fine tremble in her hand, I would have thought that kiss hadn't affected her. What else was she good at hiding? How much of that prickly exterior was just armor? "I'm taking Sawyer's dare," she announced, pulling the tequila from the shelf. "I'm daring every Reaper in this room—with exceptions"—she sent a pointed look to the guys who didn't drink —"to get over here and take a shot." She winked at me, and I dutifully took the shot glasses from beneath the bar and lined them up on the granite as she started to pour.

The guys—and some of their wives—stepped up to take their shots.

"To the newest Carolina Reaper," Echo toasted, lifting her

shot in the air and locking her eyes on mine. "Sawyer McCoy."

"Sawyer!" the guys shouted.

The tequila slid down my throat, sharp and sweet.

"So this is why you have the bar closed down," a voice came from behind me.

I turned to see three guys and a girl standing just inside the swinging door. Before I could ask who the fuck they were and why they'd come through the back door, Echo quickly put herself in between us.

"What the hell?" Echo challenged. "I'm hosting a private party, and you're not invited."

I stepped forward at her tone. As if sensing me, Echo spun and pointed her finger in my direction. "No," she said simply before turning back toward the odd group.

The woman liked to fight her own battles. Got it.

I didn't retreat, but I didn't move any closer, either.

The guy grinned as he loosened his tie. His hair was as dark as mine, but it was parted to the side and slicked in a way that told me he spent a little too much time in the hair care aisle. He was thin, but so were his friends. They all looked like they belonged to the same Izod club, even the girl who clung to the guy in the right rear, who was obviously wasted.

"Give me back that key, Chad." Echo demanded, holding out her hand.

Chad? Go figure. Guy looked like a Chad. But who the hell was he to Echo that he had a key to the bar she worked at.

"Oh come on, Echo. Honey, you know—"

Honey?

"You don't get to call me honey anymore," she hissed. "Give me back my fucking key and get out of my bar."

I heard the tell-tale sound of wood scraping on the hardwood and knew my teammates had stood from their barstools behind me.

Chad's eyes widened as he looked our direction. "Look, can't we go in the back and talk? I just came to talk to you," he urged softly. "I miss you."

He fucking missed her? Honey? For fuck's sake, she made fun of me for being straight-laced, but she'd been in a *relationship* with this country club douchebag?

"No," Echo snapped. "I told you we're done. We're not together. We're not friends. We're not *anything*." She gestured with her open hand, thrusting it toward him. "Key. Now."

He glanced my way and then his eyes narrowed like he knew I'd had my hands on Echo a few minutes ago. I lifted a corner of my mouth in a slight smirk. He might have called Echo *honey* at one point, but sure as fuck not now. The wave of possessiveness caught me off guard, but I rolled with it.

"Chad!" Echo snapped.

He tore his gaze from me and looked down at Echo, then slowly placed a key in her hand. "I'm clean," he promised.

A chill raced down my spine, sending ice through my veins.

"Don't do this," she shook her head slowly.

"I'm clean, Echo. Six months, today. That's why I wanted to see you." He stepped forward and Echo moved back.

I blinked. Her retreat told me more than enough.

"I'm glad you're clean, Chad." Her gaze cut to the others. "But if the company you're keeping says anything, I know you won't stay that way for long."

"Oh, come on," one of the guys mock-whined with a shitty little grin that was begging for my fist. "You used to like us just fine."

"Sure, in college," she countered. "But it's been what? Nine months since graduation? We're in the real world now, so grow the fuck up, Blaine."

56

Blaine. The douchebag names just kept coming.

I heard a scoff behind me and knew it had to be Noble.

"Give me a shot," Chad pled. "I got clean for *you*. A second chance—that's all I'm asking for." He reached a hand for her arm, and she backed up again—straight into me.

I didn't budge, and if the asshole reached for her again, I'd be the one he got to touch.

Echo softened slightly against me, and with the way Chad's jaw ticked, I knew he saw it. "Again, I'm glad you're clean. I really am." She sucked in a shaky breath that I felt against my chest. "But I really need you to leave."

Her voice softened in a way that told me this guy had meant something to her.

His sharp brown eyes glanced back over my team before he pursed his lips and nodded. "I can see that you're busy. Bar looks good, by the way. Let's go, guys."

The first three headed through the door. Chad looked over his shoulder at Echo. "I'll try again another time," he said with a smirking little grin that I'm sure he thought was charming. "What we had doesn't just die, Echo."

She stiffened. "It does when you kill it, Chad. Get out."

He shot me a warning look that I nearly laughed at and followed his friends through the door. Echo walked over to the window, and once she'd relaxed, I knew they'd gone.

She spun to face us, then plastered on the smile I knew so well. "Okay, so that's not up for discussion," she said with a shrug. "Langley, how about you take the truth or dare turn?"

Langley swallowed, but she nodded, agreeing to change the subject and take the pressure off her friend.

The game continued, but I stopped drinking and silently watched Echo. She diligently avoided my gaze for the remaining hour we were at Scythe. If I hadn't just witnessed that exchange, I'd have no clue that she'd been shaken, first by me, then by Chad—whoever the fuck he was.

She was a master at hiding her feelings.

I pretty much wore my heart on my sleeve. Always had.

We couldn't be any more different, yet physically, I knew I'd met my match. I'd never burned so hot, so quickly for any woman.

But with all we both had going on, the question wasn't our chemistry.

It was what we were going to do about it.

6

ECHO

*S*awyer's face filled one of the flatscreens in the corner of the bar. The place was wall-to-wall packed with customers, all Reapers' fans who'd shown up tonight to watch the game and take part in the Reaper Special—half-price beers on tap and a free appetizer. One of my best ideas yet, seeing as I had more than doubled the expected revenue for tonight.

But, despite the chatter-filled bar or the excitement over a well-played game, I couldn't *not* see the purple smudges underneath Sawyer's eyes. The way his shoulders sank with each reporter asking him the same damn questions. Grilling him on the four losses the Reapers' had suffered since he'd joined the team six games ago.

I tried not to grind my teeth. Tried not to scream at the screen *why the hell aren't you talking to Axel? The Reapers' captain?* Axel knew how to handle the vultures called reporters. Knew how to spin words to make them sound like gold. Sound like the Reapers were still an *Inevitable* team bound for the Cup.

Sawyer?

He looked burned out.

Looked like the pressure of diving headfirst into an NHL team mid-season while simultaneously moving his mother across the country had finally caught up to him.

A heaviness settled over my chest.

He needed a break. A pick-me-up. A distraction. Something.

Otherwise he'd grind out this dream-career of his until there was nothing left of him but dust.

After the interview was over, and I'd poured a fresh drink for one of my regulars, I fished my cell from underneath the bar.

Echo: Did you know that Cap'n Crunch's full name is Horatio Magellan Crunch?

Sawyer: That's a serious name for a not-so-serious guy.

I bit my lip to keep from smiling at my phone.

Echo: Right? How can you ever eat the cereal again? All the whimsy is dead for me.

Sawyer: I've always been more of a Frosted Flakes guy anyway.

Echo: Tiger over Captain. Got it. Want to grab some tonight and see how it pairs with bourbon?

I held my breath, torturing my bottom lip. I couldn't stop the flashes from the last time I'd seen him—his lips on mine, the taste of bourbon on his tongue as he claimed mouth in a way that told me exactly what he could do to my body. The way he'd lifted me without so much as a blink and took me to the kitchen...like he was as consumed by the kiss as I was. Like he couldn't take another second without touching me in private. Goddamn, the man had set me on fire. And now all I wanted to do was feel him again.

Sawyer: I promised Mom I'd stop by tonight. Just leaving arena now.

I tried to ignore the deflation inside me, tried to ignore

the smile slipping off my lips. Sawyer and I were just friends. Sure, we'd shared a too-hot-to-forget kiss. And yes, maybe I'd replayed that kiss while touching myself more than once in the past week. And yeah, maybe I couldn't get the man out of my head no matter how hard I tried, but that didn't *mean* anything. Nothing but a craving. Something shiny and new on display in my daily life. That's all.

Sawyer: Want to come with me? We could always grab Frosted Flakes after. Unless that was a joke?

In an instant, my spirit was up, and my nerves in overdrive.

It had taken Chad a year of convincing before I met his family.

But Sawyer and I weren't together. He could've just as easily asked Faith or Harper to go as they were his friends too.

Echo: I never joke about cereal. Pick me up when you're ready?

Sawyer: See you in a bit.

I tossed my cell under the bar and raked my fingers through my hair. I'd elected to just wear it down today, sans braids, because I'd been in a super lazy mood this morning. Sleep had been few and far between lately, and it had nothing to do with the way Sawyer had kissed me so much my body craved him like my next meal.

Nope.

Not at all.

Thirty minutes later, my replacement showed up, and I was in Sawyer's brand-new truck, heading to meet the most important woman in his life.

To say my stomach was in knots was an understatement.

"Are you okay?" Sawyer asked, glancing at me for a moment before returning his eyes to the road.

"Yeah, why wouldn't I be okay?"

61

"You haven't told me a ridiculous random fact since your last text."

"So."

"And you also haven't commented on my shirt."

I eyed his perfectly ironed light-blue button-down. It brought out the gray in his eyes.

"Well," I said, forcing myself to get a grip. "Now that you mention it, you do look a little stuffy."

He smiled and nodded. "There she is."

I chuckled, but the sound was lackluster as he parked in front of an assisted living facility and hurried around his truck to open my door, grabbing a bag from the back as he did.

"And she's quiet again," he said, eyeing how I wrung my hands as we stood outside his truck.

"I…" I sighed, mentally kicking myself. "I'm not used to this."

"To what?" he asked, his tall frame blotting out the setting sun as he towered over me. The heat from his body practically sizzled on my skin, a constant hum pulsing his name: *Sawyer. Sawyer. Sawyer.*

"I don't meet people's families," I said.

"That's not true," he countered, brushing back some of my purple hair. "You've met all the Reapers. They're one big family."

I nodded, unable to argue. "But meeting Axel and Lukas wasn't like meeting a parent."

Sawyer laughed, shaking his head. "No, I don't imagine it was." He motioned toward the entrance of the building.

I hesitated.

"Look, I get it," he said. "It's a big deal. And I didn't mean to spring it on you, but we were texting, and I really wanted to see you tonight. You help me…"

"Relax?"

"Yes," he said. "Something about your constant criticism or random facts puts me at ease."

"And you haven't had much of that lately, have you, Sawyer?" I dared to reach a finger up and graze the shadows beneath his eyes. He sighed under my touch.

"I'll understand if you want to wait here for me. Or call a Lyft and do something fun on your night off."

I furrowed my brow. "No, I wanted to see you too."

"So you'll come in with me?"

Heat flared beneath my skin, and I savored the sweet burn.

"Yes," I said and let him take my hand as he led me into the building.

His mother's room was on the fourth floor, though *room* wasn't actually accurate. The place was as big as a small townhome complete with a city view, a kitchenette, and spa-quality bathroom.

"Sawyer," his mother said with a grin as she ushered us inside. She was petite, almost frail, but still had a spark behind her eyes. Gray, just like Sawyer's. Her stage in the fight with Parkinson's was obvious, but she stood on her own with the aid of a handrail that ran on every wall of her apartment. "Come in. You've brought company." She nudged him with her elbow as she smiled at me.

"Echo," I said, reaching my hand toward her. She shook it and patted it at the same time before gesturing to a small gathering of chairs just off her master bedroom. Sawyer helped her into a leather recliner and then we both took seats across from her.

"I brought your favorite," Sawyer said, handing her the small bag he'd grabbed from his truck. "Want me to—" He moved forward as if to help her, but she waved him off.

She opened it, then smiled and gave him an incredulous look. "You always spoil me," she said, showing me the candy in the bag. "This is my favorite taffy from Seattle." She glanced at him, a sadness in her eyes. "You know I don't miss it that much," she said. "You don't have to—"

"I wanted to," Sawyer cut her off.

She nodded, pressing her lips together. "You just missed your aunt Nancy," she said, waving toward the door. "She's only a few hours away in Virginia," she said, mainly to me. "And she was here from breakfast until now. It was such a nice visit. Moving here has made me realize how much I miss my sisters."

"I know you do, Mom." Sawyer reached out and gently grasped her wrist. "I'm glad she was here today. I know it's been a couple of days since I've been able to get over here."

She rolled her eyes. "Sawyer, you have to stop that," she chided. "I'm not a child to be entertained. I'm fine. You're chasing that dream of yours, and I couldn't be prouder." Her eyes trailed to mine. "I've told him a thousand times he doesn't have to look after me like he does, but he never listens." She shrugged. "Though, as his girlfriend, I'm sure you've already discovered how stubborn he is."

"Oh no," I said.

"No, Mom," Sawyer added.

"We're not…" I stumbled for words. "We're just friends."

"Echo works at Scythe where the Reapers hang out between games and ice-time."

I nodded while she eyed us both.

"Oh, well, that's wonderful. I'm so glad you're making friends," she said, and it sounded so much like she was talking to a little-boy version of Sawyer that I laughed softly. The man sitting across from her was anything but little—tall, broad, muscled, and a rising NHL star. He shouldn't have a problem making friends, but the happiness in her tone made it sound like he *had* had that trouble before. "I love your earrings," she continued, eyeing the row of studs I had up and down my right ear. "I always wanted to get more piercings but...I don't know, the act simply got away from me."

"It's not too late," I said, smiling at her. "You say the word and I can make it happen. My guy is the best."

She laughed, a full, booming sound that made Sawyer's eyes light up.

"I like you," she said. "Now, you two need to leave."

"Mom!" Sawyer gaped at her.

"What?" She pursed her lips, motioning toward the window. "It's a perfectly beautiful night out there. You two kids should be out on the town. Go hook up with your Reapers and have some fun."

"I thought we were going to play cards," Sawyer said.

"Nonsense. I'm tired of cards. I'm going to go down to the social hour in a few minutes. You insisted on getting me the best living facility, and now I'm going to indulge in the amenities. You're not the only one who's been making friends." She stood with Sawyer's help, but walked proudly to the door and swung it open. "Out."

I raised my brows but did as I was told and headed toward the door.

"So lovely to meet you, Echo," she said as I passed her.

"You too," I said, biting back a laugh at the way Sawyer just stared at her wide-eyed.

"Love you, son. Have a good night." She waved him onward.

He kissed her on her cheek. "Love you too, Mom."

She shut the door behind us, and I couldn't hold back the laugh one second more.

"She's amazing," I said through my laughs.

Sawyer finally joined in as we rode the elevator down to the ground level. "She's not normally so...aggressive."

"Well," I said, walking toward his truck. "Maybe you've finally given her a place she can let loose in?"

"Maybe," he said, holding the door open for me despite my protests. When he fell behind the wheel he asked, "Where to? Frosted Flakes?"

"Let's save cereal for another time," I said. "I've got a better idea. Head downtown."

Twenty minutes later, Sawyer and I were strolling down one of Charleston's main streets, munching on kabobs from my favorite food truck.

"This is life," he said, gobbling up his last bite before tossing the skewer in a trash can on the corner.

"I know, right?" I tossed my empty skewer too. "That truck has been a favorite of mine for years."

"It must've been nice to grow up here," he said, his eyes drinking in the city at night—the historic buildings that had been converted into restaurants or boutique shops. The golden lights drenching the pavement in an amber hue that set a nostalgic tone.

I tucked my thumbs into my black thermal, shrugging. "Mostly."

"Sorry," he said. "Didn't mean to dig up the past."

"No," I said. "It's all right."

"I mean, I *have* already met a piece of your past," he continued, and I couldn't ignore the bite in his tone.

"Ah," I said. "That's a pretty direct way to bring up my ex."

"Can you blame me?" he asked as we continued to walk, taking in the sights of the busy street. "The guy was…"

"You don't need to finish that statement," I said. His run-in with Chad had been awkward, to say the least. Unexpected, too, especially since he showed up right after the mind-blowing kiss that had resulted from a dare. "I know how it looked." I sighed. "He wasn't always like that. In the beginning, we were in college, and then he was this stand-up stockbroker. We fell hard, and fast and I thought he was *it*. Then my father died—he was my world, you know. I'd already lost my mother and sister in a car wreck a few years before—it was my fault too. Dad had driven me to my piano recital, and mom was bringing my sister after she'd gotten out of soccer practice. Someone ran a red light, crushed them right into a median. If I hadn't had that stupid recital…"

I blinked a few times, a sharp gasp on my lips. I hadn't spoken out loud about their deaths—and my responsibility in it—for years.

"That wasn't your fault—"

"Anyway," I cut Sawyer off, shaking my head at myself. "After Dad's heart attack…Chad was all I had left. And when I found out he loved white lines more than me, I thought I could make him *stay* by diving into that world with him."

A muscle in Sawyer's jaw ticked, so I tugged on his forearm and settled us on an empty bench. "That bothers you, doesn't it?"

"My dad was an addict. He walked out on my mother when she was diagnosed. Chose drugs over her. Over us."

I squeezed his hand. "That's a load of horse shit."

He huffed. "Yeah."

I shook my head. "I understand, though. That pain." I took my hand back, staring out at the busy street—at the shoppers rushing this way and that, at the couples venturing to the local restaurants on dates, the street musicians playing jazz on the corner. "No one ever stays in my life. Not really. They either die or they leave." I swallowed against the old familiar pain I'd done my damnedest to bury. "I left that life behind me," I said, gathering myself. "Once I realized I was using the nightlife and Chad as a coping mechanism for losing Dad…I left. I ended things with Chad, and I threw myself into my work."

He nodded. "I've spent my life trying to make up for my dad's mistakes."

67

"You know your mom doesn't hold you responsible, right?" I asked. "I've only met her once and I can tell that."

"She doesn't," he said. "But she doesn't have anyone else."

"What about her sisters? The ones she mentioned."

"They're closer now that we've moved here," he said. "But they weren't there through my father leaving, through the diagnosis and treatment. They weren't there..." he sighed. "I'm not really being fair. They showed up when I asked them to. But...*I* was the one. The one to take it on when no one else could."

"I'm sorry you had to do that."

"I'm not," he said, shrugging. "I may still hate my father. Hate the drugs and the world he left us for. But it happened how it was supposed to. It brought me here. Brought me to my dream."

I smiled. "Well, you were brave enough to chase it."

"With a little help," he said, eyeing me.

And I could see it there, the connection leading us back to that night he walked into my bar. The night he needed the right person to tell him to stop *thinking* so much and simply *go*. There were so many things I'd love to watch Sawyer do if he acted first and thought later—like that dare. Thank God for Connell. The Scotsman had hand-delivered Sawyer to me on a silver platter and who knew he'd taste so damn sweet? So addictive. Even sitting here now, I wanted him. I could feel that low hum in my core, begging me to reach out and touch him again. Taste him again. Because he'd shocked the hell out of me with that kiss, spun my head, and set my body ablaze. It was impossible not to want more when it came to Sawyer McCoy.

"You would've gotten there on your own," I finally said, reeling in my churning desire.

He easily placed his arm on the back of the bench, tucking me in closer but not close enough to be an invitation.

A dangerous line we teetered on.

Friends, growing closer on one side.

And on the other?

A deep, intense craving to risk that friendship and devour him. To damn everything that screamed we *shouldn't* cross that line—our busy lives, the fact that he had a cleaner past than mine, the certainty that he was *going* places and I was happy standing still. All of it.

And the terrible thing?

I couldn't tell which side I wanted to win.

All I knew, with devastating clarity, was that the second Sawyer walked into my life, it got brighter.

7
SAWYER

*W*e'd fallen out of first place in the conference, and it hadn't stopped there. The point lead we'd had when I came in as the Reaper goalie almost a month ago had quickly vanished, and the team that had been nick-named *the Inevitables* was now hanging on to second place in our division by the skin of our teeth. Only the top three slots were guaranteed a place in the playoffs.

Even worse? We were six points behind North Carolina, which felt like taking the open wound and dunking it into the Atlantic.

The sound of my own voice reached my ears, and I glanced over to where two of my teammates were watching my latest post-game interview on their iPads. Thank you, in-flight Wi-Fi.

"It's just hard to believe that the simple loss of Fields, and Thurston's injury has turned this team from *Inevitable* to *Inconsequential*," one announcer said, his colleagues chuckling.

I leaned my head back and closed my eyes as my team-mates hissed.

Fuck me, I was killing this team.

"Don't let it get to you," Connell said as he took the seat next to me.

I shot him the closest thing I had to a *fuck off* look as another clip from my interview started playing.

"Turn that shite off!" Connell snapped at the guys across the aisle, then ran his hand over his blond hair in an uncharacteristic show of exasperation. "It's not easy, coming off the bench like you have and stepping into all this."

"Agreed," Logan said, looking back through the opening between seats.

"Easy for you both to say," I grumbled. "You guys were winning just fine with Fields in the net."

"And Thurston," Connell reminded me, then flinched. "That didn't come out right."

"You fucking suck at pep talks, MacDhuibh," Cannon noted from a seat right behind us.

"Have you got anything better, you surly arse?" Connell fired back.

"Not my job to babysit the new kid," Cannon answered, turning the page in whatever book he was reading.

"Nice," Connell sang in a mocking tone.

I sighed all the way to the bottom of my soul. Never in a million years had I thought that reaching the dream would be easier than keeping it.

Cannon's book hit the seat next to him, and suddenly his head appeared over the seat to my right. Jesus, was there an inch on the guy that wasn't tatted up besides his face?

"Look, rookie. You're not the only one on the ice. They got past five other players to score on you. I can tell you that Simmons and Taylor were both slow as shit tonight, and it didn't help that I got thrown out in the second period." He looked at me without pity or compassion, which was oddly comforting. "Point is, the press is picking at you because

71

you're new. The whole team has been playing like shit, and I honestly think the defense got too comfortable with Fields in net."

"Hey!" Logan snapped, shooting a glare at Cannon.

"Fuck off, Pretty Boy. Did I say shit about you?" Cannon rolled his eyes and scoffed. "Hopefully what MacDhuibh was saying is that we had two goalies rotating. You've been in net every game since you started, with Thurston playing *your* backup."

"Right. That's what I meant," Connell nodded. "He just said it better."

"You're just starting off at pre-season readiness, McCoy, and the rest of the league isn't. You'll catch on, so don't beat yourself to shit over it. We need you to build that confidence, not lose it over the fucking media. Relax. It's not like we're out of playoff contention or anything."

Without another word, Cannon dropped back to his seat, leaving us all blinking at where his head had been a moment earlier.

"Right. What he said," Connell shrugged and leaned back in his seat.

Logan turned back around, and I spent the rest of the two-hour flight looking out my window, watching the black landscape, punctuated by bright patches of city lights pass beneath us.

It was past midnight when we landed in Charleston. Exhaustion beat at my body, but not my mind.

By one-thirty, I'd gone over each of the three floorplans available in the neighborhood the team called Reaper Village and was nowhere near closer to choosing a house. By one forty-five, I nodded to the doorman and headed toward Scythe.

I hadn't seen Echo in two weeks—not since the night she met my mom. Not that I had any reason to see her. We weren't dating. My schedule was overwhelmed with practices, games, and Mom. I had zero business walking over to the bar just before closing on the chance that she'd be there.

Yet, there I was, opening the door anyway.

The inside of the bar was a little brighter than normal, and I spotted at least three workers already closing up for the night. Chairs were up on tables, and the sound of the vacuum filled the small space.

"Sorry, mister," a waitress I vaguely recognized started, only to pause mid-sentence and grin before looking back over her shoulder. "Hey, Echo, your Reaper is here."

My gaze followed hers and found Echo standing from where she'd been crouched behind the bar, no doubt putting glasses away. Her hair was down and loose, brushing over the collar of her black leather vest to curl softly around her breasts.

"Not *my* Reaper, JoAnna," she corrected the redhead before tilting her head to the side with a soft smile. "Hey there, West Coast."

"Hey." The knot that had been tightening in my chest after every loss started to loosen as I crossed the floor to her. "Looks like you're closing up."

"Yeah, the girls and I started early. It was dead tonight once the game was over. Sundays," she finished with a little shrug.

"Or the fact that I lost another game." I leaned against the bar, fully expecting her to tell me that it was way too late for a stop-over.

"I wouldn't say that *you* lost another game," she countered, drying a beer glass. "I'd say the team did."

"Doesn't feel that way."

Her eyes met mine for a charged moment and then she nodded as if she'd come to some decision. "Sarah, JoAnna, and Trish," she called past me. "Holly's done in the kitchen, so I'll lock up. Why don't you three head out?"

"You sure?" JoAnna asked, her attention darting to the clock.

"Positive. Out with you." Echo waved them off, coming around the bar to follow them out. Holy shit, she was wearing a short tartan skirt that only reached mid-thigh, and even her ripped black leggings couldn't hide the incredible length of her legs. Not that the boots were helping me there, either. Once the bar was empty, she looked back at me, assessing me with a quick swipe of her eyes. "You look exhausted, Sawyer."

"Is that a polite way of saying that I look like shit?" I asked, turning so I leaned back against the bar.

"That's a polite way of me telling you that I'm walking you home."

My brows furrowed. "Isn't that what I'm supposed to say as the guy here?"

She crossed her arms under her breasts. "Don't even get me started with that misogynistic shit."

I put my hands up and laughed. "Okay, okay, you win." I'd argue the right to walk her back later.

"Good. Wait here for a second." She walked into the kitchen, and a moment later the light I usually saw through the window was out. She finished locking up and then held out her hand at the front door. "Well, are you coming?"

I shook my head, but I followed her out the door, and she locked it behind us.

"You're just at Langley's old place, right?" she questioned as she zipped up her jacket.

"Yep. You really don't have to walk me home. I'm fully capable of making it there myself."

"Call it my public service," she answered as we began walking toward the exclusive high rise Langley had chosen as her home before she married Axel. "I'm just doing my part for the city of Charleston."

"Pretty sure putting me down would be doing your part for the city," I joked.

She narrowed her eyes. "Knock it off. You know if you stop second-guessing yourself, you'll be just fine."

"What do you mean?" I asked as we crossed the quiet street.

"I've watched you," she admitted. "You have killer instincts, but in some games, you...Oh, I don't know. I'm not an analyst, but it looks like you almost stop yourself mid-motion and do something else."

I glanced down at her and thought back through the last few games. "I don't trust myself," I admitted. "I get out there under the lights, and I'm facing down these legends that I've always worshipped, and I start to second-guess everything."

"Hmmm," she said with a nod. "You have imposter syndrome."

"Excuse me?" I questioned, beating my doorman to the door and holding it open so Echo could walk inside.

"Imposter syndrome," she repeated as she took in the marble expanse of the lobby.

I punched the button for the elevator, and it dinged immediately. Guess there weren't too many people hanging around at two a.m. "Explain," I said after I selected our floor and the doors closed behind us.

"It's when you feel like you're an imposter," she explained as we rose, the lights highlighting the floor numbers as we climbed. "You know, like you don't think you belong in the NHL."

The elevator dinged and we stepped out. "That's because I don't," I said softly as we passed by two doors toward mine at the end of the hall.

A twist of the key later, we were in my apartment—well,

Langley's—and I kicked off my shoes as the door shut behind us. Echo hung her jacket on the hooks by the door.

"For fuck's sake, this place is gorgeous," Echo muttered as she walked through the modern, minimalist living room to look out the window. "And she gave it up for Suburbia?"

I laughed as she turned and then pointed to the brochures and floorplans scattered on the coffee table. "I will be, too. A house is part of my signing bonus. I just haven't decided which one."

Her mouth dropped. "Your life is weird."

"I know. Trust me."

"You do belong in the NHL," she told me as she bent to unzip her boots. She lost about five inches as she stepped out of them and groaned when her bare feet touched the soft rug.

"Only by default," I told her, crossing to the kitchen. "Water?"

"Sure," she answered, following me. "Not by default. It's not like you were the last goalie on the planet, so they got stuck with you."

I handed her a bottle of water from the fridge and twisted the top off mine. "It's exactly like that. I didn't make a team straight out of college. I wasn't good enough. And while I'm a damn good college goalie, and better than the other guys they tried out, I'm still not up there with the Eric Gentrys of the world."

"Who?" she questioned, then drank.

"Eric Gentry? Faith's brother, and one of the best goalies in the league," I explained. He was the only reason I was in any sort of shape when Coach McPherson called.

"Oh, *Eric*! I don't believe I ever knew his last name, and they always call him Iron Man anyway," she said. "And I bet *he* doesn't second-guess himself." She shrugged like it was the easiest thing in the world.

"He has no reason to." I put my water on the counter and rubbed the skin between my eyebrows. Fuck, I was tired.

"I think I need to tuck you in."

"I'm not five."

"Trust me, I've noticed."

My gaze jerked to hers. She lifted the corner of her mouth in a smirk and looked me over.

The electric tension between us flared, and my pulse picked up. That kiss had been the best and worst thing I could have ever possibly done. The best because she tasted like the sweetest sin, and the worst because I knew it wasn't going to happen again.

I wasn't her type. We had zero time for each other. We were opposites in just about every way. There were some things in the world that even killer chemistry like ours couldn't overcome.

"Come on," she said, her tone dropping as she held out her hand. "I'm not going to jeopardize your virtue, West Coast, I promise. Those bruises under your eyes are physically painful to look at. You need to sleep." She looked over her shoulder, spotting the lone open door that led to the bedroom.

"I need to walk you back to your car," I argued even as my body moved toward hers.

"No need. I didn't drive to work. I'll grab a Lyft. Don't look at me like that. Your fancy-schmancy doorman isn't going to let anything happen to me." She wiggled her fingers until I took them in mine.

I wasn't sure if it was the smile she gave me, or the simple pressure of her fingers against mine, but exhaustion was instantly the last thing on my mind.

"You can't tuck me in," I said slowly as she tugged on my hand to follow her.

"Why not?" she asked, backing away from me with a glint in her eyes.

"Because if I get you anywhere near a bed, I'm not sure I'll let you leave it," I admitted, even as my feet moved, following her lead.

"Feeling that confident in your skills, are you?" she asked, continually moving backward.

"I remember exactly what you taste like, Echo."

She paused, her lips parting. "I said I'm tucking you in. I didn't say anything about fucking you." She lifted an eyebrow in an obvious effort to stay unaffected, but she ended with a swipe of her tongue over her lower lip.

"I didn't say I was fucking you," I answered, my eyes dropping to the rise and fall of her breasts. "But I know if I get you in that bed—hell, near that bed, I'm going to kiss you, and it would be a shame to end this night with you slapping me."

"It's not like you haven't kissed me before." She took another step, almost reaching the threshold.

"Trust me, I know," I challenged her with her own words. "But that was on a dare, and this isn't. It's on me if I kiss you again." Fuck, just thinking about it had my dick hardening.

She switched directions, stepping forward. Then she rose on her toes and kissed me softly, her lips lingering on mine just long enough to taste her.

Fuck, I wanted this woman.

"There," she whispered. "Now I've kissed you, and that's on me, not some stupid dare."

"Echo," I warned. I wasn't against one-night stands, but the problem was that I didn't *want* her to be a one-night stand.

"If you don't trust yourself, then trust me. Come on, Sawyer. You've run yourself ragged taking care of everyone else. Let me take care of you." She tugged, and I followed.

The bedroom was lit by the single bedside lamp I'd left on, casting a warm glow over the dark furnishings. Echo took it all in with a quick glance, then stopped to linger on the king-sized bed that took up the majority of the room.

"Sit," she ordered, pointing to the nearest side of the bed.

I did.

She dropped in front of me and pulled off my socks. The strange intimacy of the act caught me off guard. I couldn't remember the last time a woman had done that. If someone was undressing me, they were usually after my cock, not my feet.

She rose, and ran her fingers through my hair, watching me with an intensity that stole the oxygen from my lungs. Then she reached for the hem of my Henley and tugged.

I lifted my arms as the fabric slid over my chest, then left me bare from the belt up as the shirt hit the floor next to her.

"Whoa." She sighed in appreciation, her fingers trailing from my neck to my pecs, and down the lines of my abdominals. "You are..." She shook her head, then tugged her lip between her bottom teeth.

A smile lifted my lips. "It's part of my job to stay in shape."

"Yeah, well, good job," she muttered.

I gripped her waist and tugged her between my spread thighs. "What are we doing, Echo?"

"Whatever we want," she answered. Then she straddled me, her knees on either side of my hips. I sent one hand to the nape of her neck and kept her waist secure with the other.

Her lips crashed into mine.

She tasted like cherries again, and I groaned at the realization that she really did feel as good as I remembered.

I gave her control for as long as I could stand it—which was probably about thirty seconds. Then I parted her lips with mine and took over, thrusting my tongue against hers and claiming her mouth.

She whimpered and rocked forward, bringing us so close only fabric separated our bodies. She met me kiss for kiss, her hands tangling in my hair, her mouth slanting with mine over and over again.

Our breaths grew ragged, and even though I told myself I wouldn't take this all the way tonight, I knew kisses wouldn't satisfy either of us. I'd grown too hungry for her in the weeks we'd been apart.

I spun, flipping Echo to her back in the middle of the bed.

Our kiss broke long enough for her to gasp, and then we were right back at it as I settled between her thighs. The kiss turned carnal as her leg wrapped around my hip, my tongue thrusting against hers in the same rhythm my cock pulsed behind the fly of my jeans.

Then I moved down her neck, licking and sucking the same places she'd loved the last time as I made my way to the neckline of her leather vest.

Her hand reached between us and pulled at the zipper, clearly down with the way we were headed. Her breasts appeared as the vest fell away, perfect mounds encased in soft blue lace that seemed completely at odds with her choice of outerwear.

This woman was an enigma. Every time I thought I had her figured out, she showed me that I wasn't even close.

She shrugged out of her vest, and it landed somewhere. I didn't care as long as it wasn't covering her up.

"Damn." I cupped her breasts in my hands and ran my thumb over the pert nipples already pushing at the lace of her bra. "You have incredible breasts."

She gripped the back of my head and tugged my mouth to her nipple in answer. I obliged, using my tongue and teeth to torture her flesh through the lace, and when her fingers tightened in frustration, I rid her of the bra and worshipped her bare skin.

Then I followed the cherry blossom side piece she had inked down her right side, pausing to kiss each blossom on my path down her body. She hissed when I reached the top of her hip, and I played again at the spot until she writhed under me.

"God, that mouth," she groaned, running her thumb over my lips. I nipped the flesh, then sucked it inside my mouth to ease the sting.

"You haven't even felt my mouth yet," I told her in quiet promise, then kissed the line of smooth skin just above the fabric of her skirt as my hand swept up her thigh.

"I'm..." She swallowed when my hands reached the top of her leggings. "I'm supposed to be tucking you in and taking care of *you*."

"Trust me, you are." My eyes locked with hers as I gripped the fabric and slowly started to remove them. She nodded as the leggings slid over the curve of her ass, and my mouth watered as each inch of her skin was revealed.

Once her leggings joined the growing pile of clothes on the floor, she surprised me by pushing me to my back and then stripping off my jeans. I bucked when she traced my length with her fingertips, my boxer briefs barely containing my erection.

"Fuck, Echo," I groaned as she gripped me in her hand. Pleasure, sharp and raw, clawed through me, tightening my balls and pooling at the base of my spine.

"Not tonight," she answered with a grin. "But this?" she whispered as she slipped two fingers beneath my waistband. "This, I have to have." I arched my hips, and my boxer briefs hit the floor, leaving me naked.

Her stare more than heated my skin as she looked me over. Then she closed her hand over me, her fingers not quite meeting around my shaft as she pumped me lightly once. Twice.

I sat up before I lost all semblance of control and brought her mouth to mine, kissing her deep and hard. Her breasts rubbed against my chest with a maddening friction, and my hands reached for the zipper at her waist. Then the only thing between us was a soaked scrap of lace that served as her underwear.

"God, you're wet." I swept my fingers over the lace and her hips rocked, following the motion.

"I want you," she admitted as I rolled her over and settled between her soft thighs. My muscles locked as I fought the instinct to sweep her thong aside and plunge into her so I could stroke us both to completion.

At least I could get one of us there tonight.

I kissed her as my fingers slipped beneath the lace to find the sweetest, softest flesh I'd ever felt in my life.

She arched when my fingers found the swollen bud of her clit. Fuck, she was drenched with need, already slippery and ready. My cock throbbed against her thigh, and I cursed when she reached for me again, swiping her thumb over my head before she stroked me.

"Echo," I warned, losing myself in those desire-hazed turquoise eyes.

"Sawyer," she challenged with a smile and did it again.

I slipped one finger inside her, and that smile transformed to an O as she cried out under me. I worked her clit as I moved my finger slowly inside her, savoring the clench of her muscles around me as she rocked against me.

Then she cried out and pushed at my shoulders.

"Echo?" I immediately rolled to the side, my eyes flying to hers with worry as my hand fell away from her. Fuck, had I pushed her too far, too fast?

"You're making this impossible," she chided, pointing a trembling finger at me.

"I'm what?" I questioned, a laugh rising in my chest.

"Impossible," she muttered, urging me to my back.

The would-be laugh transformed to a groan when her lips closed over my cock.

"Holy shit," I hissed, my fingers sinking into her hair as she took me deep, sliding over me with a nimble tongue that swirled as I was engulfed by the heat of her mouth. She rose and dipped, adjusting to my size as she took me into her mouth again and again.

It was like being encased in a silk and velvet volcano—impossibly hot, and when she hollowed out her cheeks and sucked at me with each withdrawal, I had to fight the urge to come.

"Echo, you…" Fuck, she only sucked harder. "God!" I hissed. She had me so tightly strung that I knew it was only a matter of minutes.

If she didn't stop, I was going to come, and I hadn't come first since I was a fucking teenager.

I abandoned the silk of her hair and gripped her hips, swinging her with enough strength that she had no choice but to move until I had her knees on either side of my head. The sight of her drenched pussy above me was enough to send me right to the edge, but I held back.

"Sawyer?" she asked, releasing my cock just long enough for me to get a tenuous grip on my control.

"I told you what I would do to you if I had you naked." I tugged her panties to the side with my fingers and then brought her pussy to my mouth. She was sweeter than wine. More decadent than bourbon. Headier than tequila.

This time my name was a cry on her lips.

I licked and sucked at her clit as she moaned above me, rocking gently as I worked her over. Her thighs trembled as I pressed my tongue against her clit, rubbing hard where she needed the pressure only to back off and leave her keening.

She took me back into her mouth with a moan that vibrated up my fucking spine until I was certain I'd see stars in a few minutes.

The pleasure of being in her mouth, and having her heat in mine, was almost too much. My orgasm was building, spiraling with tension, and I ate at her, voraciously determined that she beat me across the finish line.

I moved my thumb to stroke at her clit as I thrust inside her pussy with my tongue, stabbing into her over and over, until her muscles clamped and she released my cock with a loud cry.

Her muscles tensed, then locked around my head as I drove her higher, fucking her in the only way I'd let myself tonight. Fuck, I loved this. I was never going to get enough of her taste, her cries, the sweet tremble of her thighs.

"Sawyer!" she screamed as she came around me, her nails biting into my thighs.

Hell yes. Pure, primal, male satisfaction swept through me as I tongued her down from her high, stroking her until the shudders subsided and the aftershocks mellowed.

Then she sucked me deep, the flat of her tongue stroking my cock as her fist worked what she couldn't take.

My back arched at the sheer pleasure of her mouth as she pumped and sucked until I felt the impending orgasm rise uncontrollably.

"Echo," I groaned my warning.

She didn't let up.

"Baby, I'm going to come," I tried again.

She took me even deeper, and when she lightly ran her nails across my balls, I lost it. I came hard, my vision tunneling as release took me over the edge.

My body shuddered as she took everything I had to give, gently swirling her tongue around me as I came back down.

I swung her hips around again, this time catching her torso and pulling her up against me. "Holy shit," I groaned against her temple as she settled against my chest.

"My thoughts exactly," she mumbled.

"Now what?" I asked, exhaustion beating down through the bliss. This couldn't be the only time I got my hands on her. This could only be the start.

"Now sleep," she instructed with a jaw-cracking yawn.

I moved us under the covers and turned out the light, then tucked her nearly-naked body against mine. My lips brushed over the shell of her ear in a soft kiss as we both drifted off.

I woke some time later. The clock read a little after four a.m.

She was already gone.

ECHO

"What do you recommend that's fried?" Sawyer asked, sinking onto the barstool in front of me.

"Long time no see," I said, my skin instantly flushed with the sight of him.

The last time he'd walked into this bar I'd taken him home, and he'd made me tremble around his mouth. Fuck, this man was a walking addiction. I saw him, and all I wanted was another hit. And the taste of him? The pleasure I took in having *all* of him in my mouth? It was the sweetest kind of desire I'd ever experienced. And I was nowhere *near* satisfied.

"Been busy," he said, a tease to his tone. "Haven't you been watching?"

"I have," I said, nodding. "And I know playoffs are coming up. How about I grab you the turkey club instead?"

"That's no more healthy than the fried fish."

"Maybe. But it's lighter. Won't sit on you as heavy. And you'll be less likely to throw it up during morning skate tomorrow."

He sighed, his head dropping into his hands. "Fine, woman. I'll take the sandwich."

I smirked and raked my fingers through his hair. He sighed with the contact, those tense muscles loosening a fraction. "Take it easy, West Coast. You're so wound up you look like you may pop." I hurried to the back, quickly throwing together the sandwich and filling the basket with celery sticks instead of fries. I had it and a seltzer water in front of him before he could even think about ordering a drink.

"Thank you," he said and dug in.

"Tough week."

"Are you asking or telling," he said after swallowing a bite.

"Both?"

"Business been tough?" he asked.

"Nah, it's golden here. Especially with playoffs coming up."

He flinched slightly, and it was the motion that made me notice the worry in his eyes. He wasn't just simply stressed, he was consumed by it.

"You okay in there?" I asked, boldly smoothing my finger over the furrow in his brow.

He closed his eyes for a moment, setting down his half-eaten sandwich.

"I don't know." The answer was a whisper that squeezed my chest.

"We went through this last time," I said, leaning my elbows on the bar. "You *are* okay, Sawyer McCoy."

He cocked an eyebrow at me. "You say that like it will change things."

I smirked. "I'm pretty powerful and usually get my way."

"Is that right?"

There.

There was that playful fire in his eyes.

"Yup," I said, leaning back to wipe down the rest of the bar. "So, you're perfect. And that sandwich will turn things around for the rest of your day."

"There are other things I'd rather be eating," he said, and those flames dancing in his eyes told me he wasn't talking about the food.

A zing of electricity stormed down the center of me as I gaped at him. The man continued to shock me with that mouth of his.

He chuckled at my stunned look but ate in contented silence. I tried and failed three times to come up with something equally as clever to say back to him, but every time I opened my mouth, only an invitation was on the tip of my tongue. To my bed. To my heart. I didn't know.

All I knew was that if I spoke, I'd say the wrong fucking thing for us both. So I kept my mouth shut and settled on not hiding the heat in my eyes every single time our gazes locked.

When he rose to stand, I was practically panting from the tension vibrating between us. He slid the empty basket toward me. "Thanks for the pick-me-up, Echo," he said. "Practice. Will I see you soon?"

I wet my lips, hating that I couldn't *wait* to see him in a non-work environment.

"We'll see when you can squeeze me in, hockey star."

He winked at me before sauntering through the exit.

At least he'd walked out with more bravado than he'd walked in with.

* * *

ECHO: Did you know that studies show that some cats are actually allergic to humans?

Sawyer: Please don't tell me you're a crazy cat lady like Langley.

Echo: She only has two cats! How does that constitute the crazy cat lady title?

Sawyer: I'm a dog person. Owning any number of cats constitutes the title.

I rolled to my stomach on my bed, laughing as I shook my head. It had been a long shift tonight with a huge rush, but I hadn't been able to even *think* about sleeping without at least texting Sawyer.

Echo: What kind of dog?

Sawyer: I'm kind of a lover of all dogs, but if I ever own one, it'll be a Golden Retriever.

Echo: Of course it will.

Sawyer: Why do you say it like that?

Echo: Golden dog for a golden boy.

Sawyer: Boy? Could a boy make you scream like I did the other night?

My toes curled under my sheets, and my fingers shook as I typed out another text.

Echo: I don't know. It's been so long I can hardly remember.

Sawyer: Is that right?

Me: That's right. Goodnight, West Coast.

Sawyer: I don't believe you. You'll be dreaming of my hands on you tonight, Echo.

I bit my bottom lip, shaking my head. This man. He was absolutely infuriating in the best possible way.

Echo: I'll let you know.

I rolled onto my back, tossing my cell to the side.

Goddamn him.

I was flushed, frustrated, and knew there was nothing in this world that would satisfy that urge between my thighs other than Sawyer fucking McCoy.

We'd long since crossed the danger line between friends and fuck buddies, and it was high time we put *fucking* in the title.

Though, I couldn't deny I reveled in this slow burn, this intoxicating back and forth.

But I didn't know how much longer I could wait for him to make his intentions known, because the last thing I wanted was a relationship, and it was the last thing he needed, too.

* * *

Echo: You looked tense today in your interview.

Sawyer: Thanks for pointing that out.

Echo: You know what studies show is the best for built-up tension?

Sawyer: What is that?

I sucked in a sharp breath. It'd been too many days since Sawyer's lips were last on mine and I was done playing the waiting game. I'd always been one to go after what I wanted, and there was nothing more than I wanted than Sawyer between my thighs.

Echo: No strings attached sex.

Two full minutes went by and not even the bouncing balls on the screen to show he was typing.

Maybe I'd scared him off. Maybe he didn't do no-strings-attached intimacy. Maybe he was busy with a bunny.

I cringed at the last thought and told myself it shouldn't matter if he *was*. He wasn't mine. I had no claim on him. The last thing either of us needed was a relationship, but...if he *did* accept my offer then I'd have to make the rules very clear.

1) Don't fall in love
2) Don't sleep with other people

That's it. Two very easy-to-follow rules. Because while I enjoyed sex and no strings, I didn't enjoy sharing.

Sawyer: Where'd you read that one?

I hurried to respond.

Echo: I didn't have to read it anywhere. I know it for a fact.

Sawyer: You're full of interesting facts.

Echo: That's it? That's all you have to say?

Sawyer: Good joke? Is that better?

I rolled my eyes and tossed my cell under the bar as a few new customers strolled through the doors. I hurried to fill their orders before checking my cell again.

Nothing.

Well, if Sawyer thought I was joking, I guess I'd just have to show him how *not* joking I was.

9

SAWYER

I loosened my tie as I dug a bottle of water out of the refrigerator.

"I'm so glad you're having a good time," I told Mom as I balanced the phone on my shoulder.

"It's so nice being with them again," she said, her voice lighter than I'd heard in a while. "Weird to be in this little town again, but I'm sure that's just because it's been so long since I've been home."

Guilt crashed through me, stealing a little of my post-win high. "I should have taken you home more often." I shut the fridge and twisted the top on the bottle.

"Sawyer McCoy, stop that. It wasn't your job to haul me all over the country at my whim. You had more than enough to handle in college. I really wish you would let some of this weight go."

"You're not weight," I argued.

"That's not what I'm saying. You are the best son I could have ever asked for, but I can't help but feel like I've done you a disservice. You have a life to lead, Sawyer, and believe it or not, I still have one, too."

I leaned back against the counter and raised the water bottle to my forehead, letting the cold seep into my skin. "I know you do. I just want to make sure you have everything you need. You've always taken care of me, and I'm just trying to do the same for you." But it was hard lately. I was only home a few days at a time, and I hated that I didn't get to see her as often as I did when we were in Seattle.

"I have everything I need," she said softly. "Now you need to make sure you have the same."

Echo's face popped into my mind. I knew she was someone I wanted but was she someone I needed? It had been so long since I'd had the space to even think about wants versus needs that I just didn't know anymore.

"Oh, we're leaving for Nancy's granddaughter's recital. I'll be home in a few days. I love you, Sawyer. Go try to relax. Enjoy the wins!"

"Love you, too, Mom." I hung up the phone and cursed my father for the millionth time in my life. If he'd been half of a man, her life would have been a hell of a lot easier.

The doorbell rang.

I discarded my jacket on the way, leaving it thrown haphazardly over the back of the sofa. Hopefully it wasn't the guys. It was only eight o'clock, and they'd said we all needed to go out and celebrate the way we'd just swept the Toronto series, but I wasn't in the mood for a crowd.

I opened the door and instantly smiled when I saw Echo standing there, holding a large bottle of Gatorade.

"I thought maybe you felt like celebrating," she said with a playful grin, wiggling the bottle.

"With you? Any time." I stood aside, and she walked in, heading straight for the kitchen. God, I'd missed her. We were texting daily—hell it was the reason I kept my phone on me—but I hadn't seen her in a week, and it had been almost three since she'd been in my apartment last.

Three weeks since I'd had my mouth on her and I swore I could still taste her on my tongue. Which was why I was pretty much in a semi-permanent state of arousal. Well, that and her smartass comment about sex with no strings.

Not that I was against no-strings sex. Hell, it might be the only thing I had time for. But I also liked...her, and the strings didn't seem so bad if they were attached to Echo. As much as I hated the definition talk, we were going to have to have it.

I followed her and leaned on the island as she grabbed two wine glasses from the cabinet. "Looks like I got here in time to see you in your post-game gear," she said over her shoulder as she poured the Gatorade into the glasses.

"Yeah, I've only been home about twenty minutes." I chuckled, looking down at my dress shirt, tie, and slacks. Coach demanded we dress to fly to and from games, and while he didn't care what we looked like on the plane itself, it was suits to and from the airport every time. "How did you know I was home? Not that I'm complaining if you've decided to full-on stalk me."

She arched an eyebrow at me as she turned with our glasses, and set one down in front of me. "Langley called, and then I saw your light on from the bar." She nodded toward the window. "I was done with my shift, so I took a chance."

"I'm glad you did."

"Me, too."

I downed the glass of Gatorade and set it back on the counter.

"Easy there, killer," she teased with a grin. "I'd hate to see you get Gatorade-wasted."

"Very funny—what the hell are you wearing?" My mouth dropped at her sweatshirt, which was cut with a ragged neckline that hung off one shoulder, revealing a bright purple bra-strap and a considerable amount of kissable, inked skin. But it wasn't the cut that had me shocked, it was the content.

"What?" she asked, backing up and pulling out the maroon athletic wear to look at the graphic that read *Respect the Cock*. "You're not a cock fan?" she challenged.

Speechless. I was completely speechless.

"South Carolina Gamecocks," she finally said with an outright laugh. "See?" She pointed to the rooster that adorned the sleeve. "It's my alma mater."

I shook my head as she rounded the island, and I couldn't stop myself from grabbing her waist and tugging her against me. "Gamecocks, huh?"

She looped her arms around my neck, and it hit me that she wasn't dressed up in her usual in-your-face style. She was wearing leggings and a sweatshirt, and her hair was swept up into some kind of knot on the top of her head. She looked like I imagined she would at home, comfortable, and all the sexier for it.

"Yep. I usually joke that I only have a degree in mixology, but that's because most people who sit at my bar aren't really looking for me to talk about myself. It's an easy way to deflect the conversation to whatever's bothering them."

I wondered how often she did that—deflected from what was going on with her in order to comfort someone else. Was it because she naturally liked people, or because she didn't want anyone seeing her scars?

"So what is your degree in?" I asked.

"Business," she answered with a shrug.

"Way more useful than exercise science."

She leaned up and brushed her mouth against mine. "But it's given you quite the body."

"Eh, I'd have to say that's more hockey, less books." I kissed her softly, careful to keep myself in check. Damn, she felt good against me.

"Whatever it is, it's working for you," she said with a smile against my lips. Then she ran her tongue over my lower lip, and I forgot all my good intentions about talking about...anything.

In a matter of seconds, I had her ass on the kitchen counter, her thighs wrapped around me, the bare skin of her waist under my fingers, and my tongue in her mouth. Our kiss wasn't pretty or delicate. It was open and hot, with nips of teeth and rubbing tongues. It was just the tip of the iceberg when it came to what I wanted to do to her, and damn if she didn't give it back just as fiercely.

What the fuck was it about this woman that drew me in like two magnets colliding?

Wait. We were supposed to talk. Right?

"Hold up." I pulled back, my breath already ragged. She was in the same state. "We need to do the talking thing."

"Later," she said, gripping my tie and pulling me back to her mouth.

I fell into the kiss, barely noticing when both my tie and my shirt hit the floor. She could do whatever she wanted to me as long as I was the only one she was doing it to.

Shit. Wait.

I broke the kiss and stepped back, putting a few feet between us.

"Sawyer?" she asked, leaning her weight back on her palms. Her lips were swollen from my kiss, her cheeks flushed, and her thighs parted, waiting for me to come back.

"Talk. We have to talk," I repeated, more to remind myself why I wasn't currently stripping her naked.

"Nope, we don't." She shook her head, losing a few strands of her purple hair from the top knot. "That's part of the whole no-strings-attached sex." Her gaze swept down my body, and I gripped the kitchen counter to stay right where I was.

"You were serious about that?"

"Hell yes, I was." She nodded just in case the words hadn't been enough.

"No relationship...no…" I shook my head, at a loss for words.

"That's the idea. Just you, me, and a lot of hot, sweaty sex that leaves us both satisfied." She hopped down from the counter and kicked her shoes off.

My cock agreed to everything she was saying, and made that fact painfully obvious.

"Come on," she said, running her hands up my bare chest. "Like you haven't had sex outside of a relationship before."

"Yeah, but not with someone I *liked*," I argued.

Her lips lifted. "You like me."

"I just said that."

She leaned forward and kissed the skin right above my heart, sending a jolt of pleasure through me. "So then what's the problem?" She started kissing her way down my chest, and I nearly forgot what I could possibly have a problem with.

I had a beautiful, funny, awesome woman offering me her body with zero attachment issues, and I was questioning this why?

"I don't want to fuck up our friendship," I blurted as I remembered. "I like being around you. We're always at Scythe. I don't want any of that to change."

She looked up at me as she kissed the line of my abs to where it disappeared in my slacks. "It doesn't have to change. We'll be friends who sleep together."

She went for my belt, and I gripped her under her arms and lifted her to her feet. "God, you're fucking distracting."

"That's the idea." She tilted her head, and a shadow passed over her eyes. "Unless you don't want me…"

"I fucking want you," I growled, pulling her against me so

she could feel just how badly I wanted her. "Feel that? It's only because of you. Trust me, right now it's taking every shred of self-control I have not to carry you to my room and fuck you so hard that you'll feel me with every step you take for the next month."

"I'm good with that plan," she replied with an impish smile. She crossed her arms at the hem of her sweatshirt and pulled it off in one smooth motion. It landed on the floor with my tongue.

"Damn it, you're beautiful."

"Don't sound so angry about it," she teased as she shimmied out of her leggings until she stood before me in just a matching bra and panty set.

God, her body was perfect. High, full breasts, a smooth, soft stomach that begged for my touch, supple thighs that topped the sexiest legs I'd ever seen. She was built for sex—to be worshipped by tongue and teeth. *My* tongue and teeth.

"Why would you agree to something like this?" I managed to ask, already mentally planning how I was about to get her off.

"Because I want you." She came close enough that I caught that vanilla scent she wore. "Because I think about you when I should be pouring a drink, or hanging out with my friends. Because I think I might actually catch fire if you don't touch me, but then you do, and I'm up in flames, anyway—even hotter than I thought possible."

"It's the same for me," I admitted, reaching for the soft slope of her waist. Her skin was as soft as satin and so very warm. "But I can never get enough of you, and our schedules are so fucked up that I lose track of what day it is."

"Exactly." She wound her arms around my neck. "That's why this is perfect. No expectations. We see each other when we can, or when we want to. No one gets hurt."

I swallowed as she lowered a hand to my buckle. When I

didn't stop her, she dropped the second hand and made quick work of dropping my pants. I kicked out of my shoes and removed my socks.

"When do you think this deal should start?" I asked.

"Right now," she answered, licking her lips when she saw exactly how hard I was. Boxer briefs weren't the best at keeping a guy contained.

Her eyes met mine and the sheer hunger I saw there nearly knocked me on my ass. My hands gripped her ass as I picked her up, and then her mouth was on mine, and that kiss we'd begun a few minutes earlier quickly spun out of control.

With her ankles locked behind my back, I carried her to my bedroom, never once breaking the kiss. I'd wanted this woman for the better part of two months, and now I was actually going to have her.

I laid her in the center of my bed and then settled between her soft thighs. Then I put my plan in motion, kissing every inch of exposed skin she had. I followed the pattern of her cherry tree tattoo with my tongue, and I kissed the swirls and dips of the lotus and lace pattern that ran down her shoulder.

She gasped and arched beneath me when I lingered on the area between her breasts, and a quick flick of my fingers later, her bra was on the floor.

"Fuck, I love these," I told her, taking the mounds into my hands and rolling her nipples. "Do you have any idea just how many times, how many ways I'm going to make you come?"

Her cry was sweet when I took one peak in my mouth.

"Wait!" she gasped.

I stilled.

"There are rules." Her chest rose and fell rapidly under my mouth, but I sat back on my knees and worked diligently to keep my eyes on hers and not her incredible body.

"For sex?" I asked. "I'll respect whatever limits you have."

She blinked. "Well, yeah, I already knew that or I wouldn't have offered you this kind of arrangement. And honestly, you can do whatever you want with me. I'll let you know if I'm not into it."

"Okay, then what rules?" My mind ran amok, thinking of all the ways I wanted to take her, but I kept myself grounded in the moment.

"No falling in love."

"Okay?" I would have grinned if she didn't look so serious. There was zero playfulness in those turquoise eyes. Since when was falling in love a bad thing? I'd only done it once or twice, but each relationship had taught me some much-needed lessons.

"I'm serious. We keep it casual. Falling in love only ends with one or both of us getting hurt, and I don't want that." Her lips flattened.

Holy shit, this girl wasn't just scarred, she was covering up some serious damage that hadn't healed. I didn't bother to argue that love wasn't something that could be controlled, nor did I point out that a lot of our friends were happily married. I simply nodded because that was what she needed.

"What else?" I asked, ignoring the way my cock throbbed for her.

"While we're doing this—" she motioned between us.

"While we're fucking?" I clarified. Her eyes flared, and her hands reached for me, but she snatched them back and gripped the comforter.

"Right." She arched an eyebrow. "While we're fucking, you don't fuck anyone else."

"Deal. Is that it?" I was already lowering myself to her breasts.

"Hold on." She wiggled back until her head reached the pillows and she ran out of room to retreat. "It's that easy? You're a big-time NHL star now. Are you telling me you're okay with turning down the puck bunnies from now on? It's not like I haven't seen firsthand how relentless those girls are at the bar."

I stalked her, climbing up the bed until I had her caged beneath me again. Then I feathered kisses down her jaw. "I haven't fucked any other woman since I got here in February," I told her between nips and caresses.

"But," she sighed, "but it's April. Are you telling me there hasn't been anyone else?"

"Exactly. I fucked my way through college, Echo. I'm not stupid enough to start that shit in the NHL. Besides, I seem to have developed a thing for smartass girls with purple hair, who literally couldn't give a shit if I'm a Reaper or not." I moved to her neck and her fingers tangled in my hair.

"Oh. God, that feels good."

"It's supposed to." I moved to her breasts and started on them again. The little gasps she gave as I sucked at her nipples had me even harder, if that was possible.

She squirmed under me, and I made my way down her belly until I had the straps of her thong in my hands, and I worked the fabric down her legs.

Finally, I had her naked.

"Fuck, you're gorgeous," I told her as I looked her over.

"You make me feel that way." She reached for me, and I covered her, hissing at the perfection of her skin against mine.

Our kiss was hotter and wetter than ever before, tinged with a crazed desperation that told me just how badly she wanted me.

My fingers dipped and found her wet and ready, and there was a loud groan. Hers or mine, I didn't know. I bit her lower lip gently as I stroked her from opening to clit, swirling around the swollen, needy flesh to wake up every nerve ending without actually stroking where she wanted me.

"Sawyer," she pled, rocking her hips against my hand.

I ran my finger around her clit. "You know it goes both ways, right?"

"What?" she asked, arching her hips.

"You only fuck me." I slipped the tip of my finger into her pussy. Her muscles clenched at me, but couldn't draw me in.

"What?" she asked again, clearly having forgotten what we were just talking about.

"You. Only. Fuck. Me." I punctuated my words with mini thrusts, only entering her far enough to stroke her sensitive flesh. "There's no one else." My eyes locked with hers, and she blinked in understanding as her nails dug into the skin of my biceps.

"Only you," she promised. "There's been no one else for...a while. I only want you."

My heart flipped, which I blatantly ignored.

Instead, I sank my finger fully inside her and kissed the cry from her lips as I worked her clit with my thumb. When she started keening, I added a second finger, pumping her hard and slow as she tensed beneath me. I kept my eyes locked on hers, refusing to miss this. Last time I hadn't seen her face, only felt her reactions.

My cock ached as her breaths came faster and her muscles locked.

"That's it," I encouraged her. "Fuck, you have no idea how beautiful you are like this, do you? All mine."

Her eyes widened, and she cried out my name as her orgasm took her, her body arching under mine in completion. I stroked her through that orgasm, and before she could come down completely, I rebuilt her pleasure, keeping her burning.

I left the silk of her body only to strip off the last of my clothes and grab a condom from the bedside table. I ripped the foil open and rolled it over my length as I settled back over her. She lifted her knees, and I almost came at the sight of her, slippery and swollen for me.

"Tell me you really want this," I ordered even as the head of my cock teased her entrance. Her hair had come undone, and I sank my fingers into it, making a fist in the silken strands. My other hand, I kept at her hip.

"I want this," she said, lifting her head to gently bite the lobe of my ear. "I want you."

God, this was such a bad idea. Agreeing not to fall in love with her when I was already crazy over her. Agreeing that we could keep the friendship and the sex and not develop strings.

But even knowing all that, I couldn't stop myself. I needed her too badly.

I sank into her kiss as I thrust slowly into her body, tunneling through her tight muscles with one long stroke until she'd taken all of me.

"Damn," I groaned against her mouth as her body clenched mine. "Echo, you feel so fucking perfect." She was tight and hot, wrapping around me like a fist.

"Move," she begged. "More." Her hips rolled against mine, and another moan escaped my lips.

Then I moved, reading her body and giving her exactly what kept her crying out for more. Harder. Deeper. We came together in a rhythm that usually took lovers months to find, our bodies recognizing its match in the other.

I took her over and over, plunging inside her heat and finding that each stroke was better than the last. The pleasure built between us until sweat beaded on my skin from holding back, from refusing to let this end. I was going to fuck this woman until we both died from it because there was no way I was ever leaving the perfection of her body. Screw the outside world. I was going to live right here with her moans in my ear and her pussy rippling around my cock.

Her hips lifted, and I felt her start to tense beneath me again.

"Sawyer," she begged, riding that edge.

"I've got you, baby," I promised, then slid my hand down her hip to lift her knee higher. Then I took her even deeper, grinding over her clit with every thrust.

That spiraling pleasure coiled within me, building at the base of my spine, each stroke bringing me closer to the moment I knew I couldn't hold back much longer.

Her muscles started to flutter around me, and her eyes flew wide as they met mine, the orgasm sweeping over her as she screamed out with pleasure. She locked down on my cock and pulled me right over with her. I came with a shout that might have been her name and rode out the mind-numbing pleasure from the hardest, longest orgasm I'd ever had.

I rolled us to the side so I didn't suffocate her, and kissed her forehead. "God, if we're that good at this the first time, how good are we going to be in a month?"

"Or two?" She kissed my chest as her breaths evened out. "Or maybe ten minutes?"

I laughed and tipped her chin so I could see her eyes. "Give me five."

"Deal," she agreed, a mischievous glint in her eyes.

By the time morning came, we'd gotten even better at it, and I knew I'd never get enough. I sneaked out of bed an hour before I was due on the ice for practice, and scribbled her a note that I left on the bedside table with a key to my apartment, asking her to either stay in that bed until I got back, or lock up when she left.

I walked out of the apartment knowing two things.

One, I wanted her in that bed when I got back.

Two, there were already strings, and I fucking liked them.

10

ECHO

I slammed the key down on the bar, right in front of where Annabelle Clarke sat with one leg crossed over the other. Her Gucci pumps made her curvy legs look ten times longer than they actually were and the Chanel skirt and blouse combo did everything but label her as Sweet Water's city clerk. Annabelle had been my best friend growing up, and while we'd remained close, distance had put a wedge between us after my father died—something I was constantly trying to remedy.

"He left me a *key*, Annabelle. A *key*."

Annabelle covered a sugary laugh with her hand, her fingers a polished pink.

"There is nothing, absolutely *nothing* humorous about a man giving me a key."

"Oh, come now, Echo, it is a tad funny." She tilted her head, her perfectly wavy brown hair falling over her shoulders. "Especially the way you're reacting to it."

I sucked in a deep breath, and I swore I could still smell Sawyer on my skin. Taste him on my lips. Feel him between my thighs. The man had sent me over the edge with just his fingers. Then he'd completely set me on fire when he'd slid that considerable length inside. God, he was like satin-covered steel, and he'd hit *every* spot my body had. He'd touched me like he'd been studying my body for years, not months. It'd been mind-blowing and terrifying and consuming and perfection all wrapped into one blissful explosion.

"Echo," Annabelle said when I'd done nothing but stare at that damn key for well over a minute. "You told me last week that you were fond of this guy."

I snapped my gaze to hers then darted my eyes around the bar like I was terrified of anyone knowing that fact. It wasn't like my regulars or our Reaper crew didn't see us together all the time, but last night had changed things, slightly. But that damn key was way over the line.

"That was before," I answered her, shaking my head. I leaned against the bar, pinching the bridge of my nose before looking at her again. "I *do* like him. We're friends."

She arched a neatly trimmed eyebrow at me. "Friends who have sleepovers?" she teased.

I couldn't help but smile at her overtly sweet suggestion. "He's a *good* friend," I said.

"How good?" she whispered the question, shifting on her barstool to draw closer to me.

"Good enough that I haven't called him to hand him his ass over this key."

Annabelle gasped, sitting up straight, her eyes shifting to that same glossed-over true-love look she always wore when we watched *The Little Mermaid* when we were kids.

"Don't look at me like that," I chided, stomping toward the bin of freshly cleaned glasses. "I don't do this. I don't do keys. I explained that. No strings. No relationship." I scooped up a tumbler and put it in its place behind the bar, then repeated the motion with the next.

"You did once before," she said, though her words were coated in acid.

I halted mid-placing a glass on the shelf. "Annabelle, you know I've apologized a hundred times for—"

She stopped me with the wave of her hand. "We're past that, honey," she said, folding one hand neatly over the other. "But you did. Once. You allowed yourself to fall for someone—"

"And look where that got me!" I cut her off, slamming the glass on the shelf a little harder than necessary. I took a breath. "Chad and I were together before Dad died," I said. "I loved him then, but after? I *used* him as much as he used me. Because he couldn't be what I needed when I lost the last of my family. And I know now that it meant he never truly loved me, just the idea of me. But…it doesn't matter. I got swept up in the numbness his world offered. I lost sight of everything."

I gave her a pointed look, knowing our friendship had suffered the biggest hit during that time in my life. Thankfully, we'd found some common ground again, but it wasn't the same. It wasn't easy like my friendship with Langley, Faith, and Harper. This friendship had been wounded, and it was still raw.

"And the minute I dragged myself away from that," I continued. "The minute I realized what that life was doing to me…" I sighed, my chest aching from the emotions storming it.

"You chased your dream," she finished for me and motioned to the bar.

"I tried to make amends," I said a bit softer as I finished unloading the bin and returned to lean in front of her.

Annabelle gripped my hand. "You've done everything right since then, Echo. Look at this place," she said, eyeing the bar again. "It's beautiful. It's everything you and your father ever talked about. And it's filled with regulars from the town you love. Filled with fans of the hockey team that is now such a huge part of your life. I've never seen you more *you* in all our lives."

I pressed my lips into a line, eyeing our joined hands. "I should frantically call you about boy trouble more often," I teased.

She laughed, releasing me. "Boy trouble? I believe Sawyer McCoy, star goalie for the Carolina Reapers is a far cry from Travis Buford."

I gaped at her. "That was the fifth grade!"

"He wasn't worth it, was he?" She tsked. "Fighting with poor Suzie May over him. You ripped her favorite blue sundress."

"She yanked out a chunk of my hair!"

Annabelle flashed me a look she'd mastered over our lifetime, the one that screamed *I should've known better.*

Story of my fucking life.

"Now," she said, eyeing me. "Is Sawyer McCoy worth all this fuss you're giving over this silly old key?" She nudged the key closer to me on the bar, and I recoiled like it was a hot poker.

Was Sawyer worth it? Worth letting someone in again?

I knew better than anyone that people never stay.

They die. They leave.

Even Annabelle left for a little while, not that I could blame her. I wasn't exactly the Echo she'd grown up with.

It'd taken hitting rock bottom, but I'd finally found myself comfortable in my own skin, and letting someone in? That had the power to rip all my progress to shreds.

Sure, I'd never gotten addicted to the drugs like Chad had, but I'd used them and alcohol and *him* to slake the pain. To numb the daily life I couldn't stand to wake up to—a world where my entire family, the three people I'd loved most in this world, were taken from me.

I'd thought I loved Chad that way.

Now I knew better.

Because he'd done nothing to save me from myself when I was drowning in grief and instead did everything to *keep* me there. Keep me dazed, keep me weak, keep me sedated enough where I couldn't *feel* the pain. Couldn't touch it enough to deal with it and work toward moving on. Work toward a better life. Work toward what I had now.

I sighed, raking my hands through my hair.

"What if he thinks after what happened last night, that I'm going to just jump up and be his beck and call girl? Like the bunnies I see here every other night? What if this key is to be used when he rolls back into town or after every home game and—" I stopped myself short. Shaking my head. "Or. *Or*, what if he gave it to me as an invitation. A silent way of saying he wants more than the no-strings-attached relationship we've agreed to."

Annabelle bit her glossed lip, tsking me once again. "Echo Hayes, I haven't seen you this torn up about a man since Dwight Pruitt."

I snapped my fingers. "Don't!" I laughed. "Don't you dare say a bad word about sweet Dwight."

She laughed so hard tears formed in the corners of her eyes. "You always stuck up for him in school, and he fell head over heels for Jessica Daniels. You cried for weeks."

"It was grade school," I said, reeling in my laughter. "And he and Jessica have been happily married for over a decade!"

"Still," she said, dabbing the corners of her eyes with a napkin. Her eyeliner nor mascara hadn't dared budge. "I've never seen you so worked up. Which leads me to believe you have actual *real* feelings for this man. More than whatever deal you've struck with him."

"I don't."

She tilted her head. "You're lying to yourself."

"What makes you say that?"

"Because, honey," she said. "If you didn't care?" She eyed the key on the bar between us. "You would've tossed that key in the garbage, had a laugh, and never spoken to the man again. Or, you would've chucked it at the man, then laughed, *then* never called. If you truly didn't want something more, you wouldn't be sitting here debating it with your oldest and dearest friend."

"Fuck I hate it when you make sense."

"Language!"

I snorted at that, shaking my head as I scooped the key off the bar. I twirled it between my fingers a couple of times as I chewed on my lip. I *had* contemplated leaving it with the doorman when I'd left this morning, but it was Langley's apartment after all, and it wouldn't hurt to have a key to the place. As long as it wasn't a key with strings.

Another sigh flew past my lips.

"I don't do this," I said again, my words a whisper.

"Darlin'," Annabelle said. "You can say that all you like and I'll respect it, but sometimes these things don't happen on your timeframe or your schedule. Sometimes life intervenes."

I narrowed my gaze at her. "Like fate?"

"No, I wouldn't dare utter such a thing as *fate* around the terrifying, doesn't-believe-in-love, Echo Hayes."

I smirked. "You think I'm terrifying?"

She held her thumb and forefinger close together. "Just a smidge. I'm just thankful you're on my side."

"Always," I said, the power in that word mending some broken connection between us. Even when I hadn't been there, I'd never *not* considered Annabelle my best friend.

"I have a grand idea," she said, clearing her throat as if something had tightened it. "Why don't you call the boy in question and ask him what in tarnation he meant by leaving you a key."

I chuckled again, the action releasing the final waves of tension coiling my body. "I'm glad you came," I said. "I needed this."

"Well," she said. "My morning was clear."

"I highly doubt that," I said. Being the city clerk of Sweet Water was a twenty-four-seven type of job. One I didn't envy her for, but she was damn good at it.

"I made it clear," she answered, and I grinned.

"Such a rebel," I said. "Clearing a schedule for a black sheep."

"Now, Echo, you know I'd never call you a black sheep."

"Of course not," I said. "You'd never be caught dead insulting anyone." I eyed her. "Unless you were Sandy Preston."

Annabelle practically hissed. "That tramp is one piece of memory lane I *don't* need to explore."

"I love it when your claws come out."

This time she was the one laughing.

And I joined her until the entrance door to the bar swung open, and one such dark piece of my memory lane strolled through it.

"Ugh," I groaned, pocketing the key, and hurrying around the bar. "You can't keep showing up like this, Chad." I stopped him before he could make it too far inside the bar.

"What?" He gazed down at me, his eyes cloudy. "This is a bar, Echo. I'm allowed to come get a drink."

"Not while I'm here," I said, my voice firm. I sucked in a deep breath, trying like hell to calm my nerves. The last time he and his friends had shown up I'd been cordial because he'd promised he was clean, but after spending more time with Sawyer, I knew I didn't want any connection to my old life. To the person I used to be.

"That's hardly fair," he said, his hands on my shoulders.

"Oh, God," I said, my nose wrinkling. "You reek of it," I said in a hushed tone. That cloying metallic scent of chemicals. "Clean, huh?"

"This is an old jacket!" he snapped. "I'm clean, I swear."

I shook my head. "It doesn't matter, Chad. I've tried to help you in the past, and you've never cared. I'm telling you now, leave this place." I spun on my heels, knowing better than to stand there and argue while I was working.

My cell vibrated in my pocket as I rounded the bar and I fished it out, winking at Annabelle as she glared daggers at Chad.

"Sawyer?" I answered, my mind reeling with blinding panic. Visions of car wrecks or bad injuries on the ice filled my brain.

"Whoa," he said. "Are you okay? You sound panicked."

"You always text me!" I didn't mean to snap, but I couldn't get my racing heart to calm.

"Well, I had time for a call. Is this a bad time?"

"You're okay?" I breathed a little easier.

"Yeah, I'm okay. I didn't mean to scare you."

I clenched my eyes shut. I was fucking losing it. This is why I never got attached to anyone. Every phone call became a trigger for the worst.

"I'm sorry. It's me. I just…anyway, what's up?"

"Honestly?"

"Always, Sawyer."

"I hadn't received a random fact text, and we're going to take ice in an hour. Wanted to make sure you hadn't disappeared on me."

I bit back my smile. "Not yet," I teased.

"Good. I was worried last night might've—"

"Come on, Echo, you know you missed me," Chad practically yelled, hanging over the bar. "Least you can do is get me a drink."

"Who was that?" Sawyer's voice had gone cold.

"No one," I said. "I'll call you after the game. Cover that net, West Coast." I quickly hung up, pocketing my cell before I calmly set my hands on the bar, eyes locked on Chad's. "I have the right to refuse service to anyone," I said, my tone lethal. "And you, Chad, have used up your charity quota with me. I'm done trying. Done paying for my past by trying to help you. You don't want my help. You want the drama that comes from hurting me. And I'm done. Leave."

He blinked a few times, his brow furrowing at my words. "Who are you?" He pushed off the bar, shaking his head.

"Echo Hayes. I don't believe we've ever truly met." I arched a brow at him and jerked my head toward the exit.

He scoffed, then swung through the door like he was trying to bust it.

Luckily for him, he didn't. Because if he'd damaged one thing in this bar I would've used the scythe on him.

"Well," Annabelle said after a few breaths. "*That* was entertaining."

I shook out my fingers which were trembling from the adrenaline it took to stand up to Chad, to stand up to my past and put it to bed. I felt lighter than I had in years.

"So," Annabelle said. "Are you going to call him back and talk to him about that key burning in your pocket?"

I parted my lips, then shut them. A surprised laugh escaped my lips as I realized I hadn't even thought about the key when Sawyer called. I couldn't see past the fear of him possibly being hurt. Though, now that I was thinking clearly, I suppose Axel would be the one to call me if he was injured, or Langley or Faith or Harper or anyone else other than Sawyer himself.

"Yes," I said, resolved. "I will call him after the game and discuss the seriousness of the situation." I held my serious face for about two seconds before we both descended into laughter.

* * *

AFTER A SECOND RUSH due to the Reapers' game my muscles were aching. Hopping from bar to tables to kitchen to bar again was an all-night affair, and I definitely had a bubble bath with my name on it.

I peeled my clothes off, tossing them into the hamper as my old claw-foot tub—my absolute favorite thing about my home—filled to the brim with steaming hot water and more bubbles than was likely necessary. I walked naked to my kitchen as the bath finished filling, pouring myself a hearty glass of red wine—my go-to relax drink.

I set it on the small wooden table next to the tub, along with my phone after I'd hit play on my favorite wind-down list. Nights like tonight left my skin vibrating with a buzzing hum as if all the energy from the bar patrons had transferred to me personally. I was beyond exhausted, but there was no way I could crash into bed yet. Not without coming down first.

The steaming water slid around my skin like a glove, the bubble's light and fresh scent surrounded me as I sank up to my neck. I leaned my head back on the edge of the tub, my hair piled high in a messy knot on my head.

A sweet sigh escaped my lips as the water did everything to help my tight muscles unwind. My playlist was shuffling to a Steeldrivers song when the words suddenly cut off, taken over by an incessant buzzing.

I dried off one hand on the towel hanging from the table and slid the bar on my screen to see the text.

Sawyer: Back at hotel now.

My eyes widened a bit, and I resisted the urge to facepalm myself. It had been an insanely busy night and I totally forgot I'd told Sawyer I'd call him after the game. Though, to be fair, I'd planned on doing it when I hit the bed, assuming he'd be out celebrating after the game.

I lifted my other hand to text back but didn't have the energy to dry it off so I hit the call button instead and brought the cell to my ear.

"Thought you preferred texting," Sawyer said by way of answer.

I tried to contain my smile at the sound of his voice. "Well, I'm soaking in the tub, so I only have one free hand."

"Is that right?" His voice went from bemused to husky in the span of a breath.

"Yes," I said, sighing as I stretched in the water a bit.

"Long night?"

"Not as long as yours," I said.

"Detroit put up a hell of a fight."

"Not as much as you," I said, my eyelids closing. "You were incredible."

"You can't say things like that when you're naked and wet."

My eyes popped open at the growl in his tone. "Excuse me? Mr. McCoy I'm allowed to say *anything* I want," I teased.

"Of course you are, Ms. Hayes," he said, trying his best to adapt my natural southern drawl. It was adorable. "But do so knowing that I'm in physical pain."

"Poor baby hockey star," I said. "Such a hard life."

"Some parts are definitely hard."

I froze a little at that declaration, a heat churning between my thighs that had nothing to do with the water.

"Is that right?" I mimicked him.

"That's right."

"Did you tell me you had a roommate on away games?"

"I did."

"Who is it?"

"Cannon," Sawyer said. "But he's out for the night."

"You're sure?"

"He always is. Never gets back until a couple of hours before we have to be on the bus."

"That's lucky."

"Why?"

"Where are you at, Sawyer?"

"I'm in Detroit. You know that."

"No, Sawyer. Where are you at *right* this moment?"

A shuffling happened in the background, and I could almost picture him sinking onto his bed.

"Laying down."

"Are the lights on?"

"No, why?"

"Turn them on."

"You're very demanding."

"You love it."

A click sounded. "Lights on."

"Good," I said, my free hand gripping the edge of the tub. "Shirt off?"

"Already done."

"Shorts?"

"Nothing but my boxer briefs."

I sighed at the mental image that burned itself in my mind. "Take those off, too."

"Echo?"

"It's only fair," I cooed. "I'm naked too."

"Done," he said, his breath hitching as he moved to do as I said.

"You know what I'd do to you if I was there?" I asked.

"What's that?"

"I'd trail my hands over your chest, down those lickable abs, and lower."

"Mmm," he mumbled. "Then what?"

"Then I'd gently grab that beautiful cock of yours and stroke and tease you until you were like velvet granite in my hand."

"Damn," he said, his tone pure growl.

"Do you feel me there, Sawyer?" I asked.

"Yes," he answered.

I bit my lip, drunk on the power of having this effect on him even miles apart.

"Echo," he said. "Do me a favor?"

"What's that?" I whispered.

"Touch those perfect breasts. Tell me how they feel."

I released the tub with my free hand and grazed my fingers over my pert nipples. "Heavy, tight."

"Yes," he sighed. "Tell me how wet you are."

My toes curled at the primal demand in his voice, and I trailed my hand lower. "I'm in the tub, so everything is wet," I teased.

"You know the difference," he said, his voice strained.

"Let's see," I said, slipping my fingers lower until I slid right where I wanted him. "Drenched, Sawyer."

"Goddamn," he growled.

"I'd grip you tighter, now," I said. "And faster."

"I'd sink so deep into you," he answered. "And you'd arch against me to take me even deeper."

"Yeah?" I said, arching as I did as he said, sliding into myself with a gasp.

"I'd slip in and out, over and over, until you were blind with need." His voice was pure lust, pure desire as he spoke.

"And I'd clench around you like a vise," I said, my breaths coming in short bursts.

"Damn, Echo," he said. "I'd slide out just enough to tease your clit, just to watch you writhe beneath me."

My fingers mimicked his words, my muscles coiling like a spring as I easily saw the image on the backs of my eyelids. Sawyer, his glorious body, those hauntingly beautiful gray eyes above me. His body playing mine like a mastered instrument.

"God, Sawyer," I said, unable to hide the breathlessness in my words. "I'd hold you with my hips," I said, never ceasing the movement of my fingers that I pictured as his. "I'd keep you right at the edge, not letting you fully *in* despite you trying. I'd repay your tease full force, only letting the tip of you touch me."

"Goddamn."

"Then," I continued, plunging deeper into myself, feeling that tightening in my core. "Just when you were mad with want. Just when you couldn't think or feel anything but wanting me. Needing me. Just when you were *begging* to get in," I moaned, "would I let you slam home." My body shuddered as I pressed against that spot I desperately wished was in Sawyer's mouth. "And I'd want you to come, Sawyer. I'd want you to come so hard you'd send me into another orgasm. Until my voice was raw from screaming your name."

"Fuck *me*," Sawyer moaned at the same time I gasped his name. "Fucking hell, Echo," he said, his breath ragged.

"Sawyer," I said, just because I could. I leaned against the tub, fully, totally relaxed now.

"You're amazing," he said.

I smiled, sighing. "You're not so bad yourself."

"Damn," he said, and I laughed.

"You should buy Cannon breakfast in the morning," I said.

"What? Why?"

"As a thank you for leaving the room empty."

Sawyer chuckled. "Fine, I will on one condition."

"What's that?"

"Don't ever say another man's name after we just came together."

Just like that, I wanted him again. The primal tenor in his voice did everything to make my skin feel electrified, ready to spark at the lightest touch.

"Sweet dreams, Sawyer," I said.

"I'll dream up something devious to do to you when I get back."

I trembled at the promise in his tone.

"Make it good," I said, then ended the call, setting my cell back on the table.

Playlist forgotten, I soaked in the tub for a few more minutes before feeling my body giving into the perfect combination of relaxed and sated. And as I fell, dry and warm onto my sheets, I realized it didn't matter that Sawyer had infuriated me by leaving me a key this morning, I'd address that the next time I saw him in person. And it didn't matter how many miles separated us. I'd *wanted* him. Wanted him so badly I couldn't have a normal conversation before I jumped him through the phone.

He'd met that jump.

Met it and matched it.

Until we'd both been left partially satisfied but wanting *more*.

But wanting more, expecting more from anyone…I wasn't used to that.

And it scared the hell out of me.

11

SAWYER

"*T*his is so awesome." Zimmerman was practically humming with excited energy as we walked off the ice after morning skate.

"Don't get too used to it, kid," Thurston growled, pushing past us both to head into the locker room.

"Give him some space." I put my hand on Zimmerman's chest, stopping us toward the side of the hallway. "Don't take that personally," I told Zimmerman once Thurston was out of earshot. They'd called the kid back to be a backup just in case Thurston couldn't hack it during playoffs, which so far, he had. I stripped off my helmet and guzzled water to make sure I'd hack it, too.

We were up three games to one against Detroit, and if we won tomorrow, we'd move on. The goalie luck seemed to have switched though—the two games we'd won, I'd been in net. Thurston had played the night we lost. The guy was hurting, and the fact that he even put the pads on was impressive, but I couldn't help but worry that it would cost us in the long run.

"What, the fact that he doesn't want me here?"

Zimmerman seethed, showing all twenty years of his maturity.

"No one wants to be replaced," Connell said as he came up from behind us. "Has nothing to do with who you are, and everything to do with how old you are."

"Some guys just don't know when to give it up." Zimmerman took off his helmet, still glaring at Thurston's back. "He's past his prime."

"Well, it's a good thing we don't let jackass kids who haven't even reached their prime make decisions like that," Cannon said slowly as he approached, giving the kid a once-over and shaking his head.

Zimmerman paled, and blinked quickly. "You're Cannon Price."

"Yep."

The kid swallowed. "It's really nice to meet you. Hey, is that the new Bauer stick? I didn't think they were out. Can I see it? I heard the flex is crazy."

This was not going to go well. Cannon loved that fucking stick.

"It is. They're not. And no. Don't even think about touching it. Or me."

I almost felt bad for Zimmerman. Almost.

"What are you guys doing?" Axel asked, pausing his own trek to the locker room.

"Trying to give Thurston some space," I told the giant Swede. "He's pretty sour on the kid."

Axel glanced at Zimmerman, and then toward Thurston's back as it disappeared into the locker room. "Good idea," he told me, pounding his fist on my shoulder pad twice. "Stop running your mouth, Zimmerman, or I'll make sure you're never called up from the farm team. We're a family here, and just like every family has its Uncle Bjorn that no one likes—"

"No one has an Uncle Bjorn here," Lukas interrupted, elbowing his best friend.

"You get the damned point," Axel said to Zimmerman. "Thurston is family."

"Then what am I?" the kid challenged. "I have a Reaper contract, too."

"For the farm team," Connell muttered, and I wondered how long it would take the kid to become a victim of one of his pranks.

"You're the annoying boyfriend who's trying to get Daddy's approval by belittling Uncle Bjorn," Lukas said with a shrug.

"You guys are assholes," Zimmerman snapped. "Thurston's just going to have to get used to me in the locker room." He pushed away from us and strode to the locker room.

"Is it wrong that I hope it smacks him in the face?" Connell asked with a grin.

"Nope," Lukas answered.

"Is he going to be a problem?" Axel asked me.

"I don't know," I answered honestly. "I get it, I do. Getting a shot like we did and landing contracts—farm team or not— it's the dream. The one-in-a-million shot. The kid is going to be a great goalie. Hell, he's almost there, but the humility could use some work."

Axel sighed and stared as Zimmerman pushed into the locker room. "Just don't get hurt on me." He glanced back at me.

"Doing my best."

I heard the rapid click of heels from the hallway just ahead about a millisecond before a woman turned the corner, hit the rubberized path, and tripped.

Cannon shot forward and caught her just before she would have face-planted and lifted her to her feet carefully.

"Are you all right, lass?" Connell asked.

The woman swept a mass of blond hair away from her face and gave a shaky smile. Talk about fairytale princess Barbie. This girl came with wide blue eyes, hair that belonged in a tower, a sundress with an actual cardigan buttoned at the top, and she couldn't have stood more than five three. Next to Cannon, she looked...breakable.

"I'm just a bit embarrassed, but I'm okay," she admitted with a sweet southern drawl. Then she looked up...and up at Cannon. "Thank you so much for catching me—" her words died and her eyes flared as she realized who he was.

"Next time don't run down the hallway in heels," he chastised.

There was a collective groan from the rest of us.

"Jesus, Cannon, can't you just say you're welcome?" Connell shook his head.

"I'll be more careful in the future." The girl's gaze dropped from Cannon to her elbow—which he was still holding.

He let go quickly.

"Miss VanDoren, you're sure you're okay?" Axel asked, which had us all looking in his direction.

"Oh, yes, Mr. Nystrom, absolutely. You're actually the reason I'm down here. Langley is running over the promotion schedule for the upcoming Children's Hospital Gala, and she wanted to make sure that you would..." Her gaze flickered past every one of us. "Ask your teammates if they wouldn't mind stopping by my office to sign the gear we're auctioning off so we can get the photographs taken? Oh, and if you knew of any players that you might be able to talk into coming?"

"You mean my wife asked which of my guys I'd order to be at her mercy?" Axel asked with a booming laugh.

"Well, yes, though it's really more at my mercy, so no blaming Langley." She flashed a smile.

"We're in playoffs, and you want us to come to a gala?" Cannon crossed his arms.

Pink tinged the girl's cheeks, but she tilted her head and looked up at Cannon. "Well, since the gala is scheduled over two months from now, you should be done with playoffs. Unless you were thinking you'd play fourteen games in the finals, instead of seven?"

Gotta hand it to the girl, she stared down the dragon without blinking.

A corner of his mouth lifted.

"I'll send the guys up, Miss VanDoren," Axel promised.

"Thank you." She smiled again, looking each of us in the eye before turning back to Cannon. "And thank you again for catching me. Those are some reflexes you have. I hope you didn't do too much damage to your gear in the process."

Cannon nodded in reply, and she walked away, her heels clipping noticeably slower this time.

"Langley's assistant gets her own office? How the fuck old is she? Twelve?" Cannon bent and picked up both his stick and his helmet from where he'd abandoned them in the rush to catch Miss VanDoren.

"Persephone VanDoren isn't Langley's assistant," Axel clarified. "She's the head of the Reaper Foundation. You know, that whole charity thing we do?"

Cannon's jaw flexed.

"She does things like organize galas to help kids with cancer, and figure out where we can help out the community. And she's not twelve. At least I don't think she is. She just graduated college. Also, you'll learn where her office is really quickly, since you'll be the first one up there to sign whatever the fuck she wants." Axel gave Cannon a grin and walked off toward the locker room.

Connell started laughing.

"What the hell is so funny?" Cannon snapped.

"You dropped your precious little stick!" The Scotsman roared with laughter as he walked by. "Not that I blame you. That lass is a beaut. Not that she's my type. I prefer my women with a little more to hold on to, but still."

Cannon narrowed his eyes on Connell's back as he followed Axel into the locker room.

"Her name is really Persephone?" Cannon questioned, looking at his stick. "Who the hell does that to their kid?"

"Don't," Lukas warned.

"Don't what?" Cannon spat back.

"Just...don't." He gave Cannon's shoulder a pat as he left for the locker room.

Cannon turned his gaze on me, narrowing his eyes.

"Hey, I didn't say shit." I tilted my head and left him standing in the hallway.

A half-hour later, I stood by the locker Zimmerman was using as he zipped up his bag. "Walk out with me," I ordered.

He followed, and we made our way out with the rest of the team, all headed for the parking lot.

"Look, you have to cool it," I warned him. "I know you're excited, and this is pretty much as awesome as it gets, but you're pissing off the wrong people." I nodded at Thurston as we passed his car.

He opened his door and swore as something fell out and rolled down the slope toward us.

Zimmerman and I both bent, but I caught it, scanning the label by sheer habit.

What the actual fuck.

"Here you go," I said as I handed the bottle back to him.

He looked at both of us and nodded his thanks, then got into his car faster than I'd ever seen him do before.

"Did you see that?" Zimmerman asked me in a hushed tone.

"See what?" I questioned, my insides curdling.

"You seriously didn't see the label on that fucking bottle?" His tone implied that he had.

My stomach flipped over.

"I don't make a habit of reading my teammates' prescriptions," I told the kid. "You shouldn't either. Remember what I just said about pissing off the wrong people."

Before he could say anything else, I got into my truck and put the key in the ignition. Thurston was using steroids. Part of me understood—he was trying to heal up from his injury and didn't want to lose his spot.

But if he got caught, chances were they'd call back any wins that he'd been in net for.

And if I didn't tell, and he took the ice, it would only increase the games we'd lose once he was found out. The bottle had felt heavy. Full. Like he hadn't been on them long.

What the fuck was I going to do?

* * *

"You seem distracted," I said to Echo as she jabbed at her steak later that night.

"Oh, do I?" She didn't look up from her plate.

Oh, shit.

"I'm sorry, am I the distracted one?" I asked softly, keeping my voice at a restaurant-level quiet. My head was still swimming with the Thurston shit from earlier that afternoon, and I still didn't know what I was going to do. "I don't mean to be," I said in way of apology.

I hadn't seen Echo in almost a week thanks to the play-offs, which also happened to be the night we'd slept together. But we'd texted back and forth, and I'd even called. Everything had seemed...fine.

She looked up at me and arched an eyebrow.

"What?" I looked down to see if I had food all over me or

something. "I told you that you look amazing, right?" Because she did. Her black dress was cut modestly in the front but left her back open nearly to the base of her spine. She was stunning.

"Yes, you did." She softened and sighed. "Look, we have to talk."

Nausea hit me for the second time that day. "We're not even in a relationship, and we have to have the talk? Holy shit, was I that bad? Because it seemed like you were enjoying yourself." Like screamed-my-name kind of enjoyed herself.

Her gaze darted to the tables around us. "Shhh. I don't give a shit what people think about me, but you're kind of in the public eye right now."

My jaw ticked.

She rolled her eyes. "Look, that was...good," she assured me. "Okay, way better than good. It was…" She bit her lower lip and looked at me like she might crawl across the table and eat me for dessert.

"Yeah, it was," I agreed. "So what's up? I know I haven't been around with playoffs—"

"We said no strings." She pointed her fork at me.

"Right," I said slowly. "And yet, I can't help but feel like I've fucked up our non-relationship somehow."

A lady at the table next to us dropped her jaw, and I offered her an apologetic half-smile.

"We should have stayed in," Echo muttered, reaching for her purse.

"If we'd stayed in, we would have skipped dinner and gone straight to bed." Fuck, maybe that's what we should have done. It was hard for Echo to be mad at me while in the throes of multiple orgasms.

"And what's wrong with that?" she hissed.

The guy at the table on my left dropped his fork.

"I need to eat," I explained slowly. "I need the protein, and I didn't feel like hauling a grill up on to Langley's balcony."

"So why don't you just pick one of their damned houses and move in already?" she challenged, fishing something out of her purse.

"That's a good question that I don't have an answer for." Part of me wondered if I was procrastinating my choice because I liked being closer to where she worked. "What are you looking for?" I asked when I couldn't contain my curiosity any longer.

"This!" she hissed, holding up the little silver key I'd left.

"My key."

She set it on the table and pushed it forward. "Yes. *Your* key. The key that opens *your* apartment."

"Has the key done something to offend you? Unlocked a door it shouldn't have? Put a hole in your purse?" I sipped at my ice water, trying to figure out what had her so frazzled.

"I shouldn't have your damned key!"

The little area we were sitting in fell completely silent for a painful moment before the chatter around us resumed.

"You're pissed that I gave you a key?"

"I'm not your little beck and call girl, and I'm sure as hell not your live-in girlfriend or any type of girlfriend, so why the hell would you give me a key?" She tucked her hair behind her ears ruthlessly and stared me down.

"To lock the door after you left," I answered, then started back in on my steak. "Didn't you read the note I left?" I asked when she hadn't responded.

"Yeah, the one that said to either wait for you in bed like I'm some kind of bunny, or lock up behind me when I left?" She smiled sweetly at me, and not in the nice way.

I leaned forward and dropped my voice. "Last time I checked, Echo, you asked for a no-strings policy. The kind where maybe you decide you want to hang around in bed and wait for me to get back so I can fuck you senseless again. Or the kind where you really need to get to work, so you can lock the door on your way out so all my shit doesn't get stolen."

Her cheeks flushed, and I saw eyebrows raise at the table next to us, despite my hushed tone.

"And that isn't a string?" she asked, pointing to the key.

"That was me not kicking you out before practice. That was me respecting you, not asking you to move in for fuck's sake." Did she really think that I was just going to forget everything we'd said the night before and key her the next morning?

"Oh," she whispered.

"Oh," I replied, and cut my steak with a little more force than necessary.

"I thought the key was, you know, a *key*," she admitted, looking more than slightly guilty. "And then you asked if I wanted to go out to dinner, and this place is totally a relationship place. I live here. I know."

My jaw dropped.

"Okay. The key was for exactly what I told you it was for, and the restaurant was because Lukas recommended the steak. I figured I'd feed us with minimal effort, and then I'd get you home and bend you over my dining room table until you came a few times. Or does that have too many strings for you?"

Her lips parted, and she shifted in her seat. Good. At least I hadn't killed off her sexual attraction to me while fucking up whatever it was we had going on.

"So this is just...dinner," she said quietly.

"Yep."

She ran her tongue over her lower lip. "And the key was just to lock the door."

"You got it."

130

"So I may have overreacted?" She scrunched her nose, and it took everything I had not to pull her across the table and kiss the shit out of her.

"Maybe a little." I gestured with my thumb and forefinger.

"And you're still on board with this no-strings thing?" She smiled hopefully.

"All about it," I confirmed as relief slammed into me with the force of a freight train. Maybe we were just friends who fucked, but I wasn't anywhere near ready to lose that yet. I liked her too much. "Are you?"

"God, yes!" Her eyes swung to the tables on either side of us before she continued, lowering her voice. "I'm incredibly on board."

"So can we finish our dinner? Because I wasn't kidding. I really do need to eat."

She laughed.

"What?"

"You don't have to give me the puppy dog face." She shook her head. "Let's finish dinner. And if it's not too many strings…" She bit her lip for a minute, and I waited, knowing if I pushed her, she'd never open up. "I missed you. I watched your games of course, but it wasn't the same as being around you."

Fuck my life, I was crazy about this girl. I cleared my throat and took a drink of water. "You could always come tomorrow night. It's a home game." I shoveled my food in quickly.

She smiled, and my heart clenched. She was so insanely beautiful.

"You don't think that's…string territory?" The hope that lit her eyes hit me hard.

"I think friends come to games. Come on. My mom will be there and everything. You'd be doing me a favor if you kept her company."

131

"I love your mom!" Her face fell. "I can probably make it, but I don't know if I have time to grab any Reaper merch after my shift tomorrow, though."

"I'll drop something off for you," I promised, barely containing a grin. I had an extra jersey in the closet that would swamp her, but I'd be damned if she was going to wear anyone else's name on her back.

Whoa, possessive much?

"Sounds like a deal. Now what about this key?" she asked slowly.

"Up to you." I shrugged. "Give it back if you think it's a string. Keep it if you think it's the easiest way to get me naked."

She picked it up and studied it like it might give her the answer while I polished off my dinner.

"It doesn't mean anything," I assured her.

"Oh for God's sake, either you take the damned key, or I will!" the woman sitting next to us snapped. She had to be in her early seventies.

We both burst into laughter, and Echo slipped the key back into her purse.

"What do you say we take dessert to go and eat it at your dining room table?" Echo asked, her voice innocent, but her eyes stripping me bare.

I motioned to the waiter and cleared my throat.

"Check please!"

ECHO

*S*awyer wiped down the bar as I locked up for the night. He'd shown up after practice and stayed throughout closing. Not to drink or eat, but just to be around me. We were still firmly agreed on the no-strings-attached deal—especially after my overreaction at dinner the other night—but I couldn't deny just how much I enjoyed his company.

When he was in town, that was. They were smack in the middle of the second round, two games up and two more to win before they could move onto the conference finals. His playoff schedule didn't allow for a ton of downtime, which would normally be my jam, but seeing as how I liked the son of a bitch so damn much…

"You know," I said, eyeing him as he shelved all the clean glasses. "If you ever get tired of being a super-star NHL goalie, you'd make one hell of a bartender."

Sawyer's grin was slow and easy sliding over his lips. He put up the last glass then leaned over the bar, our roles reversed. "You know I used to tend at a place in Seattle. Helped pay the bills."

"And look at you now," I said, sinking onto the barstool before him, content to play this game.

"Yeah," he said, that familiar weight returning to his gray eyes. "At least we're winning again."

"I figured you had a healthy dose of winning and losing in college. Shouldn't the swings hurt less now?"

"Maybe," he said, sighing. "Maybe it wouldn't hold as much weight if I hadn't moved my mom all the way out here. Hadn't uprooted her life—"

"She's happy here," I said. "You've seen her. She's told you that. And anyone can see how damn proud she is of you." I reached over the bar and cupped his cheek, the scruff from his trimmed beard scratching my palm. "You have to take ownership of your accomplishments, Sawyer. They're something to be proud of."

He leaned into my touch, nodding. A blink and the seriousness in his eyes was gone, replaced with question.

"What?" I asked, dropping my hand.

"Have you ever wanted to do anything else but be a bartender?"

I bit my lip to stop my smile.

"I mean," he continued. "I know you said you and your dad always dreamed of opening a bar together. Do you still want to? I think you'd be good at it. You practically run this place. I may even know a recently wealthy hockey star who would sponsor such an investment." The last words were part tease, part truth, and it made my heart swell in my chest.

Stop. No strings.

But friends? That was easy with Sawyer. In fact, before the sex, and hell, even after, he was one of the best friends I'd ever had. Friends were easier. Safer.

"Why are you looking at me like that?" he asked when I'd done nothing but grin at him.

I turned my gaze to the empty bar, my eyes trailing over

the custom finishes, the scythe hanging over the shelves of liquor, and back to Sawyer.

"When my father passed away suddenly," I said, speaking around the familiar lump in my throat. "He left me with some considerable money. I guess after losing my mom and my sister, he realized how unpredictable life was and took precautions...for me." I swallowed hard and ran my fingers over the smooth black granite bar. "It took me a while, as you know, to come out of my grief. But when I did?" I smiled, not ashamed of the happy tears in my eyes. "I'd heard about Silas Asher bringing an NHL team to my backyard. Once I knew the name of the team, I knew what to do." I raised my hands to indicate the building. "Scythe is *my* baby."

Sawyer's lips parted. "No shit?"

I raised my brows at him.

"I mean, yeah." He blinked a few times. "That actually makes perfect sense. You're always here. You constantly direct the staff..." he tilted his head. "Wait," he said. "You're always calling the owner a bitch."

I shrugged. "I *can* be a real bitch sometimes."

Sawyer's laugh was loud and full, and it made butterflies flap in my stomach like I was a sixteen-year-old girl.

He came around the bar, sitting on the stool next to me. "Why keep it a secret?"

"I tell a select few people," I said, tracing invisible circles on the granite. "But for the most part? It's no one's business. If someone can't respect me and like me as a bartender, then they're not worth telling I'm an owner."

"Valid point." Sawyer nodded as he glanced around the place. "Any other secrets you're keeping from me?" he asked, his eyes on mine. "You have a family of six kids I don't know about or fight crime in a costume?"

I laughed, shaking my head. "No other secrets," I said. "Definitely no kids."

He tilted his head. "You don't like kids?"

"I don't *mind* kids," I said.

"But..."

I sucked in a sharp breath. "I've lost everyone, Sawyer. My sister. My mom. My dad." I snapped my fingers. "Just like that. And that pain? I own it. It did things to me. Turned me into something none of them would be proud of for a little while. But I got out. I made it through it. But the idea of ever putting a child through that..." I swallowed hard. "I'd rather not have kids than subject them to the pain of losing me one day."

Sawyer furrowed his brow, his eyes calculating as he surveyed me. Likely putting two and two together—love, and all things associated with it, are dangerous for me. Terrified me.

You should run, far far away.

Instead, he reached across the space between us and clutched my hand. "I understand pain. Maybe not in the exact way you've carried it, but I understand, Echo." He glanced down at where his fingers trailed the inseam of my wrist. "I know my mom won't likely live to see certain milestones in my life—getting married, having kids, hell, even winning a Cup. We never know. Time is precious. But even living with that weight over my head, the never knowing if *this* day will be her last, I'd never wish her out of existence. She's made me into the man I am today, and losing her will *crush* me. But everything else? The love? That's more powerful than any grief. Even if it's just the memory of it."

A single tear rolled down my cheek, and my hands—my entire body—trembled from the terror coursing through my veins. Or it could be from the emotions I'd kept locked up for years bursting through. I wasn't sure. Whatever it was, Sawyer was at fault. His words, the man himself, had unlocked something buried inside me.

He slid off the stool, stepping between my knees as he gently brushed the tear off my cheek with his thumb.

"Echo," he said, and it was the tenderness in his tone that snapped me back to reality.

My survival instincts fully kicking in, I clutched the back of his neck and jerked him toward me, crushing my lips on his. Somehow the moment had turned from casual hangout to intense emotional bonding, and I didn't know how to handle it...so I got us back to common ground. The ground where we both wanted each other, craved each other on a physical level.

I parted his lips with my tongue, sighing at the taste of him as he kissed me back without hesitance, without restraint. He wove his fingers into my hair and tilted my head back, kissing me at a deep angle, taking my mouth like I knew he could take my body. Then he moved his hands over my shoulders and lower until he'd reached where my ass sat perched on that barstool. One motion had him hefting me up and up until I'd locked my ankles around his back. He turned, prepping to sit me on the bar, but I gripped his hair and pulled his face away enough to look at him.

"Not here," I whispered.

"Where?" he asked, setting me on my own two feet. I knew if I told him I couldn't do this tonight, he'd respect it. He'd step away and ask if I needed to talk instead. And maybe knowing that made this easier but...

"I want to take you somewhere I've never taken any man."

Sawyer visibly swallowed, but when I reached for his hand, he took it.

I tugged him past the bar, past the kitchen door, and past the bathrooms, stopping at the farthest door at the end of the hallway. I fished out my keys, my fingers trembling with anticipation as I unlocked the door.

"Is this a supply closet fantasy?" Sawyer teased, but his

laughter died as I shook my head and pulled him through the doors and *up*.

Up the wooden staircase leading to my loft above the bar.

I locked the door behind us, allowing Sawyer to walk deeper into the studio setup. His eyes took in my small kitchen, the door that led to my bathroom open and showing a sliver of that claw-foot tub I loved so much. Then he took in the lone couch next to a bookshelf and finally, my bed on the far left side of the loft.

"This screams you," he said, turning to face me.

"The cupboard above the bar?" I joked.

He spanned the distance between us, taking my face in his hands. "The home above your heart."

I pressed my lips in a line. He'd hit the nail on the head. Scythe was my heart—because it was what my dad and I had always wanted. And the place above it? It was the only home I'd felt safe in since Dad had passed.

"Thank you for showing me," he said, gently kissing my lips. "For telling me."

I tossed my keys on the kitchen counter, the words I wanted to say getting tangled in my throat. The meaning behind it, I felt it. I'd let Sawyer in, just a fraction, and it made my chest tight to the point of breaking.

Sawyer saw something in my eyes, and in a blink, his were pure mischief. He jerked his head toward my bathroom. "Is that the tub where you tortured me from a thousand miles away?"

A breath of air rushed past my lips, and the relief from his banter made my head spin.

"Yes," I said, trailing my fingers underneath his shirt, feeling the taut skin over his hard abdomen. "Later," I said at the fire in his eyes. "Right now?" I gazed up at him through hooded eyes. "I want you in my bed."

The claim was an unleashing as Sawyer grabbed my ass

with both hands and hefted me up, walking the distance to my bed. We crashed atop it in a tangle of legs, our kiss never breaking as he teased my mouth with easy flicks and sweeping dips.

I tugged at the hem of his shirt until he pulled back enough for me to tug it over his head. I tossed it to the floor, greedily drinking in the sight of his broad shoulders, his strong chest. He followed suit, pulling mine off with expert fingers, leaving my breasts covered in nothing but purple lace.

"Goddamn, Echo," he said, palming one of my breasts while his mouth covered the other. His tongue teased my nipple over the lace, and I arched underneath him, desperate to feel him.

I whimpered slightly as he pulled back, moving lower to unbutton my jeans, then his. In a few heartbeats we were down to nothing but our undergarments, and my protested growl made him laugh.

"So eager," he said, lightly grazing his fingers over the lace covering my aching center.

"So cocky," I said, gripping his hard length with a little bite between us.

He hissed and nipped my bottom lip. "You want to play?"

I practically purred at the challenge in his words.

He laughed, kissing me frantically before heaving himself upward. "You asked for it."

With one quick motion of his hand, I was flipped onto my tummy. Sawyer lightly slapped my ass, eliciting a gasping yelp from me before he hooked his fingers into the lace band and slid it down, down, until it was free of my feet. He tossed the thong to the side as I watched his movements from over my shoulder. The sight of him there on his knees—those gloriously strong thighs, those ridiculously carved abs, and

139

that hard-as-granite cock springing free of his boxer briefs—turned me molten and liquid.

But then he slid those fingers under my hips and hefted me up and up, until I was on my knees, my breasts still pressed against my mattress as he sank onto his back and slid his face underneath me.

I gasped when his warm lips met my sensitive flesh, as his tongue teased and tortured that swollen bud at the apex of my thighs. I writhed against his face as he feasted on me from beneath, the sensation so debilitating I could barely think around the feel of his tongue inside me, the feel of his fingers gripping my ass to prevent me from fleeing.

Like I ever would.

Over and over, he claimed me with strong thrusts of his tongue and teasing strokes of those fingers until I was an unbound thing writhing above him. Until I was nothing but his in that moment, his to control, his to torture.

"Echo," he moaned against my aching flesh, the vibrations from his deep voice sending me to the edge. And with one long stroke of that tongue, that flame right down the center of me ignited, and I shattered completely.

"Sawyer!" His name ripped from my lips as I came on his tongue, him never ceasing with the expert flicks and dips as I rode his face through the aftershocks. My thighs trembled from the strength of it, from the intensity of it, but Sawyer didn't waste time. No, he flipped me right over, until the cool sheets pressed against my sweat-slicked back.

He reached toward his pants on the floor, but I stopped him with a hand on his abdomen. I reached into my nightstand drawer, pulling out a condom from the box I'd bought after the first time Sawyer and I had sex. I knew, even then, that I'd let him up here. Let him in far enough to see where I *lived*.

I tried not to think on the meaning of that as I tore open the packet and rolled the condom onto Sawyer's cock.

"Goddamn, Echo," he hissed, his fingers in my hair as I teased him. A gentle nudge at my shoulder had me relinquishing control to him, falling back on the bed, open and bare and his for the taking. "Fucking perfect," he said, settling between my thighs.

The weight of him was almost enough to shatter me again.

He slid his hand down my thigh, hooking my leg around his hip, teasing me with his tip. "So wet, so fucking responsive," he growled as I arched to meet each of his sweeping teases. "And you taste like a fucking dream."

The words made me whimper, and he drank the sound with a kiss. The taste of him and me combined set my blood on fire, so much I couldn't kiss him hard enough, long enough—

"Oh, God!" I moaned as he slid in and in and in, all the way to the hilt.

He pulled all the way out just to do it over again.

And again.

And again.

Until my headboard groaned from how hard I gripped it with one hand.

Until my nails dug into his back so hard I'd practically branded him.

Until I couldn't see or think or feel around the man moving above me.

Until I gasped for breath, breaking our kiss long enough to catch those gray eyes that were locked on mine. And I watched him as he moved in me, a total and utter claiming of my body as he hit every spot I never knew I had. As he filled me so much I couldn't understand how I'd ever felt whole without him inside me.

"Echo," he growled my name, and I clenched hot and tight around him. "Fuck, baby," he said, leaning his forehead against mine. The move was so intimate it threatened to rob me of the heavenly bliss he was treating me too.

So I gripped his hips and flipped him over, never breaking our bond as I now straddled him, pinning him to the bed with my hands on his sculpted chest. I settled lower on him, this angle so much deeper than before, and then I rode him. Hard and fast, all the while those gray eyes drank in the sight of me atop him, wild and demanding and greedy with his body. Greedy with our pleasure.

And when his fingers bit into the skin of my hips, when that strong jaw of his clenched? It sent a thousand shocks of electricity whispering across my skin, bursting in my blood. Every inch of me unraveled as we came together, our breaths nearly in sync. He gently stroked my thighs as I trembled above him, the aftershocks resonating in my body long after we'd stilled.

"Beautiful," he said as I gathered my hair off my neck, needing the cool air to hit it.

"Delicious," I said, my eyes drinking in the sight of him beneath me. This incredible, strong, unbelievable male beneath *me*. I smiled at him, an easy grin, as I fell atop his chest, limp and spent.

And he held me there, stroking soothing lines up and down my back until I did the unthinkable and fell asleep.

13

SAWYER

$\mathcal{J}$ pulled my truck up the long drive and parked in front of Axel's place. Was I really going to do this? Did I honestly have a choice?

We'd pulled through the second round in a four-game sweep, and I'd been in net for every single game. Thurston had complained, but Coach Hartman told him that he wasn't willing to risk his knee while I was still holding it down. He said we'd need his experience in the division finals, then conference and, God-willing, the Cup.

But Thurston had dressed for each game, sitting on the bench and watching me, waiting for me to fuck up, or to get tired enough to need a break. But one look at Thurston reminded me that the minute he touched the ice, we were all in jeopardy. But I wasn't the only one who'd potentially seen that bottle. Zimmerman waited in the wings, growing steadily more frustrated as I saw all the ice time, and there was no love lost between him and Thurston.

I sucked in a deep breath, steadied my racing heart, and headed for Axel and Langley's front door.

He answered less than a minute after I rang the bell.

"Hey, Sawyer, why don't you come in?" The six-foot-six giant moved aside, and I walked into his house. It was one of the Tudor models in the small neighborhood we called Reaper Village. Sweet Water was a tiny town just outside Charleston, which gave the Reapers enough distance from the rink, and the fans, and when Silas won the expansion bid, he'd also bought up an entire development here so any players who wanted could live together in the community.

"Sawyer!" Langley flew down the stairs and threw her arms around me. "It's so nice to see you outside the rink." She leveled a look on me. "Maybe you could... I don't know, come over a little more often? Or even choose one of those houses just up the street that came in your signing bonus?" She arched an eyebrow.

"Yeah, you probably want your apartment back, huh?" Damn, I'd been in the thing almost three months. I really needed to get my shit together and move. But the apartment was so much closer to Mom, and she'd be nearly forty-five minutes away once I moved out here.

"Oh, no, don't even worry about that. Once I moved in with the husband here—" she looped her arm around Axel's waist, "—we decided to keep the apartment for the exact reason you're here. Just in case the team had a need. I'm just hoping you'll move out here so Faith and Harper will quit bugging me about it. They miss you, you know."

"You're right," I said, running a hand across the back of my neck. "I miss them, too. There just never seems like there's enough time right now."

Her face softened. "You do a great job balancing it all. We just selfishly want more of you."

"I'll think about it," I promised her.

"You do that. And it's not like we don't know that you're spending all your free time with a certain bartender that we happen to love. She could come around more often, too." She gave me a playful smile.

Bar-owner, I thought silently. That's right. My girl had seen a way to make her dream come true, and she'd done it. She'd made the best of an impossible load of grief and now had a place she could be proud of. A place I somehow knew her father would love. Not bad for a twenty-three, almost twenty-four-year-old.

"So, you said you needed to see me," Axel led in, his tone mellow.

I glanced at Langley, and her eyes widened slightly in understanding. "You know," she said as she scooped up a jet black cat. "Slytherin and I have a whole lot that we can get done in the office, don't we?" She finished off speaking to the cat and slipped away up the stairs.

"That bad?" Axel asked, crossing his arms over his chest.

"Yeah," I managed.

"Well, let's grab a drink and some sunshine. We're not due at the rink for another few hours." He patted me on the back and led the way.

A few minutes later, we sat on his deck, and I told him exactly what I'd seen when Thurston's door had opened.

"Shit," he muttered. "That's a steroid." He leaned back in his chair and stared up at the sky.

"Anabolic," I confirmed. "And I don't know why, but all I keep thinking about is how fucking stupid he is not just to be taking them, but to keep the bottle in his damned car."

Axel nodded and rubbed the skin between his eyebrows.

"Look. I didn't want to say anything."

His eyes flew open and locked on mine.

"I didn't," I repeated, shaking my head. "I know he's in pain. I know the knee is just fucking killing him, and I'm sure he sees Zimmerman lying in wait, and he panicked." I put my hand up to stop Axel from interrupting when he so clearly

145

wanted to. "But the truth is that it's wrong, and it's illegal, and if he gets caught..."

Axel took a deep breath. "They'll take back our wins."

I nodded. "And I wouldn't even be here, fucking telling on him like we're in grade school, except he's the one starting tonight."

The conference championships. If we won the best of these seven games, we moved on to the Stanley Cup finals.

"Fuck," Axel muttered.

"Right. I didn't just want to bust into Coach's office and lay Thurston's shit bare, but I can't let him put the entire team at risk. The only playoff game he's been in net for was one we lost, but tonight..." I shook my head, then chugged water, hoping to quench the parched feeling that had been riding my tongue since I'd been told I could rest up and not suit out tonight.

"We have to tell Gage," Axel said slowly. "We can't let Thurston on the ice."

"That's what I figured." Not that I was ever going to call Coach McPherson by his first name, but Axel had known him a shit ton longer than I had.

"I don't want to, either," Axel admitted. "Thurston's grumpy, but I like the asshole. And I really appreciate you keeping this quiet and coming to me. I know you want to protect him, but we just can't. Not with the Cup on the line. Do you think the kid saw?"

"Zimmerman?"

Axel nodded.

"I don't know. He acted like he may have seen, but I grabbed it so quickly, and he hasn't said anything since."

"Let's hope. All it takes is him going to the media, or running his mouth to the wrong person, and we're fucked."

I followed Axel's Rover in my truck, and we headed to the rink, knowing Coach McPherson would already be there.

The players' lot wasn't empty, but I hadn't hung out in the parking lot long enough to recognize whose cars were whose. We both parked, showed our badges to the guards—like we actually needed them—and headed up through the maze of hallways that made up Reaper Arena. Coach McPherson's office looked out over the practice ice, so we managed to avoid most of the staff readying for tonight's game.

Axel knocked on the thick wooden door, then swore when he glanced through the window.

"We're too late," he said quickly before twisting the handle on the door. I followed him in, then stood by his side in utter shock.

Coach McPherson sat at the head of a small conference table that sat perpendicular to his desk. Coach Hartman sat at his side while Asher Silas sat to his right. Zimmerman held down one of the seats on the side, and Thurston sat at the end, staring into space.

"So I guess I'll be going in tonight. It's not like you can have a guy using steroids in net." Zimmerman finished whatever we'd walked in on.

"Sorry to interrupt, Coach, but this is exactly why we're here," Axel said, completely ignoring Zimmerman.

"You know about this?" Coach asked, his eyes narrowing.

"Yeah, it came to my attention." Axel nodded.

"About an hour ago," I said, stepping forward. "I'm the one who knew, and I told Axel because I wasn't sure what to do with the knowledge."

"You fucking come forward!" Hartman snapped.

Zimmerman smirked.

"Coach, I held that bottle for all of ten seconds. The last thing I wanted to do was end Thurston's career based off what I thought I read. I've seen people's lives ruined by drugs, and I…" I sighed. "I knew that with him going into net

147

tonight, I had to speak up because if he's found out, we'll forfeit our wins."

"Because you want his spot tonight!" Zimmerman snapped.

"It has jack and shit to do with that!" I fired back. "I kept my mouth shut because it's none of my goddamned business what any player does in his private time. Is it wrong?" I looked at Thurston, who met my gaze with bleak eyes. "Yeah, man, you know it is. You put us all in jeopardy. And I get it. This game, it's life, right? It's the dream, and I get wanting to hold onto it as long as possible. And I'm sorry that I couldn't keep your confidence, but it's not just you out there. This affects us all."

Thurston sighed and hung his head. "I've only taken a few of them," he admitted quietly. "I started when the kid showed up. I promise."

"The drug screenings would have shown it," Coach told Silas. "He pissed clean at both the no-notice tests this year, and the last was right before we started the playoffs."

"The bottle felt full," I added. "Like he hadn't taken that many."

"Or it was just a new bottle," Zimmerman threw out.

Axel leveled him with a stare.

"Fuck!" Gage hissed and slammed his fist into the table. "Damn it, we would have done everything we could to help you," he said to Thurston. "Our hands are tied."

"I know," Thurston said quietly.

"Who else knows?" Silas asked, looking calm and collected as always. I wondered if anything ever ruffled the guy.

"Just Zimmerman, McCoy, and the guy I got them from," Thurston answered. "I kept them in the car so my wife couldn't find them. She hates my car."

"Okay, Zimmerman, Nystrom, McCoy," Gage said as he

looked at us individually. "You guys get out of here and keep your mouth shut. Axel, call your wife for me, please?"

"Absolutely," Axel agreed, his phone already in hand. If anyone could handle the PR nightmare this could erupt into, it was Langley.

"What about me?" Zimmerman snapped as he came to my side.

"McCoy, you rested?" Hartman asked, ignoring the kid.

"Yes, sir."

"You're starting tonight. Zimmerman, you're in as backup only because we don't have anyone else rostered. You came to us out of spite, not concern for the team, and that's something I'm not likely to forget."

The kid's mouth dropped open.

"I didn't want it to happen like this," I told Thurston.

"I know." His lips flattened as he nodded slowly. "I know. But you get out there tonight and kill it for the Reapers, you got me?"

I nodded my agreement and left the room with a heavier heart than when I'd entered it.

* * *

"THIS IS REALLY how you want to spend our one afternoon off?" I asked Echo as I pulled through the gates of Reaper Village. Game one was a win. Game two was tomorrow, and practice was finished for the day.

"I figured you could focus on something else for a bit," she answered with a smile, twining her fingers with mine over the console. "I know you're struggling with your mom."

My mom, who'd told me after last night's win that she wanted to move up to Virginia to be with her sisters. I'd had ash in my mouth all day.

"I don't even know what to say to her," I admitted as I

149

drove slowly up the street, careful to watch for any of the Reaper kids who lived here. "I've taken care of her for so long. My aunts—they're great, I love them—but they don't know her medical history, or what challenges she faces day to day."

"But your mom *does*," she said gently. "She knows all those things. Look, I'm not saying you should take this all lightly, but just remember that she's an incredibly intelligent woman. She had to have thought this through."

I grunted my response, unable to process anything but pure emotion over the possibility of not being there when Mom needed me.

"Oh, there's Annabelle!" Echo said, pointing to a white Volvo that sat in front of one of the houses I was here to look at. "She's the Sweet Water city clerk I told you about. The one who's here to talk you into becoming an outstanding member of this community."

"And you know her how?" I questioned as I pulled in behind her.

"We were best friends growing up," Echo said, tucking her hair behind her ears nervously. "You know, back when I had normal hair, and a mom, and a dad, and a sister, and all that normal shit."

I glanced at the woman who stood by her car and then looked back to my Echo.

My Echo? Dude, you gotta stop that shit.

Annabelle wore a pressed sheath dress, kitten heels, huge sunglasses, and her brown hair was tamed in forties-style waves. She looked like she'd just stepped out of Good House-keeping. My girl was more Rolling Stone, and they were best friends?

"It was a long time ago," Echo said quietly, glancing down at her own outfit. "Losing my Mom and sister, then losing my dad, it changed me. We don't really have anything in common anymore, but we're working on getting that back. I really do love her." She looked worriedly toward her friend, who was scrolling through her phone.

"Okay," I said softly. Then I leaned across the console and kissed her lightly. "I hate that you've been through so much, but I love who you are because of it. I'm sure she feels the same."

Echo nodded, and after another quick kiss, we both got out of the truck and headed toward Annabelle.

"Why, you must be Sawyer," Annabelle said with a wide smile and a slow drawl. "I'm so pleased to meet you."

"Same here." I shook her hand and was nearly bowled over by something—someone—hitting my back.

"It's about time you got out here!" Faith practically shouted in my ear as she clung to my back. "For a minute there I thought you were avoiding us!" She smacked a kiss on my cheek and hopped down.

"Ha. As if I could possibly avoid you." I nudged Faith with my elbow, and swept Echo under my right arm, tucking her close. "All these beautiful women here to help me house shop. I should have done this weeks ago."

"Faith, this is Annabelle Clarke," Echo introduced the two ladies. "She's one of my oldest friends and also happens to be the city clerk for the town of Sweet Water."

"Well, it's more like town clerk, since there's only four thousand of us in our little slice of heaven!" She beamed with pride over the small community.

"Annabelle, this is Faith. She's one of my closest friends and was my college roommate. Now she works with the Reapers PR team and is married to Lukas Vestergaard." Man, we'd come a long way since freshman year.

"They let boys and girls room together where you're from?" Annabelle asked with wide, curious eyes.

"Oh, no! We lived in a house together," Faith clarified. "Separate rooms and everything."

"Well, now that makes sense!" The girls shook hands and exchanged those niceties the opposite sex always seemed to remember, and then Annabelle looked at me. "I'm here to shamelessly sell you on Sweet Water, Mr. McCoy. We take great pride in having the Reapers live within our little limits and you, sir, are the lone holdout."

"Did you hear that? I'm the rebel," I stage-whispered to Echo.

She laughed, tucking in closer to my side in a way that warmed my chest.

"You are," Annabelle said with an even bigger smile. "Now, allow me to sell you on our little town as you walk through your available houses!"

"I've got the keys!" Faith announced, dangling three sets.

"We're a small town, but a pretty fabulous one." Annabelle said as we walked through the first house, which reminded me of an Italian villa. "You'll find an excellent selection of restaurants in our downtown area, which still has the original cobblestone! No chains, of course, just good local families and amazing food."

Echo watched me carefully as I took in the details of the house. It was huge, but felt too...stuffy for me.

"What about bars?" I asked Annabelle with a devious grin at Echo.

She hip checked me and then mouthed, "Oops!"

"Well, many of our establishments do serve alcohol, but we don't have a bar within town limits." Annabelle looked around the great room with an appraising eye, her brow puckering.

"Did you hear that?" Echo teased, copping a feel of my ass as she walked behind me. "You'll just have to drink at Scythe. Shame."

I rolled my eyes, but didn't let them wander too far from her curves as she followed her friend.

"It feels a little…" Annabelle shook her head, like she couldn't find the words.

"Not Sawyer," Faith finished for her. "Come on, let's check out the one across the street." She locked up, and we followed her out of the villa. "Hey, guys!" she called to the house on the right where some of the Reapers were gathered on the wide porch. I made out Cannon, Axel, Lukas, Hudson, Ward—shit I could never remember that guy's first name. He was so fucking quiet. Leo? Liam? Landon…Logan. Right. Logan Ward.

If I lived here, I'd remember shit like that because I'd know my teammates even better. That definitely fell into the plus column.

"That's Connell's house," Faith told me once we'd reached the sidewalk.

"Really? I don't see him," Echo said, shading her eyes with her hand.

"You finally joining us?" Logan asked, leaning on the railing.

"Thinking about it. What do you guys do for fun around here, anyway?" I fired back.

"A little of this, little of that," he answered with a shrug. "Hang around for a few minutes, and you'll see."

"We'll come say hi as soon as he picks a house," Faith promised, and tugged me into the street. "No getting distracted. It took us this long to get you out here."

"Yes, ma'am." I shook my head at my friend but followed her.

"As you can see, your other teammates love our town!" Annabelle said as we reached the other side of the street. "We have tons of precautions in place to make sure that you guys feel at home here."

"Precautions?" Echo asked, her fingers laced with mine.

"No reporters are allowed. Ever. You should feel just as safe walking downtown as you do in the privacy of your own home," Annabelle assured us both. "We also have strict covenants, so you'll never have to deal with unsightly messes, and our schools are highly rated."

Echo shot her a *what the fuck* look, and I nearly lost it with laughter.

"I mean, if you ever want to have kids. One day. Not soon, of course. And I'm not implying that they'd be with Echo." Annabelle blinked rapidly. "Oh, shit, not that I'm saying they wouldn't be with Echo, either!"

"Right, enough about our hypothetical suburban children," Echo said as she tilted her head at her friend, but there was no malice in her tone.

"We also have community picnics," Faith picked up as we stood at the foot of the driveway to a two-story, modern house lined with glass windows. "It's a real family feel, even for those of us who don't have kids. Everyone is so nice, and it's not like Seattle, where you walk by people all the time, and they just fade into the background. Everyone says hello. Everyone is...seen, I guess."

Annabelle blinked rapidly. "Do you really love your current job? Because I just know that you'd be perfect in the town offices!"

"I do, actually," Faith told her with a laugh.

"Well—" Annabelle sucked in her breath and her eyes widened to the size of saucers as she stared back across the street. "What in the actual hell?"

I turned to see what had her gawking and I groaned.

Connell was running down his porch steps wearing a giant hat on his head and nothing else.

Nothing.

Else.

"Good afternoon, lovebirds!" he shouted with a wave, and it wasn't just his hand waving. Nope. His dick was swinging in the breeze as he jogged over to us. "Och! I didn't realize we had company!" He quickly cupped his junk in his hands but didn't stop jogging.

"Oh my God, Connell," Faith muttered, turning her back on the naked man.

Echo sputtered into a loud laugh, and I quickly pulled her into my chest, not just to shield her, but because I didn't need her to see what the Scotsman was rocking under those hands. "Put some clothes on MacDhuibh," I shouted.

"No can do. I'm mid-streak. Cannon said I'd have to back up my claim that I have the biggest balls on the team, and maybe he meant metaphorically, but I just couldn't miss a chance to get some fresh air on my boys."

"For fuck's sake," I muttered.

"Let me know which house you choose! And who your scrumptious little friend is!" he called back over his naked backside as he jogged up the street.

"Well. I've. Never." Annabelle was full of sputters, her cheeks flushing. But she didn't look away from the naked Scotsman.

"You've never met Connell," Echo drawled.

"Now, I've met too much of him," Annabelle said with a shake of her head. "Or not enough," she muttered. "You boys are something else." She pointed her finger at me as we walked up to the second house.

"Hey, I'm not the one streaking the neighborhood."

"There's only two more houses up that way, and neither are occupied," Annabelle said, waving her hand. "He talks a good game, but if he really meant it, he'd be streaking the arena."

One of those houses had been Thurston's, and though his furniture was in it, he was gone. None of us knew where

Coach had sent him, and none of us were ready to ask. Echo squeezed my hand, as if she'd sensed the direction of my thoughts. She'd been the only person I'd told about the situation after what had gone down in Coach's office.

We walked into the house and I felt...light. It was everywhere. The ceilings were high, the windows bright, and the open floor plan made everything feel connected.

"Wow," Echo said with a little sigh as we walked into the kitchen. Gray granite over white cabinets and those same windows pouring sunshine into the room made it feel almost weightless in the way that a good *home* did. Not a house, but a place where you came home to the woman you loved. Where your bad day stopped at the door, and everything waiting for you inside made the rest of the shit outside bearable.

I opened the pantry door and eyed the rows of shelves and small counter. It was a full butler's pantry that I knew would come in handy on late nights that neither of us wanted to shop or order out. We'd be able to stock everything we could want and then some.

My heart turned over in my chest. Shit. I liked this house because I saw *her* here. Echo. I saw a life with her in the kitchen, in the sun-drenched living room, and in my bed—wherever that would be.

"That's an incredible pantry," Echo said, peeking her head around me.

I gripped her hand and tugged her into the small room, then shut the door behind us before backing her against the sturdy oak. Then my mouth was on hers, kissing her ravenously. She tasted just like sunshine. Light. Endless. Home.

Her fingers tunneled through my hair as she kissed me back. I loved that about her—the way she never held back from me. She was always in one-hundred percent, and it made it so damn easy to be open with her. Honest. Real. I

156

loved the way she kissed, the way she laughed, the way her mind worked.

I savored the way her tongue twined against mine, and as I felt my cock ready for something we didn't have time for, I pulled back from her and gently kissed her nose.

"I *really* like this pantry," she said with a grin.

"Yeah, me too." I liked who was in the pantry more than anything else about it.

We walked out of the pantry holding hands, and Faith cleared her throat from the living room. "So, what do you think about this one?"

I took one look at the woman at my side and grinned.

"I'll take it."

14
ECHO

"Y'all crushed it tonight!" I high-fived the lead singer of Starfall, the rest of the band settling at the bar for an after-hours drink. The up and coming local band had drawn in a large crowd tonight and Scythe's walls pulsed with energy from their unique mashup of southern and blues.

"The place has some killer acoustics," Morgan said, her bright red hair brushing her chin as she surveyed the bar. "I hope we're invited back," she said, turning to face me as I slid her a vodka tonic.

"Always," I said, pouring the band the rest of their drinks. "I love your sound." I grinned. "And the crowd you draw isn't too bad either."

Morgan gave me a fistbump before taking a sip of her drink. She exhaled, her eyes closing for a moment. "That's nice," she said, then eyed me. "Have a drink with us?"

I shrugged. "Why not?" I poured myself a finger of top-shelf bourbon and took a sip. The bar was already officially shut down, the last customers filing out a half-hour ago. I hadn't yet locked the doors—I was expecting Sawyer any minute—but I had turned off the open sign.

"Where are you headed next?" I asked, leaning against the back of the bar with my drink in hand.

Morgan furrowed her brow before glancing to her guitarist. "Where do we play next, Cash?"

The guitarist brushed back some of his feathered black hair. "Nashville, Mor." He gave her a lazy grin. "I swear without us you'd never know where to start singing."

Morgan just shrugged. "That *is* why I keep y'all around."

The bassist—a tall, lithe man with eyes of crushing blue and silky midnight hair—gaped at her. "Oh sure," he said. "It couldn't be for our *talents*." He wiggled his long fingers at her, his nails painted black, and she giggled.

My gaze darted between the two, my lips pressed together to hide my smile. Something electric sparked between the pair, yet they were trying to hide it.

"Maybe," she finally said, shaking her head. "*Maybe* I like your talents."

"Get a room," Cash grumbled, but there was a smile on his face too.

I watched the banter play back and forth between the bandmates through two more drinks, and joined in on occasion. I found it highly interesting how close-knit the band was, like they were family more than coworkers, and couldn't help but compare it to the relationship dynamic of the Reapers. I hadn't exactly been folded into that family yet, but with the girls' friendship and Sawyer, I was dangerously close to having my own family to claim.

A tight knot settled in my throat. Claiming family, claiming *anyone* only tripled the pain when they left in the end. Not that the Reapers would technically leave—not with their arena a few blocks away—but they could choose to leave *me*. Leave my bar and dominate another as their home base outside of the arena.

I shook my head, pouring another drink. I couldn't think like that. It only led to trouble I didn't have time for. But the more time I spent with Sawyer—talking to him on the phone, lying in bed with him when he was home, hanging here at the bar, exploring downtown Charleston, or visiting his mother—it all led me down that dangerous path I tried so hard to stay away from.

Not the danger of my past, but the new fear of my present. Getting used to him being around, being excited for his company, it made me dependent on it. And I knew exactly what it felt like when that dependency ran out. Hell, he traveled to away games more than he was home, and it wasn't like I could travel with them—I wasn't a PR rep like Langley or an apprentice like Faith. I was a bartender—an owner— but a proud bartender who had to be here to run a business.

"We're gonna take off," Morgan said an hour after our wind-down party had started. "Thanks for letting us play," she said, tapping the bar. "We'll set something up in a couple of months, okay?"

"I look forward to it," I said, raising my glass toward the band as they filed out of the entrance. I downed the rest of the drink and started cleaning up the few glasses I had left. Then I wiped down the bar and checked my cell. No text from Sawyer yet.

I pocketed my cell, cursing myself for being *that* girl.

Not only had the night been insanely busy, I'd now had three drinks, the warm whiskey doing everything to bring on the exhaustion I'd held at bay for the last few hours. But it didn't matter because here I was, finding little odds and ends to do around the bar, just *waiting* for Sawyer to walk through that door.

I couldn't remember the last time I'd been so starved for a man. And it wasn't just the sex—even though that alone was world-shattering. The mere thought of his mouth, those lips and tongue that could shatter me in a matter of minutes, made heat pool between my thighs. I always wanted him, but I always wanted to *see* him more. Talk to him. Make him laugh. Surprise him with my mouth. The shock in his gray eyes was like a drug to me.

Did that mean we really were great friends? Great friends who happened to be electric between the sheets together? Or was there something more? Could there be more if I let go of my own fear—

The entrance door swung open, stopping my chaotic thoughts. The bright smile fell from my lips when I saw Chad walking through the door, not Sawyer.

"What the hell are you doing here?" I snapped but remained behind the bar.

His footsteps were heavy, his body slightly tilted. "You," he said, his words slurred. "You're the reason, Echo. For everything. I wanted…" He closed his eyes as he stumbled against a barstool, righting himself by leaning his elbows on the counter. He peeled his eyelids back. "I wanted you. Want you. We used to be so great together."

I pinched the bridge of my nose, grabbing my cell and scrolling through my contacts. I sent a fast text to one of Chad's friends, letting him know he had ten minutes to collect Chad or I'd call the cops.

"You need some coffee," I said, turning to put on a fresh pot.

"I need you."

"No," I said, my voice firm. The machine behind me started to brew. "You need caffeine and then sleep." I caught his cloudy gaze. "You and I haven't been anything in over a

161

year. And we were different people the last year we were together anyway."

"Don't say that, Echo!" He slammed his fist on the counter, the sudden outburst causing me to jolt.

"Calm down, or I'll put your ass on the street where you belong," I put a lethal edge to my tone.

Strength. I had to show strength, or he'd pounce. He'd always loved it when I played weak in our past, it drove him crazy.

"How you gonna do that, huh? We both know you're no match for me."

"I may not be," I said, then eyed the scythe hanging right above me. "But I've practiced with that thing enough to know I could make you piss yourself." I pointed to the weapon above me.

No, I hadn't practiced with it, but he didn't need to know that.

A vibration in my hand—a text from his friend saying he was on his way. Good. At least he'd taken my threat to call the cops seriously. I didn't want to send Chad to jail merely for the fact that I knew it would cause an escalation in his drop-ins the minute he was released.

"You're cute when you get tough."

I rolled my eyes and poured the hot coffee into a mug and set it before him. "Drink that, Chad," I said. "Sober up."

He sank onto the barstool, wobbling slightly despite sitting, but he wrapped his fingers around the mug. "No cream?"

I shook my head, crossing my arms over my chest. "Don't have any."

"Sugar?"

"Nope."

"Ugh," he gurgled, but brought the mug to his lips. "Fuck," he hissed. "That's hot!" He set it back on the bar, digging in his pocket for a few seconds before pulling out a small, clear plastic bag filled with a fine white powder. "Needs sugar," he said, dumping half the contents into the cup.

"Nope," I snapped, reaching for the cup. "I can handle a drunk Chad but this is where I draw the line. Get the fuck out." My hand on the mug, I tried to pull it away from him but he clamped his hand on my wrist.

"Let go," he said, the first clear words he'd uttered.

"Get your hand off of me." I tried like hell to keep my face a mask of calm.

He tightened his grip, and my mask broke as I yelped.

"Take a drink," he said.

"No."

"Take a drink, Echo," he used the same tone he had in our past—that suggestive, demanding tone that had me giving in when we were together. Anything...I would've done *anything* to numb the pain back then. But I wasn't that girl anymore. "You know you want to," he said. "You act like you're better than me, but you're not. You're a fucking washed up bartender with no family."

I jerked my arm, trying to break his grasp. He only tightened his hold, so hard my skin burned.

"Take. A. Drink." His eyes were wholly crazed now, fueled by liquor and drugs and the anger at not being able to control me.

I gritted my teeth, narrowing my gaze at him. "You have two seconds to release me."

"Or what?"

"One," I warned.

He *laughed*.

"Two."

He twisted my arm, the tendons popping from the pressure.

I grabbed the mug with my free hand and brought it toward my lips.

Then I sloshed the contents right in his face.

He instantly let go, his hands flying to his face as he hissed.

You stupid bitch!" he screamed, knocking over the barstool as he scrambled back.

I gripped the mug above me, prepared to hit him over the head if he so much as stepped a toe near me.

"Get. Out." The demand was spoken through clenched teeth, my entire body shaking now. The skin on my wrist burned from where he'd gripped and twisted my arm.

"You'll pay for that you little cunt!" He stormed toward the bar like he was prepared to leap over it.

I raised the cup higher, ready to swing.

The entrance door swung open, two of Chad's friends instantly sprinting to him. They locked each of his arms down, holding him in place.

"Get off me!" he yelled, struggling against the two.

"Get him out of here!" I screamed.

"Echo?" Sawyer's voice broke over the shouts as he ran around the bar. "What the hell is going on?" he asked once he was at my side.

Chad's manic laughter stopped any answer I might've given. "Run, man," he said, eyes on Sawyer. "You need to run away from that piece of ass as far as you can."

Sawyer's jaw clenched and he took a step but I stopped him with a hand on his chest.

Chad turned his focus to me, no longer struggling against his friends. "She's cursed," he said, practically spitting the words. "Everyone who ever loves her either dies or ends up like me, fucking out of their mind addicted. She's to blame. I was normal until I fucked her!"

The words hit their target on my soul, each one a punch hard enough to crack.

I pushed through the pain, focusing on his friends. "Get him out of here," I said, my voice broken. "The next time he steps in this bar, I call the cops."

The guys nodded, dragging Chad back and back until they were out the door. I sprinted around the bar and locked the door with trembling fingers. My mind reeling, my body shaking, my heart fucking breaking.

Because Chad may have been high out of his mind—he may have been drunk too—but he'd been right about me. There were three gravestones ten miles away to prove it.

"Echo," Sawyer said, his voice like a lightning strike in the now quiet bar.

I spun around, the tears unstoppable as they rolled down my cheeks. The sight of him—sober at two a.m., his perfect polo shirt unwrinkled, his khakis just as crisp—I couldn't take it. Couldn't stomach the idea of tainting him. Cursing him. Ruining something so good and wonderful.

"You need to leave," I said, my heart splitting with my words.

"What?" Sawyer came around the bar, his arms reaching for me. I took a step back, and he halted. "Echo, tell me what happened. *Talk* to me—"

"No," I cut him off. "You need to leave, Sawyer! Get out!" I tossed my keys at his chest, and he easily caught them. I didn't have the strength to unlock the door, too terrified Chad would be out there waiting.

"Echo—"

"Don't you see?" I yelled, the pain in my chest doubling. "Don't you see?" I motioned to myself, then him. "We're from different worlds. You keep coming around me, and you'll lose *everything*." I palmed my cheeks, trying to stop the tears.

"That's not true."

"It is. Look at us! You're in the middle of Division Finals," I said, rubbing at my chest. "You fly out in the morning for game three, and you're here at two a.m.! I'm ruining you!"

This...this pain, I *knew* it. Heartbreak. Which meant...

Sawyer.

My heart belonged to him.

I'd fallen for him despite trying not to.

And now I would ruin everything.

To keep him safe, I would destroy us.

"Chad was right," I said, completely defeated.

"You did *not* just say that stupid prick was right."

"He was," I said, cradling my arm that hurt like a bitch. "I'm cursed. You need to run. Far away from me. You'll end up dead or get swept up in a dark world you were never meant to see."

Sawyer took one step toward me, then another.

I hoped he was heading toward the door behind me.

But he stopped in front of me.

I refused to look up.

Refused to meet those gray eyes.

"Echo." His voice was soft, calm, but held a power enough to give me pause. He tilted my chin up, forcing me to meet his eyes. "I'm not scared of you," he said.

I clenched my eyes shut. "You should be."

"I'm not," he said, smoothing his thumbs over my cheeks, wiping tear after tear away. "I'm not scared of your past, either."

I peeled my eyes apart, searching for any sign of deception. I only saw the truth in his eyes, the hope, and the compassion.

"You're too good for me," I said, and meant it.

This incredible man who'd spent his life taking care of his mother, putting his dream on the line to ensure her comfort. The man who supported his team and worked hard and played hard and listened when I spoke and never judged me for any dirty detail I'd told him about my past.

This man...

"Echo," he chided, cupping both cheeks in his hands. "You are amazing. And wild. And smart. And funny. And..." he sucked in a sharp breath, his eyes churning with too many emotions to read. "And you're *mine*."

More tears slipped free at the declaration, at the idea that someone as *good* and decent as Sawyer McCoy would ever claim me.

"And what am I to you, Echo?" The question was a whisper between us.

My eyes cleared as I locked onto his gaze, looking up at him with my heart fully exposed.

"Everything, Sawyer," I whispered. "You're everything."

The admission was an unleashing because one second I stood there gazing up at him and the next he'd swept one strong arm underneath my knees and cradled me to his chest. He grazed the tip of his nose over mine and slowly, softly planted a kiss on my lips. The motion restrained of the fierce hunger we had for each other and replaced with something infinitely more intimate. Powerful. Consuming.

I wrapped my arms around his neck, kissing him back, gently exploring his mouth, letting my lips and tongue silently tell him the words I couldn't dare speak.

I've fallen for you.

Don't break me.

Sawyer smiled against my mouth, pulling back to catch my eyes.

"Can I take you home, Echo?"

The question was so polite, so unnecessary, that I let out a tear-filled laugh. "Yes, Sawyer. Please, take me home."

Another quick kiss and he carried me through the

167

hallway and up the stairs until we stood at the threshold of my loft.

And for the first time since I could remember, I was nervous.

Nervous about sleeping with a man who owned my heart completely.

15

SAWYER

I set Echo down only long enough to run her a bath. Once the water ran hot enough, I dumped in whatever girly bubble stuff she had sitting on the edge of the clawfoot monstrosity and went back to where she sat at the kitchen table.

"Tell me what I can do," I said, kneeling down so I was at her eye level. "That guy has no right to rip into you. No right to even set foot in the bar. No right to crawl into your head."

She swallowed and ran her fingers through my hair. "There's nothing you can do. Chad is his own worst nightmare. He'll complete his self-destruct cycle at his own pace."

"I don't know how to help you."

"You can't," she said softly.

I stood, then walked back to the bathroom to check the water level while my head spun. Helping was what I *did*.

Dad walked out? I stepped up and became Mom's proxy.

Faith had a broken heart? I bought ice cream.

Harper needed extra study space? I'd cleaned out the spare bedroom. Helping was the one thing—besides hockey

—I was good at. So how the hell was I supposed to stand by and watch Echo go through some shit like this and *not* help?

How was I supposed to let Mom move up to Virginia next week and simply hope that my aunts knew everything they needed to? Hope that she had everything she needed and access to the right doctors?

What the hell was with the women in my life that they wouldn't just let me fucking help them? And fuck that no-strings policy Echo insisted on. She was in my life, and she wasn't going anywhere if I had anything to say about it.

The water rose to what I guessed was the right level, and I shut it off, trying to do the same to my raging emotions.

The last thing Echo needed was me piling my shit onto her while she was emotionally raw. I took two steadying breaths and tried to stuff all my issues back into a metaphorical jar. Maybe I couldn't knock off the ex-boyfriend and dump his body in the Atlantic, but I could take care of my woman.

I walked back out into the kitchen to find Echo exactly where I'd left her.

"Come on," I said gently, holding out my hand for her.

Her lips parted, and her forehead creased for a second, but she stood and took my hand. "I got nervous that you'd leave," she admitted as I led her to the bathroom. "I know you don't do well with feeling helpless."

I turned and cupped her cheeks in my hand. "One, you know me a little too well. Two, I'm not helpless. Three, I'm not leaving. You can't scare me off." I bent and kissed her slowly, leaving her tilting her head for more when I pulled away.

Wordlessly, I stripped her, pausing to kiss and caress her skin with each bared inch, leaving her erogenous zones untouched. Her legs trembled by the time she stepped out of her thong, and her hands gripped my shoulders to stay upright.

I helped her into the tub, and she groaned as she slipped beneath the bubbles. "This feels like heaven," she said, leaning forward to hug her knees. "Get in here."

"Not sure if you've noticed, but the water is pretty much at max capacity." I nodded toward the bubbles.

"The bubbles are deceiving," she argued. "Plus, I had the tub put over a floor drain because I like my baths like I like everything else." She arched an eyebrow.

"And how is that?"

"Deep. Hot. Consuming. You know."

Our eyes locked, hers already going hazy with want. Far be it from me to deny Echo anything she wanted. *Anything.* Shit. I meant that.

This woman could ask me for the contents of my bank account, the deed to the house I hadn't yet moved into, or even a fucking ring, and I wouldn't say no. It wasn't just the drive to make her happy, though that was strong. It was because seeing her happy made *me* happy. In that way, it was almost selfish to want to see to her every need, whim, or desire. The fact that I knew she'd never abuse the power was as intoxicating as the shit she kept on the top shelf downstairs.

I stripped my clothes carefully, holding her gaze the entire time. By the time my boxer briefs hit the ground, she was gnawing on her lower lip and looking at me like I was dessert. I stepped into the tub behind her and slid down until my back rested against the curve of the tub. Then she moved back and pinned my erection between us.

I hissed at the contact, but being hard around Echo wasn't exactly new.

"This tub is huge," I said as I ran my hands down the slippery skin of her shoulder.

"It was my splurge," she admitted as her head rested against my chest. "I probably spent more than I should have on it, but I'm a sucker for a good bath."

I reached for the soap and then began to wash the patches of skin I could see—her shoulders, her knees where they popped up above the water, and finally her collarbone. She arched as I passed above her breasts, and the blatant sensuality of the movement made lust wash over me, even hotter than the bathwater.

"I love the way you make me feel." She tilted her head and looked at me, her eyes big and bright, and full of something that felt a lot like a string.

A string I wanted.

"I love everything about you." The admission slipped from my lips in a gravel-worn voice I barely recognized as my own. The words were true. I was crazy about her—loved every little thing that made up this complicated woman I'd fallen for.

Shit. I'd fallen for her.

Three months. That was all it had taken. I loved her.

She turned slightly and brought her mouth to mine. Then she kissed me, taking it light and slow. She opened under me, and I took the kiss deeper, stroking my thumb down her neck as I melted into everything she was.

I craved this woman on a level I'd never experienced before.

The kiss turned passionate, and soon lazy sensuality was replaced with a primal heat that sent my hands to her breasts. I broke my mouth away and twisted her so her ass was against my groin again. "Just relax," I whispered, lightly nipping her ear.

She shivered.

Then I sent my hands questing, first to her breasts and those velvety hard nipples, then down her ribcage. I traced the curve of her hips, then lifted her so she sat in my lap, her thighs spread over mine.

"You're so fucking beautiful," I growled at the sight before me as the bubbles faded.

"Sawyer," she squirmed against my cock. "Touch me."

The bathwater was comfortably hot, but her pussy was even hotter, enveloping two of my fingers in a slippery, silken grip as I thrust into her.

She cried out, arching against me, and I nipped at her neck where it met her shoulder.

"Is this how you touched yourself that night on the phone?" I asked.

"Mmmmm." She nodded. "You're better at it, though."

"Touching you?" I grazed my thumb over her clit and thrust my fingers inside her again.

"God, yes." She rocked her hips, taking what she wanted from my fingers. "You somehow know what my body wants before I do."

I flexed my jaw, beating back the impulse to lift her a few inches and replace my fingers with my cock. This wasn't about me. This was about her.

"You know what I think?" I asked softly between open-mouthed kisses on the side of her neck.

"Hmm?"

I withdrew my fingers slowly, and when she whimpered in disappointment, I thrust in again, then curled my fingers at her G-spot and rubbed. Her nails bit into the back of my neck, and I felt her moan in every inch of my dick.

"I think you like the loss of control." I kept pumping at that spot, and her breaths changed, coming shallower and faster. "You see, when you're touching yourself, you know exactly what you're going to do." I flicked her clit with my other hand, and she gasped.

"Sawyer!" she demanded, her voice pitching higher.

"I fucking love the way you say my name. Half-plea. Half-demand. All mine." I rubbed her clit hard for two, three seconds, and her back bowed as she cried out. "See, you like my fingers better because for once in your life, you're at someone's mercy."

I stilled completely, and she gasped.

"Please." She turned and brushed her lips across mine.

"You're at my mercy," I whispered, then slid my fingers inside her again, stroking her deep. She fluttered around me, her muscles pulling at me in desperate need of release. "You melt for me because you can trust me." I wasn't sure how many people she could say that about in her life, but at that moment, it was more important to have that trust than the body that was driving me insane with lust.

She stiffened slightly, but she was too lost in her passion to fight me on it—if she even would.

I curled my fingers again, giving her what she wanted, but I gently stroked her clit, backing away when she'd rock for more pressure. "Say it."

"Sawyer!" My name was a hot pant of breath against my own lips as hers trembled.

"Say it." I swirled my fingers over her, pumping my other hand inside her.

"I trust you," she admitted softly, and I saw the truth of it in her eyes, even with the desire thick enough between us that I knew it had the chance to bind us for forever.

I kissed her deeply and gave her the pressure she wanted. She came apart in my arms with a scream, her pussy gripping my fingers so tight that I almost came against her back—I was that close.

Fuck, I needed to be inside her. Needed to feel her pulse around my cock, not just my fingers. Needed to come inside her so deep that she'd feel me even when I wasn't with her. Because I couldn't be with her every day. Hell, I was leaving in a few hours. All we ever had were stolen hours, and it wasn't enough. I needed more. I needed *her*.

She twisted in my arms and straddled my thighs. I'd expected to see some of that fire banked in her eyes now that she'd had a release, but as usual, she demolished my every expectation.

Her mouth met mine in a kiss that cost me my common sense. Or maybe it was just Echo. Either way, her arms looped around my neck, her tongue tangled around mine, and I forgot everything outside the incredible woman in my arms.

Need raged inside me, demanding I thrust inside her and take us both to completion again. But something kept me from sliding her down over me and doing exactly just that. I was simply too lost in kissing Echo to remember exactly what was stopping me.

She rocked forward as the kiss took on that sweet edge of desperation, and I knew she was right there with me.

"God, I need you inside me," she groaned against my lips.

Her ass filled my hands, and I jerked her against me, until my cock slid against her pussy. She was slicker than the water, and my dick pulsed in time with my heartbeat as I rested at her entrance.

"Sawyer, please," she begged, resting her against mine.

Our breaths were ragged, our bodies so hot the cooling bathwater felt even better against my skin. Above me, she was silk and fire, and everything I'd never realized I'd been missing in my life. The wild in her called to me, broke the restraints I kept not on my body—but my heart.

And I loved her.

God, I *loved* her.

"Give me a second, and I'll get you to bed," I promised.

"I can't wait." She shook her head. "Baby, I can't wait!"

Maybe it was the way she'd called me baby, or simply the

urgency in her eyes, but I gave her what she needed. I arched my hips and drove into her with a long thrust, groaning as she rippled around me, taking every inch of me until her ass rested against my thighs.

"Holy shit, you feel incredible." The pleasure was so intense that I had to take a few breaths so this could last. She was hotter, tighter than ever, and so wet that I felt every inch of her as I glided again, pulling out slightly only to thrust deeper.

"Yes!" She arched, throwing her head back as I thrust again, putting her breasts right at my mouth. I licked and sucked at her nipples as she started to ride me, rising on her knees and taking full control.

She took me shallow, a wicked gleam rising in her eyes. When I rubbed my thumb across her clit, she sank down again, taking me deep. Then, playtime was over as she locked her mouth to mine and fucked me hard, sloshing the water over the sides of the tub with each rock and swirl of her hips.

The tight heat drove me mindless, and when she started to tense above me, and I felt that clench in her muscles, I gripped her hips and held her still as I thrust up deeper, harder, faster, until I managed to press on her climax-sensitive clit with a thumb and she came around me.

Pleasure gripped me tight and wouldn't let up, pulling my orgasm from me in a rush of ecstasy so fierce I let out my own shout as I emptied into her in what felt like the longest, hardest orgasm of my life.

We held onto each other as we both came down from the high. Holy shit, I'd never felt anything like that in my life.

"Echo, that was…" I shook my head, trying to think of anything I could say that would come close to explaining my feelings. "I love you."

Well, that wasn't what I'd planned on.

Her eyes flared, but instead of climbing off of me and

screaming that we'd agreed to a no-strings...whatever, she simply smiled at me, more beautiful than I'd ever seen her.

"Good, because I love you, too, and I didn't want to be the only crazy one."

Joy hit me so hard and fast that I felt drunk with it. "You're not," I promised her, then kissed her hard. "But as crazy as we both might be, I need to get you out of this water. It's not exactly warm anymore."

She laughed, and the sound cracked open the last of my restraint when it came to her.

"Is crazy okay?" she asked with a lopsided grin.

"Crazy is the best."

I groaned as she slid off me, and then flinched as the cold water hit my cock. I used the sides of the tub as leverage and then stood, quickly getting out and locating a towel for Echo. Once she was out and wrapped up in thick terry, I took one for myself and wrapped it around my hips.

That's when I realized *why* the sex had felt even better than before.

"Holy shit." My gaze jerked to meet Echo's.

"What's wrong?" she asked, reaching around me for her brush.

"We didn't use a condom. Echo, never in my life have I *ever* forgotten to put on a condom. Not once." It was as habitual to me as putting on my seat belt in the car.

She looked at me with wide blue eyes and then smiled. "It's okay, West Coast. I'm on birth control. We're covered."

"But I wasn't!"

She put the brush back and wrapped her arms around my waist. "I'm clean, Sawyer. It had been a year since anyone before you. Is that what you're worried about?"

"What? No." That thought had never crossed my mind. "If anything, you should be worried about *me*. Aren't you?" Sure,

I'd always used a condom, but it wasn't like I kept a book with the names of every girl I'd ever slept with.

"Are you clean?" she asked, not a single hint of worry in her voice.

"Of course I am! But you didn't know that!" And I hadn't protected her.

"I already knew you were," she answered with an easy shrug.

"How?" Damn it, if she didn't stop rubbing against me like that, we were going to end up on the bathroom floor, not the bed.

"It's like you said. I trust you. Remember?" She kissed me lightly, then spun and walked out of the bathroom.

I watched her walk away with a sense of awe. *Never fuck without a condom.* That was the first advice I'd been given by my coach in the locker room my freshman year. Too many girls wanted the pro-athlete life, and they were willing to get knocked up to get it.

But even the thought of Echo pregnant didn't turn me off. It revved me up higher in some primal way. Not that I wanted a kid now, or anything. I just knew if I was going to have one, I'd want Echo to be its mother. Not that it mattered, either way. She was on the pill.

"Hurry up, and I might just show you how much I trust you again before you have to get on that plane," she called after me.

I spent the next three hours buried inside of Echo, twisting her into every possible position that would give her an even better high. She was insatiable, and by the time I crawled out of bed around six-thirty, I'd rung so many orgasms from her that she was finally sleeping.

"Are you leaving already?" she asked, peeking up at me with sleepy eyes.

"Yeah. The Thurston thing freaked Coach out, so we have

to get to the rink an hour earlier for every game and every flight to test. No biggie." I kissed her forehead.

"Okay. Good luck. Save pucks. Have a good flight. All of that," she murmured, already closing her eyes.

"I love you," I whispered at her temple.

"Love you," she replied, slipping into sleep.

I kissed her forehead one more time before finding my discarded clothes. By the time I reached the rink, I felt oddly energetic instead of exhausted.

We had a conference championship to win.

16

ECHO

*T*he boys were Conference Champions, headed to
the Stanley Cup Finals in the next couple of days,
and it was time to celebrate.

A line of people wove around the brick building, the
golden streetlamps casting the historic jazz club in a warm
glow. The night sky was clear and peppered with stars, the
air warm and full of that ancient breeze only downtown
Charleston could manage.

"Whoa," Faith said, her arm interlocked with mine as we
walked past the line. "You said this place was popular, but I
didn't realize..." she halted, tugging me to a stop. "Shouldn't
we head to the back of the line?"

Langley clicked up with Harper in tow. "Yes, Echo, I'm all
about using the Reapers for good press but I don't want to
drop the boys' names just to get into a club." She motioned
behind her, where a trail of Reapers followed us like little
ducks. I chuckled at the image, since they weren't *little* at all.
In fact, each NHL star looked downright intimidating as they
followed our lead.

"Really, Langley?" I shook my head. "I know the owner," I

180

jerked my head toward the building. "She has free drinks at Scythe for life so I can come here whenever I want without the wait."

Langley nodded, impressed.

"Now that I'm not using the Reapers' name to get into this place, let's use *me* and have a good time!"

The girls cheered with me and within minutes we were strolling through the doors of one of the oldest jazz clubs in Charleston. Ownership had changed throughout the years, as did the name of the club, but one thing that stayed the same? The quality of local music played live on the same historic stage as when the building was erected.

"This is the closest thing Charleston has to a speakeasy," I said into Faith's ear to be heard over the band.

"Hey, Echo!" Coraline hustled out from behind her elegant mahogany bar, the liquor bottles back-lit by warm red lighting. "You came with a crowd this time?" She eyed all the Reapers and their queens behind me.

"Sure did," I said. "These newbies needed a taste of real Charleston."

"No place better," she said, winking at me. "Hold on a sec, honey." She hurried and grabbed one of her waitresses and brought her back to our group. "Take this crew to the balcony lounge," she said to the waitress. "Bottle service?" She eyed me.

"Definitely," I said, speaking for everyone.

"Have a good time, sugar!" Coraline called as we followed the waitress through a mishmash of tables and high-tops until we reached a set of roped-off stairs. Two minutes and we were upstairs settling into the vintage couches and chairs Coraline had decorated the area with. The balcony over-looked the stage, creating the perfect view for the show.

"This seat taken?" Sawyer asked, eyeing the empty space next to me on the small, lush sofa I'd sat on.

"It is," I said, arching a brow at him.

"Who's the lucky asshole?"

"Oh, he's not an asshole," I cooed. "He happens to be the smartest, sexiest, *sweetest* boy I ever did meet." I stood up, trailing my fingers over the soft-cotton T-shirt that stretched tight over his muscled chest.

His hand easily slipped around my waist and to the small of my back. "That southern drawl, Echo," he practically growled. "It *does* things to me."

He did things to me.

Had done things to me.

Turned me into a love-struck swooning woman.

Two weeks of nothing but pure bliss and this man still sent my heart racing whenever he was within five feet of me.

"What do you think of the place?" I asked, tugging him to sit next to me.

Cannon, Logan, and Connell had taken over the two Victorian couches at the farthest end of the balcony, the Scotsman already sipping his first drink. Lukas, Faith, Noble, Harper, Langley and Axel were scattered among the chaises and high-backed chairs in the middle of the balcony, accepting the champagne Coraline had sent up. Laughing and talking and applauding as the band wrapped up another number.

Not one stranger in here would be able to look at the group and see anything other than one awesome unit—a family chosen not by blood, but by bond. Brothers of the ice, sisters through marriage—it was beautiful, breathtaking. And I was beyond lucky to get a taste of it.

Because it won't last.

I flinched against the traitorous voice in my head. Cringed against the bitch who had tried to ruin these past two weeks for me. Tried to tear down my happiness by reminding me over and over again that Sawyer's world wasn't mine—wasn't anything close to what I was used to—and I didn't belong in his.

"It's incredible," Sawyer whispered in my ear, answering the question I'd already forgotten I'd asked, but successfully grounding me in the present. Taking me away from the darkness in my mind. "I wouldn't expect anything less from you."

I smiled, easy and helpless against Sawyer's charm. He never made me feel self-conscious, never criticized me or spoke down to me. He built me up whenever I doubted myself, and he drew me away from the edge when I was certain I'd topple over. I'd never had that before, let alone the full family support that came along with him. It was...other-worldly almost. But something I knew I could sink into, if I let myself.

"How old is this building?" he asked, tucking me into his side after we'd both accepted a flute of champagne from our waitress.

"Over eighty years," I answered before taking a sip of the bubbly.

"Nice," he said. "You know all the best places around here."

I shrugged. "Comes from growing up here and never leaving."

He furrowed his brow. "You don't travel?"

"I have," I said. "But not as much as I probably should've before opening a bar."

He smiled. "I know it's your baby, but the bar isn't like an actual baby, you know? You *could* hire a manager to run things if you wanted to go on vacation. Or, say, see an away game. Or any game at all."

I gaped at him before lightly shoving his chest. "Game nights are my most profitable nights!"

"Same for me," he teased.

I sighed. "I'm sorry I couldn't make it the last time you invited me. Hayley was sick, or I would've shown up. I'd love to see you on the ice someday."

His gray eyes flashed. "I like the sound of *someday.*"

Sawyer knew me down to my core—knew I was still getting used to this relationship thing. Still opening up to the idea that I'd fallen for him on a level that terrified me. Scared me because everything I'd ever loved had been taken from me or had chosen to leave. Hell, that was the main reason I never left the bar. I had a great staff and at least three employees that I could promote to manager but I was afraid if I left for too long, I'd come back to nothing but ashes.

"Does it bother you that I don't come to your games?" I asked. "Bother you that I'm not in the family box with the other queens? Wearing your jersey?"

He shifted against the sofa. "You wearing my jersey any time would be hot," he said. "And no, Echo, it doesn't bother me. I respect your business. I understand how much game nights bring in. And I take great pride in knowing how much me being on that screen distracts you from all your hard work."

"Someone thinks mighty high of himself," I play shoved him again.

"Hard not to with you at my side."

I leaned into him, drinking in his cinnamon scent, and let the sounds of the piano and symbols and sax soothe that traitorous voice in my head. Settled myself in the moment—this rare moment where the team didn't have practice until the afternoon, so they could let loose tonight. And I'd *wanted* to bring them here—all of them. Not just Sawyer, but the whole crew. Wanted them to see and experience a place that meant so much to me. A place draped in history and alive with music and food and drinks.

It was a marvel I could choose to do anything else over

being with Sawyer alone, at his new place or mine. The time I'd seen him in the past two weeks since we'd become *official* had been spent tangled with his body. His lips on my skin, his fingers coaxing moans from my mouth, the weight of him a delicious craving I never could slake. And in between? We talked and laughed and simply *were.*

Sawyer's knuckles grazed my cheek, his eyes churning as he watched me. "Where is your mind at?" he whispered in my ear, and chills burst along my skin.

"You," I said, trailing my lips over his in a featherlight touch. "Always you, lately. I think you've properly driven me crazy."

"Oh, Echo," he said. "You have no idea."

I grinned at the tease in his voice, at the promise of what was to come. And I couldn't wait to see what he had in store.

"You have to have a reason," Logan said an hour later, eyes on Connell who leaned against the balcony railing, switching from watching the band play to conversing with the rest of us. We'd long since rearranged Coraline's balcony furniture so we could be closer together and mingle. We'd also long since lost count of how many bottles we'd shared.

"What makes ye say that?" Connell asked.

"Because," Logan said. "No one loves pranking people that much. No one outside of grade school," he joked.

The Scotsman held his drink up to him, narrowing his gaze. "I resent that," he said, though his blue eyes were nothing but tease.

"Come on," Logan urged. "Spill."

Connell shook his head, his blond hair messy in that perfect way. "There doesn't have to be a reason," he said, his accent thick, but surprisingly I was getting better at interpreting him. He pointed to where Cannon sat on the edge of the couch, sipping a dark amber liquid from a glass tumbler, having foregone the champagne. "That's like saying there has to be a reason for Cannon to be so angry all the time." Connell held out his arms. "Sometimes things just *are*."

Cannon flipped him off, but there was a crackle of something behind his dark eyes—amusement, maybe. I was a hardass when I wanted to be, but even *I* wasn't about to cross the line to get Cannon to open up. It had taken me a month of seeing him at Scythe to work up the courage to comment how fond I was of his tattoos, and all I'd gotten was an appreciative grunt and a kind request for another drink. Good luck to the girl who was currently perched on his lap.

"One day," Lukas chimed in, pointing at the Scotsman. "One day you're going to pull some shit on the wrong person, and it's going to bite you right in the ass."

"Speaking of ass biting," Connell said. "I quite like a good risk. That's the fun of it, isn't it? And the laughs."

Noble tsked him. "Yeah, we'll all be laughing, buddy, when that day does come and someone hands your ass to you."

The laughter drained from Connell's face, his arms dropping to his sides, his drink clinking near his hip. "You'll all still have me back, though, right?"

"No question," Axel said, standing up to clap the Scotsman on his shoulder. "But we'll still laugh our asses off."

That was met by laughter from all of us. I set down my empty flute, wiping the tears from the corners of my eyes.

Sawyer grinned at me. "You're beautiful."

I rolled my eyes. "Please," I chided. "I'm sure I've laughed off all my eyeliner. I probably look like a raccoon right now."

He shook his hand and tugged me to standing. "You're beautiful," he said again then moved his cheek to mine, his lips at my ear. "And you're mine," he whispered, sending a trail of warm chills in his breaths' wake. He pulled back slightly, his head tilted. "Dance with me?"

I wetted my lips, my mouth suddenly dry, but managed to nod.

Sawyer interlocked our fingers, leading me down the stairs and onto the crowded dance floor, the band switching to another number. This one slow, sultry, and electric.

The music pulsed around us while Sawyer slid his hands over my hips, taking the lead as he moved us in slow dips and swaying steps. I wrapped my arms around his neck, pressing my chest against his as our bodies writhed to the intoxicating music, every inch of me alive with the feel of him against me, the heat from his body, the intensity in his eyes.

He spun me in his embrace, keeping my arms hooked around his neck as my ass now ground against him in beat to the music. My blood warmed at the hardness I felt pressing into me from behind. Instantly liquid, my head spun with wanting this man. My muscles went tight and loose all at the same time as his expert hands moved over my skin, down my sides, across my hips. He twirled me to face him again, his gray eyes churning with want.

Without opening our mouths, we *spoke*. All the things we wanted laid bare and crackling between our bodies. It didn't matter that we were surrounded by people. Didn't matter that we were in the middle of an outing with more than a half dozen of our closest friends. In that moment, I was consumed. We both were, if Sawyer's sudden urging me off the dance floor was any indication.

I followed him like a starved woman, blindly going wherever he led. I felt *that* safe with him, the sensation hitting me like a blow. When I caught on to his destination—the darkened hallway where the bathrooms waited—I tugged on him until he leaned closer to my mouth.

"I know a better place," I whispered into his ear and winked at him as flames danced in his eyes. I took the reins, bypassing the bathrooms and guiding him farther down the hall and to the left, where I knew Coraline kept a private room for VIP banquets and the like.

Lucky for me, she didn't lock it up.

Though Sawyer locked the door behind us as soon as we entered the dark room.

Big enough to house two banquet-size tables, the room was thankfully empty save for those and the chairs stacked in two neat rows along the back wall.

I jerked Sawyer's head down, reaching up on my tiptoes to meet him in a crushing kiss. I swept my tongue past his lips, drinking in the taste of him before pulling back. I smirked and turned, moving to grab a chair.

Sawyer hauled me against him before I could reach for one. "Too far," he growled, claiming my mouth in a fierce kiss, all the while spinning me until my back was pressed against the door he'd just locked. He gathered my hands and pinned them above my head with one of his own, his other freely roaming down my neck, over my aching breasts, and lower, teasing me over my black skirt.

"Sawyer," I sighed, unable to contain it as he slid his hand underneath the skirt and continued his exploration over the fishnet stockings I wore.

"You have another pair of these, right?" he asked against my mouth as he tugged on the fishnets.

"Yes," I gasped. "Why?"

Sawyer released my hands he had pinned, using both of his to dive under my skirt. A quick jerk from him and a loud rip sounded. Another heartbeat and he'd pushed my thong to the side, his fingers met with my warmth.

"Fuck, Echo," he said, his mouth and tongue never ceasing their teasing of my lips, my neck. "You're so wet. So ready for me." With a few expert moves, his pants and boxer briefs were down and bunched around his ankles. "I need to feel your warm pussy around my cock."

"Goddamn!" I practically screamed as he hiked my leg around his hip and thrust inside me. The motion was pure delicious heat and unbridled desire as he seated himself to the hilt. My spiked heel dug into his ass as he dragged himself out in one slow motion only to ram home again. "Sawyer. *Fuck.*" My eyes rolled back in my head from the sensation of being absolutely fully clothed, and yet I could feel him bare inside me. Hard and strong and hot, filling me so much I could barely breathe.

"So damn tight," he growled against my neck, pumping over and over and over. "Perfection."

I dug my nails into his strong shoulders, holding on as if I might fall off the edge of the planet.

"Don't let go," he said, then shifted his hands behind my ass and lifted until I'd locked both ankles around his hips. The man didn't miss a beat with the set change, and the feel of his hands on my ass through the fishnets? That was enough to have me clenching around his cock like a vise.

Energy built like a gathering storm, each of Sawyer's thrusts, strokes, or kisses enough to set me off. But he kept me there, at the edge of pleasure and pain until I was *dying* for him.

"Sawyer," I moaned. "Please," I begged. "Never stop. *Fucking* never stop." I never wanted this to end. Never wanted to leave this place of pure ecstasy and ultimate unleashing. I may not have gotten addicted to the drugs in my past, but I sure as hell was addicted to Sawyer McCoy.

"Never," he said, his tone a promise, a brand on my soul as he upped his speed.

A loud knock on the door, the vibrations hard enough to jerk Sawyer and I both back to reality. To the very *real* reality of being in a very public place.

"Coraline?" a waitress yelled from the other side. Another knock. "Coraline?"

I pressed my forehead against Sawyer's, his body a statue as we waited. "Stay with me," I whispered, and then *moved* on him. Used every ounce of strength in my thighs and core to lift up on him and rock down. Slowly. Torturously. Until Sawyer's fingers dug into where he held my ass.

"Always," he whispered back and used that leverage on my ass to move me himself. Up and down, slow and steady, until we heard footsteps leading away from the door—the waitress likely running off in search of where Coraline actually was.

But I didn't care.

I wouldn't have cared if she'd pounded on the door the entire time.

I rode Sawyer like we were the only two people in the club. Reveled in the way he made my body sing, made me come alive with sensation.

"Harder," I demanded, gripping the back of his neck.

Sawyer obliged, pistoning his hips with deep thrusts that raked through the heat of me until I was slick with him and me and moaning his name so loud I was certain our friends in the balcony could hear.

But as I hurtled over that sweet, sweet edge, my body trembling as he shattered me completely, I didn't care who heard or who knew—Sawyer McCoy owned me. Body and soul.

Despite my no-strings insistence.

Despite my pathetic attempts to protect him from me...I loved this man.

He held me as we both came down, our bodies trembling with pleasure. Slowly, he slid me down his body, readjusting my panties and setting me on my spiked heels.

"I get it now," I said, smiling up at him.

He tilted his head.

"I didn't before," I said, cupping his cheek. "That night.

Truth or dare," I said, grinning. "When you spoke about being so consumed by someone you didn't care where you were, you just simply *had* to have them."

A mischievous grin shaped his lips. "Feel free to use this as an example the next time Connell makes us play."

I bit down on my lower lip, lost in those gray eyes. "You're so bad," I teased.

"You love it."

"I really do," I said, dropping my hand to unlatch the lock, leading us through an unknowing crowd and back up the stairs to the balcony and a group of friends who kindly didn't remark on the length of our absence.

The next afternoon, I hurried out of Scythe, Sawyer's warm-up jacket in hand.

"You're sure you don't mind?" Sawyer asked into my ear where I held my cell.

"Of course not," I said. "I got Hayley to cover for me. She can hold down the bar for a bit."

"Thanks," he said. "I didn't realize we needed the jackets for a group promo pic today."

"Part of me wants to keep this just to see how hard Langley lays into you over it," I teased, rounding the building toward the back lot.

"Not funny, Echo. Her husband is the scariest mother-fucker in the league."

"Axel?" I laughed. "He's a teddy bear."

Sawyer huffed. "If he's a teddy bear then what the hell am I?"

"A sexy, perfect specimen."

"You're too good to me."

"I'll try to fix that," I said. "See you in a few." I ended the call, reaching in my bag for my keys without watching where I was going.

"Heading to see your new boyfriend?" Chad's voice halted my steps, and I whipped my head up to find him leaning against my car. He pushed off of it, his hands raised in defense. "Don't call the cops just yet," he said. "I came here to apologize."

I narrowed my gaze. His eyes were still cloudy, but not as badly as last time. My body surged with adrenaline, every danger instinct on full alert. Inside my bar had been one thing, but here? In the back lot where no one would likely happen upon us? I was exposed. Vulnerable.

"Fine," I said. "I have to go." I made to move around him, but he stepped into my space, close enough I could smell that metallic tang of drugs that always followed him. "Chad," I warned.

"You're in such a rush to go see him? To be his little puck bunny?"

I glared up at him. "Apology is going splendidly."

He sighed. "Right. I didn't mean for the other night to happen." His eyes trailed to my wrist, the one he'd hurt. "Are you okay?"

"I will be," I said. "Once you decide to leave me alone."

"Fucking hell, Echo. We did spend almost three years of our lives together, you know? Can you really just throw that away for some perfect bullshit hockey player?"

I scoffed. "You left me long before I left you, Chad. And it doesn't even matter. We're done. We've been done. There is no *us* anymore."

He nodded, the muscle in his jaw clenching. I moved to go around him, but he stopped me again, this time so fast I dropped Sawyer's warm-up jacket.

"Sorry," he said, darting to pick the jacket up before I could move. I held his gaze, not wanting to lose sight of his eyes in case they switched from cordial to lethal.

"Give that to me," I said, each word slow and clear. "And move."

He handed me the jacket after another breath and backed away. "No one is perfect," Chad said. "Someday you're going to remember that." He turned his back on me and headed around the building. "I'll be waiting for you when you do."

My hands were still trembling when I parked outside Reaper arena, which was a too-quick drive from my bar. I sucked in a sharp breath, held my chin high, and rushed Sawyer's jacket inside minutes before the shoot.

"You're lucky your girlfriend cares about you," Langley chided Sawyer as I made my way toward the exit of the arena.

I winked at Langley, blew a kiss to Sawyer, and got out of there as fast as I could. I couldn't dare let Sawyer see the fear in my eyes. The anger and the exhaustion over the one piece of my past that wouldn't stop haunting me.

Because the last thing I ever wanted it to do was to start haunting him too.

17

SAWYER

*H*oly shit, we were really going to the Cup.

"Well, we're not here for fun," Cannon said without looking up from another book.

"Guess I said that out loud?" I questioned as our bus pulled into the private airport we usually flew out of.

"That or I'm now a mind reader."

The 737 was parked directly ahead of us, and the bus turned to stop just outside the small trailer that served as security.

I swung my backpack over my shoulder as we filed out of the bus. Just ahead, the box truck carrying our equipment was open in the back as several of the equipment managers and a few airport staff quickly unloaded a mountain of gear.

"Gentlemen!" Coach called as we gathered on the asphalt outside the security building, a sea of black warm-up jackets and ties. Thank God Echo had brought mine this afternoon, or Langley would have forced me into something awful just to prove a point.

Echo. God, I already missed her. She'd raced over as the team was loading the bus so I could sneak in one last kiss before the trip, but it wasn't enough. I thought about the wives flying out commercially tonight, and a stab of jealousy hit me in the stomach. I loved that she worked so hard for the bar, but there was a part of me that longed to see her at the game now that we'd made the finals.

"Let's get through the checkpoint as quickly as possible and get you into the air," Coach shouted above the noise. "It's a four-hour flight to Vegas, and I want you in bed early. No gambling, no booze, no women, nothing. You understand?"

"I play better when I get laid," Cannon grumbled next to me.

Connell laughed from his other side but kept his mouth shut for once.

After we all muttered the expected, "We understand you," Coach led the way into the trailer.

"This time tomorrow night, we'll have won Game one," Connell predicted, nodding his head like it was already a fact.

"Next time we'll have to charter a bigger plane to fit your fucking ego." Cannon shook his head and closed his book. The title made me raise my eyebrows. Somehow I expected a guy with his temper to read books on serial killers or murder mysteries, not *Atlas Shrugged.*

"Jesus," Connell's accent drew the word out. "They're taking this drug thing a little far, don't you think?" He nodded toward where a K-9 unit entered behind the coach.

"Can you blame them?" Ward asked from my other side. "They can't afford to take any chances."

The line started moving forward, though we were regretfully in the back quarter of it.

"Just do us all a favor and take your damned sunglasses out of your pocket before you go through the metal detector this time, McCoy. No one needs to get held up again."

Connell winked because he'd put them in there to begin with.

"You're not getting me this time, asshole," I said with a grin shoving my hands into my warmup jacket. No sunglasses. I felt something odd in my right pocket, and pulled it free, holding it between my thumb and forefinger.

Looking down, I saw a small, plastic bag half-full of white powder.

What the fuck?

Keeping my hand low, I tested the texture of the powder, rolling my thumb over what felt like baby powder under the plastic. But I didn't use powder, or keep it in anything like that...

"Holy shit." Cannon fisted his hand around mine as the line moved forward again, bringing us closer to the door. "What the fuck is that?" he questioned lowly, so only I could hear.

"I don't know. It was in my jacket."

He flipped my hand over and opened it. "Motherfucker," he hissed, then closed my fist over the bag again. "Damn, dude," his voice rose. "I have no clue if they brought your favorite fucking stick. Didn't you leave it in the rack like usual?" His eyes narrowed pointedly at me.

"Uh, I don't know..."

"Jesus, rookie. Okay, come on." He tugged on my arm. "We need to check equipment for a second," he shouted up to Coach Hartman, who stood at the door.

"Don't take too long!" he called back.

We walked out of the line and headed along a line of hedges that bordered the small security checkpoint, toward the equipment truck.

"Give that to me right now," Cannon ordered.

I gave him the bag, and he cracked it open just long enough to sniff above it lightly.

"Why the fuck are you carrying coke?" he growled, zipping the bag shut.

"That's cocaine?" I stared at the bag.

"White powder, little bag, chemically sweet smell?" He looked at me like I was a moron.

"How the fuck would I know what cocaine smells like? I've never touched a drug in my life that wasn't prescribed," I snapped.

He tilted his head. "Know anyone who has? Or still does this shit?"

"No," I protested immediately. Wait. Echo *had*, but she swore to me that it had been during a time where she'd been grief-stricken, and hadn't touched it since.

Cannon sighed, taking in my fallen expression. "Okay. Follow my lead." His eyes darted to our surroundings, and then he started walking.

"Hey, Marcus!" Cannon shouted at one of the equipment managers. "Did you grab McCoy's favorite stick? He's freaking the fuck out."

Marcus hopped out of the truck as another bag was passed down. "We grabbed the stick he starts with and two backups from the rack. Plus Bauer is sending another four directly to Vegas. That sound like enough?" His eyebrows rose.

"I told you," Cannon growled at me before turning back to Marcus with a sigh. "Sorry man. Didn't mean to offend. Rookie's got nerves, that's all."

Marcus eyed me but finally nodded. "Don't you worry about us, McCoy. We've got your gear. You just worry about those Golden Knights."

"Yes, sir," I said to the man who was easily a decade my senior.

"Thanks, man. Say hi to Kim and the kids for me," Cannon said in farewell, edging us toward the opposite end

SAMANTHA WHISKEY

of the truck. He turned on me, staring me down with a glare that sent chills down my spine. "Don't you ever fucking question something like that again!" he shouted, coming at me with deliberate steps.

I backed up with each word he said, unsure if he was putting on a fantastic show, or if he was really that pissed. "Okay, I'm sorry," I said, meaning every word.

"You make us look like motherfucking divas when you pull shit like that!" He poked me in the chest. "You want to go all rock star in public? Fine, but not in our house!" He flung his arms out, indicating both where the team stood to our right, and the truck waited on the left.

If I hadn't been watching his hand, I would have missed it. The baggie fell just a few inches into the large, black metal-lined trash can he'd managed to maneuver us to.

"You understand?" Cannon barked.

"Yes, sir." I stared in awe at the man who'd just saved my ass.

He nodded, and turned, leaving me to trail after him back to the line, where only five or so of my teammates were waiting to enter the checkpoint.

My heart pounded as we came up to Coach Hartman, who simply raised an eyebrow at me.

"Fucking rookies," Cannon muttered. "Don't be too hard on him, Coach. He's nervous as a virgin on prom night."

Hartman shook his head at me, then looked at Cannon. "You were hard enough on him for the entire coaching staff. See you boys on the plane."

Cannon grunted, and we headed into the checkpoint. My heart didn't cease its chaotic beat until we'd checked in for the manifest and passed the dog.

"Look, I don't know what the fuck is going on, but you almost just cost us the Cup," Cannon said quietly as he took

198

the seat next to me on the plane. "You honestly think that Zimmerman kid can pull us through? Because I don't."

"I have no idea how it got there," I said quietly, my mind reeling.

"Anyone else worn it?" he questioned. "Or kept it for you?"

I nodded slowly, unwilling to say it, or even believe that the woman I loved was doing drugs. Not when she knew how they'd fucked up my life.

"Shit. You'd better get some answers from that bartender of yours when we get home," he said, already pulling out his book. "But for now, you keep that shit out of your mind and get your head in the net where it belongs."

But keeping Echo out of my head had never been my strong suit.

We fell three to six in game one.

* * *

Echo: Have you landed yet? I've missed you.

I stared at the text message as I sat outside Scythe in my truck, trying to organize my emotions into some recognizable, logical box.

I loved this woman.

I needed to know the truth.

Sawyer: Just pulled up.

Firing off the text, I got out of my truck and locked the door. The bar had the average number of Saturday afternoon cars, but I knew tomorrow night it would be packed with fans as we played Game two just down the street.

I opened the door and barely made it past the first table before a flash of purple appeared from my left. Then Echo was in my arms, her arms tight around my neck and her face against my throat.

My arms closed around her, holding her to me in what I knew might be the last time depending on what she said. God, even if she was using again, could I walk away from her? Could I bail at the first real test of my loyalty?

"I missed you," she admitted, kissing my throat lightly.

A quick glance told me she had three waitresses on duty for a reasonable crowd. "Can we go upstairs? I need to talk to you."

She pulled back to look up at me, confusion causing the skin to wrinkle between her brows. "Sure. Everything okay?"

"I hope so," I said gently, unwilling to lie even to settle her nerves.

She nodded and took my hand, then led us through the kitchen and up the steps to her loft. The door closed behind us with a click, shutting out the noise from the bar. Silence stretched between us.

"What's going on?" She reached for my hand, but I stepped back, almost hitting the bookshelf that served as a room divider.

"I love you." That was the most important thing, so I said it first.

"And I love you…"

"When I got to the airport—heading to Vegas—I found a bag of cocaine in my pocket."

She gasped. "You what?"

"Jacket. Cocaine. Pocket." I wasn't sure I could say the whole sentence again.

"What were you wearing?" she questioned, her eyes flying wide with worry.

"My warm-up jacket. The one you dropped off to me." I tried to keep my voice soft but damn it, my stomach was flipping over, and nausea was quickly taking control.

Her mouth dropped open. "But you don't use. Do any of the other guys?" She pushed her hair behind her ears.

"No. There's no chance of any of the guys using. Especially with the drug tests we've been subject to since the shit with Thurston."

She nodded, then stilled. "Wait. You...You don't think it was mine, do you?"

Choose your words carefully, McCoy.

"I don't want to," I said softly.

She flinched and crossed her arms under her breasts. "You don't want to, but you don't know?" Her tone was hurt, not defensive, and it ripped right through me.

"I don't know what to think! I got to that airport and just happened to check my pockets before going through the security checkpoint—the checkpoint that happened to have a drug dog at it, I might add." I walked forward and turned my back to the kitchen, needing the space to breathe.

"Oh my God. What did you do?" She stepped toward me in concern but stopped herself before coming too close. "Are you okay?"

"Cannon handled it. I was fine physically, but..." I raked my hand through my hair. "I didn't want to have this conversation over the phone or in a text, and—"

"And you were distracted during the game," she assumed, her shoulders dropping.

"Sure, a little, but I'm certainly not blaming our loss on this." I sucked in a full breath and steadied my nerves, knowing I had to directly ask what she hadn't directly offered. "Echo, was it yours?"

"Are you fucking kidding me?" There was zero hurt in her tone there. Nope, that was pure rage.

"Look. I love you no matter what you answer, but I have to know. You're the only one who had my jacket. You've told me that you'd used it in the past. You know what that shit has done to my life—to my mother's. I have to know." I slipped my hands into the pockets of my slacks. I hadn't bothered to change after getting off the plane an hour ago.

Her face twisted, as if she couldn't believe I'd actually asked, and for a moment, I thought she might not answer. "No. It's not mine. I told you I used it a few times after my dad died, but that's it. I didn't like who it turned me into, and I pulled myself out of that life."

I sighed, and my entire posture relaxed, releasing a tension I hadn't realized had even been there. "Okay."

"Okay?" she snapped. "You just asked me if I left cocaine in your jacket, and you think it's okay?"

"No! I think this is the furthest thing from okay! But what am I supposed to do? I left my jacket here without cocaine. You brought it to me, and then there are drugs in my pocket. What am I supposed to think?"

"You're supposed to trust me!"

"Easy to say when you're not the one about to be arrested by the K-9 unit, and subsequently cost your team the Stanley Cup. Oh, and wreck your entire career!"

She flinched again, and I cursed my stupid temper.

"Echo," I said softly. "I do trust you. If you say it's not yours, then I believe you. And even if it was, I still love you. We'd work it out. But it's a big fucking deal to find out whose it is and how the hell it ended up in a piece of my uniform."

"Even if it was mine, you'd stay with me?" she asked, her voice breaking.

God, the look on her face ripped me open like nothing else could. I crossed the distance between us and pulled her against me, then pressed a kiss to the top of her head. "I wouldn't leave you over a drug problem. I'd insist on rehab and pray it never happened again, but I wouldn't walk away if you needed help."

Her shoulders shook with a wry laugh, and she pulled away from me, bracing her fingers at her temples like I was giving her a headache. "Of course you wouldn't. Sawyer McCoy doesn't walk away from a woman in need. He steps right up and mends whatever's broken."

My eyes narrowed. "What do you mean?"

She let out a guttural sigh and rolled her head back, loosing her frustration at the ceiling. "I know *exactly* how that cocaine got in your jacket."

I stilled.

"Fucking Chad."

I didn't question the order those two words came out of her mouth. That would have been madness, right? So I stood there silently and waited for her to explain what she meant.

"Chad was outside the bar when I left to bring you your jacket." She brought her gaze back to mine.

"And you're just now telling me this?"

"You're just now telling me you had drugs in your pocket two days ago?"

"Fair point. So how exactly does Chad play into all this?" I folded my arms across my chest, needing something to do with all the pent-up frustration.

"I dropped the jacket. He picked it up and handed it to me. Then I took it to you. He must have put them in the pocket. He knew it was yours." She closed her eyes.

"Awesome. So your ex planted drugs on me so what? I'd take them? I'd get caught with them? What?" My body was practically vibrating with tension.

"Either result would have been a win for him. He knows that if you started using I'd kick your ass to the curb, and he probably figures if you get caught, then you'll probably lose your contract with the Reapers—"

"There's no *probably* about it."

"—and he thinks you playing hockey has some appeal for me."

"Well, we both know that's not true considering you've

never even been to one of my fucking games." Shit, now I was the one cringing.

Her eyebrows shot up. "Right. I wondered when that was going to come back around and bite me in the ass."

"Shit." I raked my hands down my face. "I'm sorry. I shouldn't have said that. I know how hard you work, and I respect it."

"You just wish I also showed up at the rink with your name on my back like one of those good little women whose lives revolve around their boyfriends?"

"No! Maybe. Shit."

"Sorry, West Coast, but I'll never be one of those women who wrap my entire world around a man. I might love you, but I'll be damned if you become my center of gravity just so you can eventually leave." Her eyes hardened.

"Who the hell said anything about leaving? I just told you that even if the coke was yours, I'd still be here!" What the fuck did she want from me? What did I have to prove to her?

"You'll leave!" She threw her hands up. "Everyone does. You'll eventually get traded, or you'll decide I'm not right for your photo op, or that seeing each other at two a.m. after closing just isn't good enough."

"Not good for my photo op? When the hell have I ever acted like that shit mattered? You're beautiful, and I could give a shit what the media or fans want to know about the woman I'm in love with. That's up to you. Public, not public, I don't give a shit as long as I get to come home to you, so don't you dare lay that at my feet. And second, yeah, the two a.m.'s are getting old—"

"See!" She pointed a finger at me.

"So maybe I sleep here during the off-season, or hell, maybe you hire someone to close more than twice a week. Or maybe you even decide to move in with me so we can see each other in the sunlight every once in a while." I shrugged.

She scoffed, but there was so much conflict in her eyes that I couldn't even begin to guess at her emotions. "Move in? You think I want to move into that chunk of suburbia?"

"One, I think you actually like that house, and two, it's better than never leaving work. Jesus, Echo, you literally *live* at work. And I know this place is your dream, but it can't be your *only* dream."

"Why not?"

"You're seriously going to tell me that at twenty-three years old, you have everything you've ever dreamed of?"

"The big NHL star is going to use that line on me?" She shook her head. "You're twenty-three too, remember?"

"And this isn't my only dream! Sure, it was the biggest one, but I'm hanging around the guys, and I'm realizing that maybe it's about the bigger picture, too. It's about kicking ass on the ice, and coming home to the woman you love. It's about not just building a career, but building a life!"

"How can you have a life when you're either at the rink, on a plane, with me, or at your mom's? Sawyer, you're so busy fixing everyone else's life that you hardly have one of your own, so please don't lecture me on where I choose to live mine."

I sucked in a breath.

"Mom is moving to Virginia after the finals are over," I said slowly. "I'm allowed to reexamine my life now that I have options for the first time."

Her face fell. "I didn't mean it that way. The way you take care of your mom is so amazing."

"No, it's not. It's what a son does. It's what you would have done for your dad if you had the chance. It's not some huge feat or something to be praised for. You show up for the people you love. You make the sacrifice because, in the end, it's only the love that matters."

Something changed in her expression, and suddenly she felt further away than the night I'd met her.

"Look, if we can just figure out how to keep Chad from trying to fuck with your life and mine, this will be fine," I assured her. "Everything will be fine. All this shit doesn't need to be sorted out in an instant."

She shook her head and looked away. "It won't be fine."

My stomach tightened. "Yeah, it will. We'll figure it out."

"No, we won't," she said slowly, and brought her eyes back to mine. "You and I...what were we thinking?"

"That we love each other," I answered instantly.

"Since when is that ever enough?" Her voice rose, and she backed farther away as she started pacing. "We should have kept it at no strings. Why didn't we keep it at no strings?"

"Because I love you! And you love me!" Heat flushed up my neck.

"So what?" She stopped and threw her arms out. "Look what love has done to us! My ex is so jealous that he nearly ended your career, and it wasn't just you he could have hurt. He could have taken down your whole team. Do you want that on your head?"

"Echo—"

"No!" She put her hand out when I started to move forward. "Think about Lukas and Axel. About Logan and Connell. Hell, even Cannon. You really think they'd accept, 'But I love her' as the reason they lost the Stanley Cup?"

I swallowed. She was right in that one regard. Chad could have damaged way more people than just me.

"You think you didn't lose a game here and there because of exhaustion with *my* hours? Sawyer, we are a train wreck waiting to happen. Hell, that's already happening. We have to stop this before we end up hurting everyone around us, too."

Bile rose as my muscles locked, as if in protest to what she was saying.

"We're not breaking up because we had a fight," I told her slowly.

"We're not breaking up because we were never together," she countered, squaring her shoulders. "We agreed on sex. Our emotions got involved. Our agreement is over."

I looked down to see if I was bleeding because it felt like she'd just sliced me to the core. "You...you can't just decide that shit got complicated and end this."

"But I can." That hard-ass exterior I now knew she used as a mask clicked back into place. "It takes two people to be in a relationship, and I'm pulling out."

God, the arch of her neck, the way she tilted her head in that haughty way...I almost would have believed we meant nothing to her if not for the stark pain in her eyes.

"Why are you doing this?" I walked forward, but she retreated until she hit the back of the couch. "You know you love me."

"Yeah," she admitted with a smile that didn't reach her eyes. "And that love is killing you. I can't be responsible for pulling you under, and you can't make me settle down. Bird and a fish. Whatever. It doesn't matter. We're over."

"I don't accept this."

"You don't have a choice."

We locked eyes across the five or so feet that separated us, and I felt it—her withdrawal. She was locking herself up behind those walls that I couldn't crack unless she let me. She was the strongest woman I'd ever known, and she was using that strength against me.

"Echo, what do you want me to do? I love you. I'll get a restraining order against Chad. I'll hire bodyguards for the bar. I'll sell the house in Sweet Water and buy a condo in Langley's building. Tell me what you need."

"I just need you to leave." Her eyes fluttered closed. "I'm not one of your problems to fix."

"Echo—" I shook my head.

"Stop making this harder than it has to be and get out!" she snapped, pointing to the doors as two tears tracked down her cheeks.

Pain. There was so much pain in that cry, but she wouldn't let me soothe her. I'd done everything to prove to her that I would stay. That I wouldn't abandon her, and it still wasn't enough. I wasn't enough for her.

"You know what your problem is?" I asked softly, but she didn't open her eyes. "You love me, and it scares the shit out of you. You're so focused on your fears that you've locked yourself away."

She stood there, tears tracking down her cheeks with her eyes squeezed tightly shut.

My heart shattered as I realized there was nothing I could do.

I finally nodded and made my way to her door. The handle felt cold, just like the rest of me. "When you look back on this, and I know you will, you'll see it differently. You'll tell the next guy that you were too much for me. That I wanted a different life than you did, so I walked out—I left you. And physically, I guess you're right since it's your house and I can't exactly force you to let me stay. I actually have to *walk* away. But you're not alone because people leave you, Echo. You're alone because you make it impossible to stay. You push everyone away, and that's on you."

I mentally gathered what was left of my broken heart and did exactly what she'd demanded.

I walked away.

18

ECHO

"Well well well," Chad droned as I approached him with clenched fists. "Look who it is. Ms. Holier-than-thou decides to finally slum it again?"

I rolled my eyes, drawing in a long breath to calm my racing heart. It hadn't taken too many guesses for me to find him. It was Memorial Day, so naturally his family was having their regular barbecue. I should have been spending the day in the solace of my loft, mourning my family in a quiet, calm, respectful way. And quite possibly mourning my own soul since I'd shredded it by pushing Sawyer away two days ago. But I was too enraged for that. Too angry at everything the man before me had cost me.

"You're an idiot, Chad," I said, seething. "You were a *stock-broker.*" I pronounced the word slow so he would understand. "You were the one slumming it with me. Don't get it twisted." I shook my head. "I can't help what you've become because no matter how blue collar I was compared to your family…" I eyed them all in their finery, holding champagne flutes and gaping at me like they didn't *love* a good scene. "I wasn't the one who turned you into what you are. Poison."

Chad swallowed hard, glancing over his shoulder at his gawking family before pulling me off to the other side of his house. "What are you doing here?"

"Not fun, is it? Having your past show up where it isn't wanted?"

"What's your issue?"

I scoffed. He had some fucking nerve. "My *issue*?" I laughed a manic laugh. "My issue is that *you* cost me everything!"

He tucked his hands into his pockets. "Finally realized what you let go of?"

"Not you," I snapped. "Sawyer."

He flinched, his eyes flaring a fraction. "I can't be blamed if he up and left you because he finally realized what trash you are."

I cringed, pure disgust rolling through my veins at the man standing before me. He wasn't who I'd fallen for all those years ago. He never would be. And that stupid notion of hope had kept me cordial with him for far too long. Kept me wishing I could help him get better so we could go our separate ways as better people.

"You planted drugs in his jacket," I said, my tone a hiss. "He could've lost his contract! The Reapers' could've lost the Cup!" Maybe they still would, seeing as they'd lost again last night. If they lost two more games, they'd be out.

"You've lost it," he said, but there was fear in his eyes.

"Come on, Chad. Let's not play dumb."

He shrugged.

"I have proof."

His entire body stilled, his lips parting, a plea or a denial I couldn't tell.

"You lie."

I tilted my head. "You think I'd open a bar and not have

the place covered with security cameras?" I glared at him. "You think I'm that stupid?"

He swallowed hard. "What are you going to do?"

"It's not about what *I'm* going to do."

"What?"

"It's about what *you're* going to do."

He pursed his lips but remained silent.

"You're going to leave me the hell alone," I said, ticking off the first item on my finger. "You're going to leave Sawyer alone. You're going to leave anyone I fucking know alone." I raised my brows. He gave me one nod. "You're going to stop showing up at Scythe." I ticked the next item off on my next finger and received another curt nod. "And you're going to forget you ever knew me." I dropped my hand, my limbs shaking. I took a deep breath and let it out slowly. "There was a time when I thought if we stayed in contact, maybe I could help you get out of that hole. That maybe I could help you get clean. But you don't care what I think. You don't care what anyone thinks. I've tried to get you professional help so many times I'm sick with it. And what you did? What you've done these past few months? You've made it incredibly easy to let you go. To give up." I shook my head. "You're a poison. And I'm not going to let you hurt me or the people around me one second longer. You understand?"

Another nod as he crossed his arms over his chest.

"Because, Chad?" I made sure his eyes were solely focused on me. "I swear to *God* if I see you or hear about you trying to fuck with my life or any of my friends' lives again I will use the security footage to put you in jail for a long, long time."

And that's likely where he belonged. Maybe that's the place he'd get clean. Maybe I should've already turned him in. But I couldn't be that girl. His family needed to deal with him. *He* needed to deal with himself.

"If Sawyer's contract would've been taken from him?" I stepped closer to him, letting him see the rage in my eyes. "I would've already turned you in. Got it?"

"I got it." He had the audacity to sound pissed.

"Good. Then we're done. Forever." I turned my back on him, stomping away from his family home, my chest a bit lighter with each step. I saw the fear in his eyes—he cared about himself and his habits more than anyone, and jail was the last place he wanted to end up. Finally, I'd clipped the chain off my ankle that was Chad.

I fell into my driver's seat, my lungs tight with tension as I breathed in and out.

Sure, I'd rid myself of Chad. Sawyer wasn't in trouble.

But I'd lost him.

You're not alone because people leave you, Echo. You're alone because you make it impossible to stay. You push everyone away, and that's on you.

I cringed against the memory of his words. The sight of him so utterly disappointed and wrecked. But I *had* to push him away. Being with me...it had nearly ruined his life. Almost cost him everything. I wasn't worth that. I had to end things so he could have the life he deserved—one without drugs and darkness and the baggage I carried.

Guess it was only a matter of time. Thanks, bitch.

I rolled my eyes at the traitorous voice in my head, hating that it still had any sway over my thought process. Sawyer had already broken me with his instant assumption that the drugs were mine. That I would ever put him or his dream career, or the Reapers at risk. And even after he believed me, I'd done a full shredding of my heart by ending it between us. Because he fucking deserved better.

But...he made me want to *be* better.

God, did I want to be the woman he'd spoken of—the woman to come home to. His home, *our* home. I may love the loft I lived in, but it wasn't roots. Wasn't like what I'd had growing up. And with Sawyer? It wouldn't matter where we lived—loft or condo or a house in Reaper Village—it would be *home.* Because even if I'd pushed him away for his own good, he still owned my heart.

Part of me ached to reach out to him. To call him. To send him a random text and pretend like nothing had happened between us. To hit the rewind button and go back to that blissful piece of paradise we'd lived in a week ago.

Too good to be true. People die. People leave.

And the only thing that remained constant was the strength I had to muster to put myself back together. But this time? This time was a different kind of breaking. One I'd never experienced before. This one felt like I'd never actually been whole—not really, not without him. And now he was gone because I reacted to my survival instincts and cut him out of my life for his own good.

I loved him so much I wanted what was best for him… and I wasn't it. Not with how much he'd nearly lost because of me.

I'd been foolish to think I could ever be good enough for him.

I drove away from Chad's family house, cruising the streets in a daze. My mind chewed on all the things that had gone wrong with Sawyer, and I wondered if striking up a friendship with him had been the thing to damn him. If we hadn't gotten along so well, hadn't had that instant connection, maybe we'd both have been spared this pain.

The love? That's more powerful than any grief. Even if it's just the memory of it.

Sawyer's voice echoed in my mind, the words he spoke to me with such passion all those months ago.

I pulled over and parked on a side street, needing a

second to collect my breath. To stop the tears that kept on coming, despite me thinking I'd used them all up.

A few deep breaths and some agonizing back and forth and I reached for my cell, my thumb hovering over Sawyer's name.

I chewed on my bottom lip, wanting to scream at him, wanting to cry at him, wanting to simply *hear* him. Wanting to confess to him that I hadn't meant a word of it. That I didn't mean to break us. Break him. Wanted to tell him that he was right—I did push people away, but he was the first one I actually wanted to stay.

I hit call.

It rang.

And rang.

And rang.

And went to voicemail.

I didn't have the courage to leave a message. Didn't have the words or time enough to speak the truth slicing through my heart.

So I hung the phone up, wiped my eyes, and pulled back onto the road. Ready to drive home and sleep for the rest of the day. Or the week. I hadn't decided, yet.

I crept to a stop at a red light, my stomach swirling until I thought I might vomit. I cranked my air conditioning, letting the cool air ease the nausea. I hadn't eaten this morning— nothing had sounded appealing, and I'd been so focused on ridding my life of Chad forever that I didn't think about it. It was well past lunch. I'd have to eat something as soon as I got home.

The light turned green just as my cell vibrated in the cup holder. I instantly answered, putting my cell on speaker as I slowly accelerated into the intersection.

"Sawyer?" I gasped.

"Echo, I—"

Screeching tires covered whatever he was about to say.

A hard, fast, something slammed into the passenger side of my car.

One second I was there.

The next I was rolling.

Flying.

The sound of crunching metal.

Shattering glass.

A stuttered sob.

Then darkness.

19

SAWYER

"*E*cho?" I called out, but the line had gone dead. I lowered the phone from my ear and stared at it, willing her to magically appear on the other end again.

What had that sound been before we'd lost service?

I called her back, but it rang four times and went to voicemail. Just the sound of her voice on the stupid message had my heart aching. Finally the beep sounded. "Hey, it's me. I'm not sure why you called, but I'm glad you did. I miss the hell out of you, and I'm hoping you were calling to say the same thing, but even if you weren't, I still miss you. I still love you. Call me when you can."

I hung up and slipped the phone into my back pocket. Then I went back to boxing up Mom's books.

"Who was that?" she asked, walking over slowly.

"Echo, but we got cut off." I quickly took her elbow and helped lower her into the recliner she'd sat in the same night she'd met Echo.

"Well, that's too bad. I'm hoping you two will patch things up, you know."

"Yeah, well, that's really up to her." I turned and lowered another set of books into the open box.

"Is it?" she asked in that tone of hers, the one that told me I should rethink what I'd just said.

I blew my breath out slowly and faced my mother with a calm smile.

Her gray eyes narrowed, and she tilted her head so the light caught the silver streaks in her black hair.

"I want you to take this recliner with you. I'll worry less if you do." It was the one I'd bought her when I got my signing bonus, the one that mechanically tilted and lifted to help her stand.

"I'll take the chair, but no changing the subject." Her words were slower today, but she was also tired.

"What do you want me to do, Mom?"

"I want you to fight for her!"

"How?" I turned and grabbed another stack of books to pack. "She doesn't want me around. She threw me out of her house. She said we were over. How exactly would you like me to fight for her?"

"You show up and don't leave!" she snapped.

"Well, they call that stalking." I slid another stack of books into the box.

"Sawyer McCoy, you damn well know what I mean. You've got a stubborn streak a mile wide. I want you to use that to your advantage."

"I tried."

"Try again."

I sucked a breath in through my nose and let it out through my mouth. I loved my mother more than my own life, but she was sucking all of my patience dry. "Can't we talk about something else? I don't have much time before I have to leave for the plane."

My suitcase was already in the truck, packed and ready to

217

go. The flight for Vegas left in three hours, where hopefully we'd win a fucking game.

"I'm worried about you," she said quietly.

I stilled.

"Sawyer, once I'm with my sisters, and off-season is here, what are you going to do?"

"Oh." I laughed, thinking she'd meant something else entirely. "I don't know. Work out. Hang with friends. Call you." I shrugged. "I'll be okay."

Her face fell. "You won't. Honey, you've been hiding for so long that I'm not sure you even know what to do with yourself."

I crouched before her. "Hiding?"

She put her hands on my face. "The moment your father walked out, you stood up and started taking care of me."

"Of course—"

"Shhh. Listen. You didn't scream at him, or cry, or act out in the normal way teenagers would. You hid every emotion behind this to-do list that never ended. You never sat still long enough to process any of it. Between your insane hockey schedule in college and checking in on me, I'm surprised you ever had time to forge any real connections."

"I had relationships, Mom. It wasn't as bad as you think it was." Women I'd dated, and a couple I'd fallen for.

"Every girl you dated needed something from you. A shoulder to cry on, a steady hand, someone to hold her up. I've never seen someone care for *you* until Echo."

That crushing pain awoke in my chest. "Well, look how that ended." I forced a smile.

"I love you, Sawyer, but you're about to be out of excuses. I'm moving, and you know I'll be happy. Your season is about to be over, win or lose the Cup. And then what? What will you find to do that will keep you from going after the woman you love?"

My forehead wrinkled.

"It's time to figure out what life looks like when you don't have me burdening you."

"You're never a burden!" God, I hope she knew I meant that.

"Fine. It's time to figure out what life looks like now that you're going to put yourself first. Because that's what you have to do. You have to figure out what you want. You're not obligated to me, and this summer you're not obligated to the Reapers. What you are obligated to is your own heart."

"The heart that belongs to the woman who doesn't want it?"

"She called. She wants something."

"She probably wants me to bring back the cell phone charger she left at my house," I joked.

"Then take the charger and plead your case. And if she won't listen, you plead it again until she does."

Before I could answer her, my phone buzzed in my pocket, and I quickly yanked it out, praying it was Echo calling back. The number wasn't familiar, and I nearly sent it to voicemail, but it was a local area code, so I took a chance.

"Hello?"

"Sawyer?" a teary southern drawl asked.

"Yes? Who is this?" I stood as the hairs on the back of my neck prickled.

"It's Annabelle. Look, I'm on my way to the hospital. Echo's been in an accident."

* * *

"Where is she?" I asked the second Annabelle came into view.

She stopped pacing the fluorescent-lighted hallway and turned to face me. "Mom, I'll call you back." She dropped her phone in her purse and headed my way. "I'm glad you came. She might not be, but I am."

"Where is she?" I repeated as if I was only capable of those words.

I'd driven like a maniac to get here, bloody scenes playing in my head the whole time. What if she was badly injured? What if—nope, not going there. I refused to even imagine a life where she wasn't alive.

"Hold on. I'll tell you, I promise just—"

"Where. Is. She?" I growled.

"Stubborn one, aren't you. Fine then, it's your funeral." She gestured to the door across the hall, and I strode to it without another word.

I knocked three times just in case—oh, like it fucking mattered. I was going in no matter what.

"Come in," she said, and I ripped past the curtain and immediately stilled.

She was in a hospital gown, with a white bandage that went from wrist to her upper bicep. Her face was bruised in places and scratched up in others. She was pale as hell but alive.

"Sawyer?" She stared at me like I was the one banged up.

"Are you okay?" I walked to her bedside but didn't know if I could touch her safely or if she'd even give me permission to do so.

"I'm a little shaky, but so far, I'm okay. How did you know I was here?" She tilted her head and glared at something— someone behind me.

"I called Scythe, and JoAnna gave me his number," Annabelle answered from the doorway.

"JoAnna?" Echo challenged.

"Yep. She said you gave it to her just in case she needed you, and you weren't picking up your phone?" Annabelle's voice was sugar sweet, contrasting Echo's narrowed eyes.

"Don't you think I would have called him if I wanted him to see me like this?" she snapped, then winced and lightly touched her forehead.

"Sure, if your phone hadn't been pulverized by that truck," Annabelle answered.

"Your phone was pulverized? Jesus, what happened?" I braced my hands on the rail of her bed to keep from reaching for her.

Echo sighed. "You can leave us now, oh meddling friend."

"Pleased to be of service!" Annabelle shut the door on her way out.

"She's listed as my emergency contact," Echo grumbled in explanation as she plucked at the hospital gown with her good hand.

"I'm kind of losing my mind here, and I know that's selfish seeing as you're the one in the hospital bed, but could you please put me out of my misery and tell me what happened to you?" If I gripped the rail any harder, I'd bend the damn thing.

"Guy in an F-350 ran a red light and plowed right into my passenger side. Good thing it wasn't the driver's side, right?" She brought her gaze slowly to mine with a shaky smile.

My knees went weak, and I grabbed the nearest chair, then scraped it across the floor until I sat as close to her as possible. "That was the sound."

"Sound?" she asked.

"When you called me, there was a sound, and then the line went dead."

She blinked rapidly but finally nodded. "Yeah, I guess so."

Why had she called me? The question was pressing against the roof of my mouth, but I bit it back. None of that mattered if she was hurt.

"How hurt are you?" I leaned forward, resting my elbows on my knees.

"I'm okay," she promised. "You didn't have to come."

"For fuck's sake, of course I came. I'm in love with you!" I snapped.

Her eyes softened.

So did my tone.

"How hurt are you, Echo? Broken bones? Internal?" My mind spun with the awful possibilities.

"Laceration up my right arm." She pointed to the bandage with her left hand. "Cut goes from my wrist to my shoulder, and I lost count of the stitches after seventy."

"Oh, baby," I whispered before I could stop myself. "What else?"

"Bumps, bruises, minor concussion. Nothing you need to worry about." She leaned her head back against the pillow but didn't look away.

"Of course, I'm worried. If it were nothing, you'd be out of here already." My phone rang, and I silenced it without looking to see who it was.

Worry shadowed those turquoise eyes, but she shook her head. "There's nothing. They put me in a CT scan, and I'm just here waiting for the results. I'm fine. It's my passenger seat you should check up on."

I laughed despite the situation. I both loved and hated how she could always do that. "You called me," I said softly, now that I knew she wasn't in any mortal danger.

"I called you."

Two breaths passed. Three.

"Why? You have to tell me."

She bit her lip, then winced when she aggravated a little cut at the corner of her mouth. "Because I missed you. Because I like your house."

"I miss you too—wait, what?" I leaned forward until we were only a foot or so apart.

"I like your house," she repeated quietly. "I *hate* the whole suburban vibe. You know that. But I like your neighborhood —that it's full of your friends. Our friends, I guess. And I like all the light from the windows, and I love that landing when you first walk in. You should get a piano for that space, but paint it pink or something."

"You can paint the entire house pink if you want to." My eyes searched hers as my heart thudded to life.

"You don't want a pink house."

"I want you." My phone buzzed again, and I silenced it once more.

"And I want you." Her admission was a whisper, but it screamed through my entire being.

"Then have me," I offered.

Her face fell, and took my heart with it. "I think our timing is off."

"How?"

She looked up at the ceiling, and the tear that fell from her eye broke me all over again. "What you said about me pushing everyone away—"

"I'm sorry for saying that."

"No. You were right." She swiped at the tear with her good hand and met my eyes again. "It's easier to force you out than to wait for you to realize how wrong we are for each other all on your own. I saw what Chad did to you—and what he could have done, and I took the chance to push you as far away from me as possible."

"What Chad did isn't your fault. And I don't see that we're wrong for each other." I leaned over and brushed away another tear with my thumb. "We're opposites, sure, but do you really want to spend your life with someone who's exactly like you? I'd be bored out of my mind, and you'd end up insane."

My phone rang again, and I turned the ringer off.

"You'd better answer that," Echo muttered.

"Nothing else in the world matters," I countered.

"I hate how you do that!" she cried, covering her eyes with her good hand.

"How I don't answer my phone?"

"How you make me feel like I'm the only person in the world for you. You melt all of my fucking defenses when you say shit like that!"

"Good!"

She shook her head. "It's not good. Maybe we are the right people for each other, but it's the wrong time. I have to trust myself enough to be with you."

"And I have to figure out how to live without the responsibility of my mom on my shoulders," I added.

She moved her hand and looked at me, her lips parting.

"Yeah, I'm not blameless in this," I said with a nod. "I've taken care of my mom since I was fifteen. In every other relationship I've had, Mom was still the number one girl in my life. She had to be. But now she's taking off to live with my aunts, and part of me is scared shitless, and the other part is…" I sighed. "I'm relieved," I admitted. "As shitty as that makes me, I have this feeling of excitement that maybe there's this whole world waiting for me where I don't have to freak out about doctor's appointments or her schedule. I don't have to spend hours in the car every week traveling to see her. And I'll miss her—holy shit will I miss her—but I also feel…free."

She listened without judgment or condemnation in her eyes.

"And that makes me think of all the time I'll have to prioritize you—when you're ready. I don't think our timing is off. I think we can go through all of this together. But if you do, then I'm not going to force you into something you don't want."

"You're not?" Her eyes widened.

"I'm not." I shook my head and stroked her cheek with my thumb. "What I'm going to do is wait. If you have shit you need to figure out, then figure it out. I'm not afraid to wait for you. I love you more than I've ever loved anyone, Echo. I'll wait."

Her lip quivered. "But you'll find someone else in the meantime. I mean, look at you. The women will be lined up, and they'll all be a better fit for you than I am."

That right there—that's what she had to work on, and it killed me that I couldn't fix it for her. I couldn't help.

"East Coast, there is no one in this world who fits me better than you do. We're both fucked up puzzle pieces—all jagged and torn. But somehow, we fit. And the truth is that I don't think anyone else ever will—for either of us. So I'm going to wait until you're just as certain of that as I am. Until you're certain of *me.*"

"Sawyer McCoy!" a voice boomed down the hallway.

Both Echo and I turned to the door just as it was thrown open. Lukas and Axel marched in, both gawking when they saw Echo in the bed.

"Holy shit. Echo, are you all right?" Axel asked.

"Car accident," she answered with a shrug. "Let me guess, you guys totaled your passenger seats, too?"

"What?" Lukas asked, managing to close his mouth. "No, we came for dumbass over here." He jerked his thumb in my direction. "You're okay?"

"I'm fine," she answered.

"How did you know I was here?"

"After you didn't answer your phone the first nine calls, I called someone who did pick up—Faith," Lukas answered. "Apparently you three have had a tracking app since something she referred to as *the spring break incident of sophomore year*, and since Harper has her nose in the lab, Faith tracked you for me."

"I've been a little busy," I snapped.

"You're about to miss the fucking plane," Axel growled. "So if your woman is okay, then kiss her goodbye and get in the goddamned car so we can get to the airport before they leave us here."

I blinked. Holy shit. I'd forgotten that we were leaving for Vegas.

My eyes flew to Echo, and I saw my panic reflected in her smile.

"It's okay. Go."

"I can't leave you. Not like this." I shook my head.

"You can, and you will." She reached for me with her good hand, and I took it. "This is where you prioritize *you*. Well, you and the other Reapers."

My heart and my brain warred with each other. I couldn't leave her, especially not without her CT results back yet. But I also couldn't let my team down.

"Go," she urged.

"Echo…"

"You can wait for me in Vegas just as easily as you can moping around here." Her smile was shaky, but it was there.

"Three minutes," Axel warned, then hauled Lukas out of the room.

"I don't want to lose you. I'm terrified that if I get on that plane, I'll lose any chance I have of keeping you—getting you back, whatever." I rose, only to sit on the side of her bed.

"We're not going to fix what's wrong with us in the next three minutes," she said softly. "I love you. That won't change. So you go. We'll talk after you win the Finals."

"It's only game three!" My voice broke like a teenager. "We'll talk when I get back in two days."

"No," she said, shaking her head. "You focus on you. I'll focus on me. This is one of the biggest moments in your life, and I refuse to be a stress. So just know that I'll be around, loving you."

"Sawyer!" Lukas barked.

"And I'll be playing the games of my life. Loving you."

She smiled. "Something like that."

"I meant what I said. I'll wait as long as you need me to."

Her eyes drooped with a sadness that made me almost change my mind.

"Well, the fucking plane waits for no one!" Lukas yelled through the door.

"Go. I'll never forgive myself if I ruin this for you, too," she begged.

I brushed my lips across her forehead. "I love you."

"I know. Now go. And I expect you to kick some ass."

"Yes, ma'am," I replied with another soft kiss on her brow.

It killed me to leave her, but I did it.

She wasn't the only one depending on me.

2 0

ECHO

I watched Sawyer walk out the hospital door, and my broken heart sighed a little at the balm he'd offered it.

I'll wait for you.

Sawyer didn't do anything lightly, and saying he'd wait for me? For the first time in my life, it felt like I might be someone worth waiting for.

If I could sort out my demons first.

"Great news!" My nurse from earlier came through the door, a massive smile on her face.

"CT results show I'm sane?" I tried to joke, but it fell flat.

"Still waiting on those results," she said, rolling in a mobile computer and locking it next to my bed. She clicked on a few things, then faced me. "Your blood work came back, and we believe the baby is okay."

I blinked.

And blinked again.

"Excuse me?" I whispered, certain I'd misunderstood her.

She tilted her head as she grabbed a small blue tube with one hand and an intense-looking wand thing with the other.

"Can you lift your gown please?" She eyed my abdominal area, the insistence in her eyes assuring me this wasn't some terrible joke. "We need to ensure the heartbeat is strong."

I lifted my gown on autopilot, my mind spinning in disbelief.

She slathered some goo across my lower stomach before she pressed the end of the wand there. A few hard passes, and then she paused. With her free hand, she clicked some keys, and then...

A whirring sound stopped my breath.

Stopped my heart.

Stopped my mind.

Everything narrowed to that steady sound.

Tears filled my eyes as I gasped for breath.

"It's strong," she said, smiling as she focused on her screen. "Looks like you're around eight weeks."

I swallowed the lump in my throat, my mind racing backward in time.

Sawyer. A bathtub. The feel of him bare inside me.

That was about eight weeks ago...

"But I'm on birth control," I said, my voice frantic. "I've been taking it. I took it this morning! Did that hurt our baby?"

My soul shifted with the deepest terror I'd ever known—the idea that I'd hurt the baby or the realization that the car wreck could've taken another loved one from me.

Love.

I was overwhelmed by it within the span of a few heartbeats.

An uncompromising love I'd never known.

"It's okay," the nurse assured me. "This happens. Stop taking the medication now, and we'll go over any others you're taking and discuss whether they're safe."

The nurse continued to speak about precautions and

what to expect as she wiped the goo off my stomach and packed up the rolling computer cart. My entire world flipped as she spoke, as every heartbeat solidified my love for this person I'd never met.

"Do you want me to call the father?" she asked as she headed toward the door.

A bucket of ice-water crashed over me.

Sawyer.

Not twenty minutes ago, he'd told me how relieved and hopeful he was at finally being free. Finally, being able to put himself first, for once. To explore life without the burden of hospital visits and worrying constantly.

"No," I said a little too quickly. "He's...busy." I didn't want to explain just how important the next two weeks were for him.

"Okay," she said. "Is there anything I can get for you while we wait for the CT results?"

"No, thank you," I said. I wouldn't know what to ask for right now even if I did need something. I was too busy watching a life flash before my eyes—one that held so much promise and was *nothing* like I'd ever planned.

* * *

I smoothed my good hand over my stomach an hour after the nurse left, my injured arm stinging something fierce. Annabelle perched on the chair across from my hospital bed, quiet, reflective.

"I never thought..." I started to say then my airways clogged. I cleared my throat and tried again. "I never thought I could feel this way." I focused on Annabelle, on my oldest friend, to keep me from spiraling.

Pregnant.

I was pregnant.

With Sawyer McCoy's baby.

The universe had a sick sort of sense of humor. Giving me a piece of him when I couldn't have the whole.

"I never...never wanted this," I said, but couldn't stop myself from protectively laying my hand over my still-flat stomach.

"I know you didn't, Echo." Annabelle sighed, not a hair out of place. "But you know I've always said that nothing happens on our own timeline."

"I know," I said. "Fate. You're a strong believer in fate."

"And you're telling me you aren't?" she asked, eyeing my tummy. "How could you not be? With a miracle like that growing inside you."

"I don't like the idea of *not* being in control of my own life anymore, Annabelle. I've had enough of that with losing my own family. And now..." Tears coated my eyes. "Now this speck of life inside me means more to me than my own soul. How do you explain that?"

"Easy," she said, tapping her perfectly pink nails on the bar. "Love."

I nodded. "You're right about that." This—what I felt for this baby—it was the purest love I'd ever experienced. I loved Sawyer with my whole entire heart, but this? This baby beat him out tenfold. Now if I could've had them both, the world might've burned from the happiness pouring out of me. But that wasn't in the cards for me. Sawyer may love me, but he'd just gotten to a place where he was finally putting himself first. And he deserved that. He wouldn't want this life.

I'm sorry, baby.

"When are you going to tell him?" she asked.

I shifted in the uncomfortable bed.

"You do know you *have* to tell him, right?" she asked when I hadn't said anything.

231

"I know I have to. He has the right to know. But he doesn't want this life, Annabelle. He's on the road—"

"There are a ton of hockey players with kids and happy marriages, Echo Hayes," she cut me off. "So don't go using that excuse. Sawyer McCoy's own coach is a prime example."

"I know. I know," I said, slightly delirious. So much had changed in my life and I'd only known about the baby for an hour.

My world completely turned on its head.

Because of Sawyer.

First, he got inside me—showed me what real love felt like.

Second, we'd broken each other's hearts.

Third, I'd nearly died, and when I came to...I wasn't alone anymore. It wasn't just *me* I had to live for anymore. It was *us*.

"I'll tell him. After the Cup," I said. "I'll be likely to get more than five minutes with him then." I was a tad bitter. I could taste it on my tongue. I'd been close enough to happy to *feel* it, and now...now it didn't matter.

This baby did.

Sawyer's baby.

Mine.

Ours.

"That's not far away," she said. "What will you do until then?"

I laughed a dark laugh. "You know a place I can order a onesie with the Scythe logo on it?"

* * *

"I HAVEN'T HEARD a peep from you since the accident, and then you call out of the blue begging for Lukas' jet?" Langley chided me as I followed her into the family-guest box of the arena.

"I didn't beg," I said, taking a seat next to her, Faith and Harper already seated and glancing at me with too-knowing eyes.

"We've been so worried," Faith said.

"It was bad enough we had to see you in a hospital bed, but then you ghost us?" Harper finished.

"I'm sorry," I said, wrapping a Reapers hoodie emblazoned with *McCoy* on the back tighter around me. One of the items Sawyer had left in my loft. I shouldn't have worn it. It still smelled like him. But I needed something warm for the cold arena, and I'd be lying if I said it didn't feel good to be drenched in his scent, even if it was fading.

Langley narrowed her gaze, then pursed her lips. "I've never seen you leave the bar for more than a few hours," she said. "And now here you are in Vegas."

I nodded, swallowing hard.

I couldn't wait anymore. Each day was a battle between the love bursting from me for our baby to the constant anxiety over not knowing what Sawyer would say when he found out. Tonight was game seven of the Stanley Cup finals —the biggest game of his life—and I'd always wanted to watch him play. I wouldn't distract him with the news before the game, but after?

God, my heart raced just thinking about uttering the words to him.

Because I would support him, I knew that. If he decided he still needed time to sort himself out. To be on his own and not be responsible for another person for once. I loved him enough to want him to take care of his own heart, but I couldn't help the hope that he'd want to choose us. That he'd want to *stay*.

"I've had to sort some things out in my head," I finally

said, my heart racing as the time ticked on. Sawyer would be on the ice within minutes. "I will explain everything to you all soon. I promise. But for now...I need to speak with Sawyer first."

"He's been a miserable prick, you know," Langley said, accepting my words and moving right along without pushing. "Can barely stand to be around him."

"It hasn't affected his game, has it?" I asked. I hadn't been able to watch him since I found out.

"No," Langley said, sighing. "Somehow, they have the ability to keep their game and their personal life extremely separate." She waved her hands in the air. "Different breed, the lot of them."

"But a good breed," Faith said.

"One worth a little struggle," Harper chimed in.

"I get it, queens. I really, *truly* get it."

They eyed me, but let me sit in silence while the announcer went through the process of identifying the teams, the players, the packed stadium going absolutely wild.

The breath stalled in my lungs.

There he was.

The first I'd seen of him since he'd visited me in the hospital.

It didn't matter that he was covered head to toe in bulky gear. He was *there,* and my heart did all those stupid flutter beats like it was trying to fly right out of my chest and join its other half on the ice.

Sawyer fucking McCoy.

My stomach swirled, a wave of nausea crashing over me. I quickly rested my elbows on my knees, taking deep breaths and praying the girls thought I was emotional over seeing him. I wanted to tell them about the baby but now wasn't the time. Sawyer needed to know first. Then I'd let the girls know.

Sorry, baby, I said internally, nearly smirking at the thing's attitude. Clearly it didn't like me thinking about its father that way.

"Echo?" Faith asked, her hand on my back. "You all right?"

I sat up straight, nodding. "Yes," I said, sucking in a slow breath. "I'm fine."

The game crackled through the crowd through each period and Sawyer was perfection on ice, not that I'd ever doubted that. It was one thing to watch him on television and another thing entirely to see him in person. He was magic in front of that goal, a powerful force to be reckoned with. Here was the man who could wipe my tears away with gentle fingers, yet catch fast-flying pucks like it was nothing but air.

Beautiful.

He was absolutely beautiful. And brilliant. And my heart ached so hard I was shocked it was whole enough to hurt so much.

And just as third period started, he looked to the guest-family box. Spotted me there, standing as the game churned on. The first game I'd ever shown up to, and likely the last. It didn't matter that it was for a blink. That his head was back in the game in a second flat. In that moment, I'd *felt* him there.

And it broke me.

"I'm sorry," I said as I moved past Langley. "I have to go."

"Echo," she called after me. "Do you want us to go with you?"

"No," I said, shaking my head. "You three stay. Enjoy the game. I'll be at the hotel. I just...I just can't do this." I hurried out of the arena before they could stop me.

Hurried so fast it was like I was being chased.

And it wasn't until I'd gotten back to the hotel and in my room that I took a full breath.

I'd never outgrow the love I had for Sawyer, no matter how much I knew we didn't belong in each other's worlds. I would only bring him down in the end, and now that I was a mother-to-be, I couldn't play second best to anyone. I had to be the best for this baby.

And in the end, I suppose that is all that truly mattered.

Regardless of how bad it hurt.

21

SAWYER

I must have been hallucinating. One moment I could have sworn I saw Echo standing in the family box, and the next time I had a chance to look up—she was gone.

There was no way she'd come all the way to Vegas, not when that meant leaving Scythe for more than a few hours. And my mind must have had a good time playing tricks on me because I knew there was no fucking way she'd show up in my Reaper hoodie. No way she'd actually put my name across her back.

Jesus, I missed her so badly that I was hallucinating about her during the biggest game of my life.

"You okay?" Axel asked over the roar of the crowd.

"I'm good." I had more than enough adrenaline to finish out the game, much to Zimmerman's frustration. Guy had been chomping at the bit to get out here.

"Two more minutes, McCoy. Just hold them off for two more minutes." He dropped his fist twice on my shoulder pads and skated off to center ice for another face-off.

We were up by one.

I blocked it all out. The noise from the crowd. The bright lights. The hammering on the glass behind me. The fact that in two minutes we'd either be devastated, headed into overtime, or Stanley Cup champions.

As much as I knew I should memorize everything about this moment—chances were it would never come again—I also knew that letting my thoughts drift from the game would ensure our loss.

The puck dropped, and my world narrowed to the ice and the game I'd always loved.

For the first minute, we were on the offensive, and the puck stayed in the Las Vegas zone. I kept my attention on their forwards, knowing that the game could change in a flash, and they could be on me in less than ten seconds.

The whistle blew again, but my heart didn't ease up. The atmosphere in the arena was electric, and I let myself glance up at the clock. Fifty seconds to go.

Puck dropped in their zone. Cannon sent someone into the boards. Axel took the puck. Lukas caught the pass.

Las Vegas stole it right off his stick and came at me.

I came out of the net at his approach. Ward challenged and lost. Connell was on the other side of the ice, charging hard as the crowd started to count down the ten-second mark. The forward swept behind me, and I pivoted to keep track of the puck. Connell checked the guy hard, but he fired off a pass just before he hit the glass.

Another Las Vegas forward spun around Ward, caught the pass and fired in the time it took for my heart to beat just once.

The puck flew so fucking fast.

I reached out with my glove, knowing that every millimeter mattered.

The buzzer rang.

The arena fell silent as seventeen thousand fans waited, their eyes solely on me.

I rotated my wrist, dropping the puck from my glove to the ice outside my net.

Roars filled my ears. Arms engulfed me. Helmets and gloves flew.

"Holy shite! We did it!" Connell's voice was accompanied by so many others they crashed into me, sending us all—including the net—into the boards.

The joy was indescribable, pulsing through my veins like a drug, swelling my heart until I knew that this moment would be one I dreamed about for years to come.

The shouts died down, and when I had enough space to move, I took off my own helmet.

What followed was a blur. Someone handed me a hat. A shirt was thrown over my shoulder. Axel hoisted the cup. My smile was so wide I thought my jaw might crack as I laid on my side to take the team picture.

It was heaven. Pure heaven.

Eventually we came off the ice.

The guys were met with enthusiastic embraces from their wives. Their girlfriends. Their families. And the small, irrational part of me that had hoped she'd come, overtook the joy until it all felt empty.

I missed her so much that I'd imagined she was there, standing proud. The reality was sobering, heartbreaking even in the midst of so much joy.

"You're sure you don't want to come out?" Connell asked in the hotel lobby. "It's not every day you can tell a woman you've just won the Stanley Cup." He grinned and threw a

239

wink at two blondes passing us in the tight space by the elevators.

Truth was, I did want to celebrate. But I didn't want anyone but Echo, and since she wasn't here, going out with Connell wouldn't really solve my problem.

"Yeah, I'm good," I promised and punched the button to call the elevator.

"Sawyer!" I turned at the sound of Harper calling my name as she pushed through the crowd. She hugged me tightly, and a little of the numbing chill I'd felt since leaving the ice dissipated. "I'm so proud of you!"

"Thanks. You know your husband is a badass, right?"

The elevator opened behind me.

"Don't tell him that, or his ego will never deflate." She grabbed my hand just as I was about to back into the elevator, and pressed a key into it. "Room eight thirty-seven."

"Uhhh," I mumbled. "You know I don't..."

"Oh, shut up!" She shoved at my chest. "Just trust me. Eight thirty-seven."

The doors shut, leaving me in complete, blissful quiet. I punched my floor—thirteen—and leaned back against the elevator wall. As the elevator rose, I studied the key in my hand and then pressed the eighth floor just in time. Maybe Harper had known I wasn't feeling in the mood for a crowd and this was a private Reaper party.

The elevator dinged, and I stepped out, keeping my head down as I passed a group of people headed into the elevator.

"Holy shit, you're Sawyer McCoy!" one of the guys said.

I startled, realizing I'd become the guy I used to idolize.

"Yeah, I am," I answered with a quick, tight smile.

"Amazing game tonight, man!" he congratulated me as they filed into the elevator.

"Thanks," I answered, offering a wave as I turned to head down the hallway.

I found eight thirty-seven and put the key to the lock, half expecting it not to open, but it did. "Hello?" I called out as I walked into the strange room.

Then I was speechless.

Echo stood in the middle of the room, right by the foot of the bed as if she'd jumped up when she'd heard the key in the lock. Her hair was up, and she really was wearing my Reaper hoodie. She was here. She'd been *there*.

"Hi," she said, wringing her hands in front of her.

"You were there?" Not my smoothest line, but it was all I could manage to get out.

"Until you saw me in the third period," she admitted with a nod.

My eyes widened. "And then you *left*?"

"Yeah. Probably not the most supportive thing I could have done, but I didn't want to distract you, and..." She blew out a long breath. "And the truth is that it was hard to see you out there, all fast and crazy-good, and know that I can't have you. And the moment you saw me, I felt it—that pull that's always between us, and I couldn't breathe, and I figured if I couldn't, then maybe you couldn't either, and I needed to go before you got all distracted and blew the game or something."

By the time she'd finished her ramble, my jaw was nearly on the floor. "I don't even know where to begin with all that," I muttered, shaping the bill of my hat.

"You aren't supposed to be here," she blurted, shaking her head.

"I'm sorry?"

"You're supposed to be out partying with your friends. You won the Stanley Cup! Aren't there parties and stuff? Why are you staring at me like that?"

"Harper gave me a key and told me to come up to the room." Was I in the Twilight Zone? First the woman shows up to the first game—ever, then she leaves when I realize she's there, and now she was telling me that I wasn't supposed to be here with her?

"Fucking Harper," she muttered with a shake of her head.

"Let me get this straight," I bit out, annoyance getting the best of me. "You flew all the way out here, but didn't want to see me? Harper wasn't supposed to tell me that you're here?"

"Yes, but no...and yes." She went back to wringing her hands, and it was all I could do not to cross the floor and kiss her stupid just so she'd have something to do with those hands.

Also because I was desperate to taste her.

"Echo, you're a lot of things, but indecisive isn't one of them," I ground out. Was it her mission in life to drive me insane? Because she was accomplishing it with a gold star.

"I know." She rubbed the skin between her eyebrows. "I just wanted to be here. I wanted to see you. I wanted to watch you play. I know what a big deal this is for you, and I wanted to support you, but not interfere with it."

"Interfere with it?" I practically yelled. Jesus, she was going to be the fucking death of me.

"Right. Like right now. You're supposed to be out celebrating the most amazing night of your life, not fighting with me in a hotel room!"

"Why is that?"

"Because this is a moment you'll never get back! You're supposed to be out there!" She pointed out her window.

"Will you please stop telling me where I'm supposed to be?" I stalked toward her.

"Well, you are!" She didn't back away, and within a few steps, I was close enough to catch the warm vanilla of her scent.

"You wanted to see me?" I wrapped my hand around her waist through the bulk of my sweatshirt.

"Yes."

"You came all the way to Vegas just to watch me play?" My other hand rose to the nape of her neck.

"Yes," she admitted, her lips parting.

"You still love me." It wasn't a question.

"Yes," she whispered.

I kissed her before she could say anything else, or spout off another ridiculous reason that she needed to push me away. God, she was wearing that cherry gloss again, and the taste immediately rushed to my dick, hardening me to near pain in the breath of that kiss.

She melted, and I surged, unable to hold back after weeks of being denied even the sight of her or the sound of her voice. I took her mouth until she whimpered and returned the kiss stroke for stroke, until her hands knocked my cap loose to fist in my hair.

"I've missed you so fucking much," I managed to say between kisses. I wanted to eat her alive, to worship her thoroughly, to drench her with so much pleasure that she'd see that we weren't an inconvenience to each other. We were air.

"God, I've missed you," she admitted as I set my lips to her throat. "Every minute. Every day. You're all I think about."

I groaned and pulled her tighter against me. Then I gripped her ass and lifted her. She locked her legs around me, and I kissed her with stark relief. "Tell me you're done denying this," I demanded.

"Sawyer…" She silenced me with a kiss, nearly bringing me to my knees with her deft tongue and passionate response.

I pinned her to the wall and kissed her until I was drunk on her, until she filled every sense.

"Damn it, Echo." I ripped my mouth from hers and tried to clear the fog of lust that clouded my judgment. "Tell me we can be us. Tell me you didn't fly all the way here just to leave me again."

Her breath was ragged as she searched my eyes. "I love you."

I would have taken that answer as an affirmative from any other woman but the complicated vixen in my arms. "Baby, please."

Her expression softened. "Don't you want to go party with the guys?"

"I'm exactly where I want to be." My thumb stroked the soft skin of her cheek. "Having you here with me makes this the best night of my life. I thought my mind was playing tricks on me when I saw you in the stands, and then when we won, and you weren't there..." I kissed her softly. "None of this matters if I don't have you. You make everything in my life sweeter."

"I make everything in your life more complicated," she answered with a brush of her lips on mine.

"In the best way." I rested my forehead on hers. "I don't want to go another day without you, and I know you feel the same otherwise you wouldn't be here."

"But we both have so much growing to do," she protested, but her thighs locked me in place.

"Then we grow together," I answered. "We both have baggage, Echo. We just have to help each other unpack that shit. You have to help me loosen up and learn to balance my personal life with my professional one. I have to help you learn to trust that I'm not going anywhere."

"Right—" I kissed her silent, unwilling to let her get up in her head again.

"Baby, I can't learn that stuff without you, and you can't trust me not to leave if you don't give me the chance to stay. And I know it's scary. I know that trust is expensive, but you have to give a little upfront. I'll earn the rest for the rest of my life, I promise. Just don't do this to us. Don't ruin the best thing either of us has ever had, because you'll ruin us both."

She swallowed, and I could almost taste her fear.

"I love you, Echo. I'm never going to hurt you. I'm never going to walk away. I'm never going to forget just what a lucky bastard I am to have your love, and I'll never let you regret giving me your trust, I swear. I'll find the nearest Elvis right now and marry you if that's what it takes for you to believe it."

Her eyes flared, and I lifted just enough to look into her eyes without going cross-eyed. "You'd marry me?"

"In a heartbeat."

"You've known me for four months." Her words were a little harsh, but there was a plea in her eyes that sliced me to the quick.

"And that's long enough to know that you're it for me. That's long enough for me to add you to the deed to my house so you'll know that you have a home and roots if you want them. That's long enough to—"

"You did what?"

If it wasn't for the raging demand of my cock, pressed right up against her cleft, I might have laughed.

"I added you to the house. I figured it was one way I could show you that I wasn't going anywhere."

Joy sparked in her eyes, and then her mouth was on mine, kissing me with a hunger I felt in the depth of my soul. She was a force in my arms, and our kiss spun out of control, our mouths only parting to remove clothing, until we were both naked and desperate.

I backed up to the bed and sat on the edge as she straddled me, her naked breasts pressed against my chest.

"I love you," she whispered as she lowered herself onto me, taking me inch by inch. She was so slick that I slid easily but groaned at the exquisite friction.

"I love you," I replied, thrusting up to take her to the hilt.

Then our words were gone, our breath used in sighs and groans as we made love. Each time I sank deeper inside her, and she moaned even louder, swirling her hips over mine the way she knew would take me to the brink.

We both came hard and fast, as though our bodies were as unwilling to wait as our hearts had been. I'd never been swept away so quickly in my life and thanked God that she'd been right there with me, just as desperate as I had been.

She rested her head on my shoulder as we both gasped for breath. "You're serious about the whole wanting me thing, right?"

"You have no idea." I ran my hand down her spine, already hardening inside her again. I was going to spend the entire night with my mouth and cock between her thighs, making her come until my name was the only word she could speak.

"Good." She sat up and looked me in the eye, running her tongue over her lower lip nervously. "Because I'm pregnant."

Everything in me stilled.

"I'm not saying you have to follow through on the whole Elvis thing. I'm not really a big Elvis fan anyway, but it's good that you have that big house, right? Because I don't want to raise our baby above a bar," she babbled.

Our baby. A surge of protectiveness, hell, even possession, swept through me. Echo was pregnant with my baby. We were going to be a family. *Our family*.

"Say something," she pled.

"This is the best night of my life." My fingers tunneled through her hair as my arm wrapped around her waist.

Her smile was bright. "You're sure? I know it's a lot to take in, and we're so young—"

I kissed her, letting all my love and joy shine through. "We're young, so we'll be able to keep up with her easier."

"Or him," she laughed.

"And yeah, it's a lot, but I'm…" I couldn't even think of a word. "God, I can't wait to see you holding our baby."

She grinned. "That means you'll be stuck with me forever. You know that, right?"

"Looking forward to every single minute of it," I replied, flipping her so she was under me. I withdrew from her and slid down her body, pressing a kiss against her flat abdomen. It was insane to think our baby was in there.

"I'll never be the perfect suburban mom," she said as I kissed her belly again.

"No, you'll be the exact mom our baby needs," I assured her, sliding over her until I met her lips with mine. "She'll know her worth from birth. She'll never gawk at tattoos. She'll know that beauty is individual and subjective. She'll know her brain is the most valuable part of her body. She'll know how to throw a mean right hook."

"Or he will," she reminded me. "What's that grin for?"

"Little tiny baby skates," I answered with glee.

"You're such a kid," she laughed.

"You feeling okay?" I paled, thinking that I'd just tossed her around like a rag doll.

She arched against me. "Perfect. I'll be even better once you make me come a few more times." A wicked smile played over her face.

"I love you so much."

"Yeah, I know. Now show me." She pulled me into her kiss, and I did just that.

I'd show her for the rest of our lives.

EPILOGUE

ECHO

Seven Months Later

"*A*re you sure that's close enough to our bed?" I asked, watching as Sawyer tucked the newly constructed bassinet next to our bed.

Our bed.

Our home.

Us.

I smoothed my hand over my giant stomach, my lower back aching something fierce.

"It's as close as it's going to get without me actually putting it *in* our bed," he said, smiling at me as he rose from his crouched position. He walked the distance between us, cupping my huge pregnant stomach. "Everything will be perfect," he said, leaning his forehead against mine. "I'll take care of you both."

My heart swelled, my mind spinning with happiness

despite the aches in my body and my general constant state of uncomfortableness.

"We'll take care of each other," I said, arching a brow at him. Just because I was madly in love didn't mean I'd lost my sense of independence. Though, I had loosened the reins on my control a tad bit since this basketball started growing in my stomach. I hired one of my best staff members, Hayley, to manage Scythe while I was on maternity leave, but I'd worked up until this last month. That was a comical sight, a pregnant woman slinging whiskey sours and vodka tonics to customers.

"Now," Sawyer said, massaging my tummy. "What else can I do to make you feel ready?"

I grinned at him a little sheepishly. I was in full nesting mode. I knew it. He knew it, yet he was too damned sweet to comment on my slightly hysterical need to have our home perfect for when the baby showed up.

I tilted my head, going over the mental checklist in my mind. "I think you've covered everything, Sawyer McCoy." I smirked. "But there is one last thing I want."

"What's that?"

"A kiss," I said, crooking my finger for him to come to me. I had long since lost the ability to reach up on my tiptoes to try and meet him halfway. Poor Sawyer practically had to bend in half to reach me.

"Always," he said, lowering his face until his lips brushed over mine, soft at first then hungrier as he explored my mouth.

Seven months of living together, being together, and the man still took my breath away. Still ignited a fire inside me like nothing else. And we'd done our fair share of mentally growing and bonding too—without him, I'd never have the sense of trust and happiness that I did now. And without me, he wouldn't have learned the importance of *self*-care, but I ensured he prioritized himself now too.

He tilted my head back, getting a deeper angle as he claimed my mouth with sweeping passes of his tongue, reminding me exactly how he felt between my thighs.

"Ow!" I jerked away from him, my hand flying to my lower back as a pain settled there. A much deeper, more intense pain than I'd been dealing with on the regular.

"What's wrong?" Sawyer asked, concern flashing in those gray eyes as he looked me over.

I took a deep breath and shifted my weight, hoping that would alleviate the pain.

It didn't.

This time, a powerful surge of searing fire wrapped around my hips and circled to the source, my lower back. A deep cramp settled there, so much I could barely breathe.

"Echo?" Sawyer demanded.

I locked on his gaze and then smiled a near panicked smile. "It's happening."

He tilted his head for a second, then realization clicked, and he jolted. "It's happening?" He gasped, then jumped into action. "It's happening!" He raced out of the room and was back with the go-bag slung over his arm in five seconds flat —I'm not even sure if he moved that fast on the ice.

"Here we go!" Sawyer had his arms around me in an instant before he lifted me and cradled me to his chest.

"Omigod, Sawyer, I can walk!"

"You can waddle," he said. "And that isn't quick enough." He hurried us through our home and settled me in his brand new Rover, a rear-facing car seat already expertly installed in the back seat.

"Slow down," I said, cringing through what I now knew was another contraction. "You're going to scare everyone in Reaper Village."

"Oh, right," he said as if I'd suddenly reminded him of something. Then he laid on his horn in a weird succession of honks.

"What the hell?"

He gave me an apologetic look before returning his eyes to the road. "Lukas worked that out with me a few weeks ago. So anyone home would know it was happening."

I gaped at him.

"I'll text him when I get you to the hospital," he said. "Just in case he didn't hear that."

"Honey," I said, trying to laugh but failing because of the sheer pain ripping through my lower half. "Everyone in Reaper Village heard that."

"It's happening," he said again, a crazed kind of smile on his lips.

"Breathe, baby," I said.

"Shouldn't I be saying that to you?" He teased, but took a deep breath.

Ten minutes later, I was in a wheelchair being ushered to the room our baby would be born in.

An hour later, I was in the worst pain in my life.

But nowhere close to having our baby.

"You sure you don't want me to call the nurse?" Sawyer asked, pressing a cold wash cloth against my head. "We can get you the drugs."

I shook my head. "I want to wait," I said.

Sawyer sighed.

"What?" I breathed. "I don't want it to wear off when the big show happens!"

Sawyer bit back a laugh, and I glared at him but chuckled through the pain.

"You're the strongest person I've ever met," he said.

I cringed against another wave of knives stabbing my

lower back. "You take beatings on the ice all the time," I ground out.

"That's nothing compared to this."

I sighed as the contraction ebbed. "You know, you're right. It totally isn't."

Sawyer laughed, and I managed a weak one myself.

The door to our room swung open. "Do we have a wee baby yet?" Connell said, coming into the room. Logan and Cannon followed in behind him. The two looked terribly uncomfortable while the Scotsman looked like he could check to see how dilated I was if we needed him to.

"Not yet," Sawyer said, eyeing the yellow balloons Cannon held.

"What?" Cannon said, shrugging. "We don't know what the Reaper baby will be."

Sawyer grinned at his teammates. "Thank you for coming."

Cannon set the balloons on the table across the room that was already peppered with other gifts from our friends.

"And now they're leaving!" Lukas' voice boomed through the room, and I shot him a good glare. "Sorry," he whispered, then eyed the guys. "Give them some space." He waved them toward the door.

"Good luck," Logan said, flashing us a soft smile as he filed out the door.

"Awh, but I didn't even get to tell Sawyer about the time I helped a cow give birth on the farm back home," Connell whined as Lukas all but shoved him from the room. "It's nearly the same thing..."

"Think the baby will come out with ink?" Cannon joked as he followed Connell out of the room.

I laughed even though it hurt.

I had such a beautiful, terribly overprotective family.

"You two need anything?" Lukas asked from where he hovered in the doorway.

Sawyer glanced down at me. "I've got everything I need right here."

I smiled up at him.

"God, that was saucy," Lukas said, shaking his head.

"*Cheesy*, honey," I heard Faith say from outside the door.

I craned my head to see her there and smiled at her.

She waved, tugging on Lukas' arm. "We'll be respectfully waiting in the sitting area!" she called. "You're amazing, Echo!"

"Thank you," I said to her just before the door gently shut.

A happy sigh released from my lips. "How'd we get so lucky?"

"Fate?" Sawyer asked.

I narrowed my gaze at him. "Now you sound like Annabelle."

He shrugged. "I don't care how we got here, Echo. I'm just glad as hell we did."

I reached for his hand, interlocking our fingers. "Me too."

Four hours, some *beautiful* drugs, and hard pushing later, Sawyer and I welcomed Sadie Jean McCoy into the world.

An hour after that, our doctor came in to check on us as I held my sweet, warm, sleeping bundle against my chest. Sawyer a constant show of support and strength by our side.

"You two are doing beautifully," the doc said, her tone lowered since Sadie had fallen asleep.

I could barely tear my eyes away to look at the doctor. Sadie was the most beautiful thing I'd ever seen, though it felt like I'd known her my entire life. My soul glowed with warmth and love and all the things I never knew I needed.

"I'll let you two rest but will be back to check on you in

another hour. Be sure to hit the call button if you need anything at all."

"Thanks, Doc," Sawyer said, his hand softly touching Sadie's head.

"Oh, and I'm not sure if you're aware," the doc continued as she headed toward the door. Her tone had both Sawyer and me snapping our eyes to hers. Panic flooded me like there was some *huge* thing I'd missed during birth. "There are more than half a dozen NHL players in the waiting room looking like they're about to burst from anticipation." The doctor smiled at us, a laugh on her lips. "Something I don't see every day. You all must be really close."

"We're family," I said, returning my gaze to our sleeping Sadie.

The doc nodded, then gently closed the door behind her.

I glanced up at Sawyer, exhaustion hitting my body. "You want to hold your daughter, Sawyer McCoy? I'm afraid I'm going to fall asleep with her in my arms."

Tears glistened over his gray eyes. "Absolutely," he said, his voice pinched as he easily took her from my arms, so smooth she didn't even stir.

I felt the absence of her slight weight like an empty spot on my soul, but the sight of him holding our baby like she was the most precious thing in the world? That was enough to send my heart soaring.

My eyelids drooped, my body wrecked. "I wonder," I said a bit sleepily as I gazed up at him.

"What?" he whispered.

I took a slow, steady breath. "I wonder if it's legal to have six sets of godparents?"

Sawyer clamped his lips shut, but his body trembled in a silent laugh. "I guess we're going to find out," he whispered and returned his focus to our daughter.

"Sadie McCoy," I whispered. "The first Reaper baby."

"Has a nice ring to it."

"Hey, West Coast?" I said, my mind already succumbing to sleep.

"Yeah?"

"Thanks for giving me everything I never knew I needed."

A slow smile shaped his lips as he bounced gently in place with our daughter cradled to his chest. "This is just the beginning."

I couldn't imagine life getting any better than this moment.

But with Sawyer at my side, I was certain that every day would be better than the last.

THE END

Did you love Sawyer? Find out what happens when a prank goes wrong, and Connell is sentenced to six weeks community service under none other than the sexy, rule-abiding, smart-mouthed city clerk of Sweet Water— Annabelle Clarke. Sparks fly in this enemies-to-lovers hockey romance! Download CONNELL today!

CAN'T GET enough sports romance? NFL quarterback Nixon Noble hasn't been able to forget—or find—the woman he spent an earth-shattering night in Vegas with...until Liberty shows up with the ultimate shock—a pregnancy test with two pink lines. Their chemistry is undeniable, but he's bound by contract, and her post-masters dream job is a continent away. Read Nixon, the first book in the Raleigh Raptors series here!

. . .

WANT MORE HOT HOCKEY ROMANCE? The rink gets steamy when star NHL player Gage McPherson falls for his bff/nanny—click here to read their story and binge the whole Seattle Sharks series today!

NEED SOMETHING A LITTLE MORE WILD? Something with a bite? Text VAMPIRE to 77222 to be the first to hear about my upcoming steamy vampire romance! The sexy alpha males of the Onyx Assassins are heading your way soon!

GRINDER SNEAK PEEK

If you loved Sawyer, you'll love Gage! Turn the page for a peek at the first chapter of Grinder and learn how the hottest player in the NHL became the Reapers' coach!

GRINDER

GAGE

Getting a three-year-old to sleep should be an Olympic event.

"Is that better?" I asked Lettie, smoothing back her thick brown hair from those summer blue eyes as she drained the small glass of water. She nodded, her smile full of tiny, gapped teeth as she settled back against her pillow.

If hockey was my world, where I made my living breathing the game, the ice, the needs of my team, then Lettie was my sun—the only thing in this universe that thawed my heart.

She was also the only thing I'd ever be caught waxing poetic about, but I couldn't help it, I was owned by a tiny three-year-old.

"Thank you, Daddy," she said, but the way she plucked at her covers and wiggled her tiny feet told me there was something else on my daughter's mind.

"What's up, sunshine?" I asked.

She looked up with excited eyes. "I like that Bailey is here."

"Me too," I said, unable to stop the smile that spread across my face at her happiness.

"I like Bailey."

A small chuckle rumbled through my chest. "Well, me too," I said, ruffling her hair.

"And now she's here all the time? Mornings and everything?"

"Yep," I answered, reaching for her bedside table. Bringing Bailey to live with us as Lettie's full-time nanny was a no-brainer. As often as I'd need her to travel with me for away games, and with the unpredictability of my schedule, it was really the only way for her to have a life...for either of us to. She'd been doing the job for six months already, but with the season starting up, it was the right time.

"So when I get up she'll be here?"

I paused before turning out the light and took a deep breath. "Yes, but Lettie, let's wait until the clock has a seven on it, okay? Not everyone likes to party at five a.m."

She bounced slightly, her eyes lighting with mischief. "I just can't wait to see her."

"You just saw her, remember? She tucked you in," I said, bringing her covers back up to her chin and urging her to lay down.

"I know, wasn't it amazing?"

I leaned forward, kissing her forehead. "Yes, it was amazing. And it will be amazing again tomorrow night."

"She's the best," she said, her eyes as wide as her smile. "Maybe she wants to see me before the sun is up!"

I pursed my lips, fighting the laughter that came so easily around my daughter, but only her. "Scarlett McPherson, you leave Bailey alone until morning. Do you understand me?"

Her lower lip extended in the cutest damn pout. "Yes, Daddy."

"Okay. I'm going to run for a little bit, so if you need me I'll be in the gym, okay?"

She nodded and flung herself forward, hugging me tight.

I held her close, savoring the smell of her strawberry shampoo, and the simple joy she emanated. Everything was simple in her world—her daddy loved her and Bailey adored her.

For the first time since she was born, there was a sense of stability in this house, and by God, I was going to keep it that way.

"I love you more than the stars," she said with a hard squeeze.

"I love you more than the moon."

"The stars are prettier," she argued.

"Well, the Earth needs the moon, so I love you more."

Her face scrunched momentarily before she shrugged. "Okay. But only because you need a win."

I hugged her again and put her to bed, silently cursing Rory for saying that yesterday when he was here, arguing to let Bailey move in.

I turned off Lettie's light and shut her door softly behind me.

My watch read 8:15 p.m. I could get in a couple miles and then meet the guys for drinks. Or I could get a couple miles in and maybe chill for the night.

Yeah, the second was probably the more responsible of the choices.

The refrigerator shut as I passed the kitchen, and I turned to see Bailey unloading a bag full of groceries. Her top was perfectly respectable, but the slight dip in her neckline gave me a mouth-watering glimpse of her cleavage.

Don't look at her like that, you asshat.

"Hey," I said, instead, as smooth as a fucking seventh-grader.

"Hey," she answered with a bright smile as I leaned across the island. "So I picked up some more of that Greek yogurt you like, and some stuff for cupcakes tomorrow. I figured I'd bake with Lettie to kind of celebrate our little..." she gestured around her, "arrangement?"

A corner of my mouth lifted in a smile. "Bailey, you're living with us. There's nothing illicit going on."

Pink stained her cheeks and damn if it didn't make her even more beautiful. Not that Bailey needed the help. She was petite but packed a powerhouse body that had found itself under mine in a few of my more drunken fantasies. And that face? Damn, she was perfection—huge hazel eyes, thick lashes, and olive skin with the most kissable mouth I'd ever laid eyes on.

But that was all I was ever going to lay on her.

"Well, yeah," she said, pulling her long, dark brown hair into some kind of knot on the top of her head. "It's just a transition."

"Hopefully a good one." It had to be. Lettie adored Bailey, and we'd been friends since we were kids, so it wasn't like I could afford to piss off Bailey...or our mothers.

"It will be," she promised. "Besides, I was practically living here anyway. Now I don't have to drive back to my place in the traffic."

"Agreed." Seattle traffic could be a nightmare.

She paused, leaning back against the opposite counter, inadvertently putting those lush curves on display.

Fuck my life. If I didn't get out of here I was going to sport wood harder than the fucking floor.

"I'm going to go get a couple miles in," I told her, pushing back from the island.

She reached over and into the fridge, then tossed a bottle of water my direction. "Have a good run. Oh, and I heard Rory and Warren talking today while we were moving in. If you want to grab a couple beers with the guys, I'm totally okay here with Lettie."

"Thanks. I'll think about it, but I'm pretty sure I'm just going to turn in." *And get the hell away from you before I lose my nanny to sexual harassment.*

"Okay, well the offer always stands. I don't mind." She crossed her arms under those perfect breasts. "It's not like I have a boyfriend or much of a social life outside Jeannine and Paige."

I opened the water bottle and took a few quick chugs. "Yeah, and your friends are always welcome here. Seriously. This is your house now, too."

Her smile was small but genuine. "That means a lot."

I nodded awkwardly. "I'll catch you later."

"Later."

I ran out of there so fast the room may as well have been on fire and headed down to the lowest level of the house until I got to my gym. The floor-to-ceiling windows opened up to a view of Lake Washington, where the sun was in that last moment of setting.

I powered on the treadmill, slipped my earbuds in, turned up the Eminem and hit it. My heartbeat was steady as my feet pounded at the machine beneath me, my breathing even. Maybe I wasn't that badly out of shape after all.

After taking most of the last season off when I tore the fuck out of my shoulder, I wasn't sure I'd ever get back to the Sharks, but the coach kept me on the roster, and I was still leading for my position if that baby of a rookie didn't beat me out for it.

Fuck that, it's mine.

Yeah, six months ago I couldn't have run at this speed without screaming in agony. Six months ago I'd still been in a sling, still broken as fuck from the way Helen left us.

And then Bailey had walked back into my life, fresh out of

her graduate degree at Cornell. It wasn't fate, I wasn't fucking stupid. It was our mothers pushing us together, not romantically—they weren't stupid either—but I needed help, and Bailey needed a job until she figured out what the hell she was going to do with her life...and her double degree in Art and Philosophy.

It had been perfect until I'd seen her again. The girl she'd been while we grew up, while I went to college at U-Dub and she went Ivy...well, she was long gone. It wasn't like she'd had one of those chick-flick makeovers, no, she'd always been pretty, doe-eyed, and just as beautiful inside than out. But now...

Fuck, now she was a knockout and seemed unaware of it somehow.

And worse, it was like my body had fucking Bailey-radar. She came into a room, I got hard—even when I reminded my body that she was a no-go.

It wasn't that I didn't like sex.

Fuck, I loved sex.

I adored women.

I fucked a lot of women.

Then they left.

The first woman I'd ever loved had left while I begged her to stay...

Now they left because I told them to...Let's be fair, it's not like they didn't know that was part of the package while I was dropping their panties.

I said I fucked women...I didn't fuck *over* women.

There was a difference.

Of course, they were all blonde lately. Anyone blonde or red-haired, but never brunettes. Never anyone I could accidentally mistake for Bailey.

I was never going *there*, and it didn't matter how badly my dick begged otherwise.

If she wasn't off limits because we'd grown up together—our mothers were best friends—she was definitely unfuckable because at the heart of everything, she belonged to Lettie.

And I didn't steal anything from my daughter.

Hell no, she deserved the world, and that was exactly what I was going to give her.

At mile number three, I ripped off my shirt, wiping the sweat off my forehead before tossing it and hitting two more miles. Nothing like a little run to get out some sexual frustration.

It would pass. I'd get used to having Bailey here. She'd become like a sister, and all these sexual urges would fade. It wasn't like she had them. Fuck, then we'd both be in trouble.

But it was just horny-as-hell me, lusting after the girl I'd never had, and I wasn't a little boy anymore. I was a full-grown man, a forward for the Seattle Sharks NHL team, and the best damned grinder in the league. More importantly, I was Lettie's dad, and since her mother had about as much maternal instinct as a fucking rock, I was all Scarlett had.

I had to be enough.

Better than enough.

I had to be everything.

Mile six sounded, and I lowered the speed of the treadmill, rolling my shoulders and stretching out my muscles before I headed up to the shower.

That was exactly what I needed. I congratulated myself for running out my baser needs instead of jumping my nanny as I walked up the stairs. Look at me, all civilized and shit.

I was so focused on my feet that I didn't realize Bailey was on the steps to the third floor until I nearly ran into her.

"Shit, I'm sorry," I said, catching her very smooth, very bare shoulders.

"Oh, my fault! Lettie asked for more water, so I took her up a glass," she said, but I barely heard her.

Fuck my life. Is that what she slept in? The light purple silk shorts barely covered her thighs and the spaghetti straps on the matching top looked flimsy enough to break. With my teeth.

One. Good. Bite.

"Gage?"

My eyes slid shut. Why did my name sound so damn good coming from her mouth?

I felt her fingers softly graze my sweat-dampened skin.

"Hey, are you okay? Is it your shoulder?"

I swallowed and opened my eyes, shaking my head with a forced smile. "Nawh, I'm okay."

Her eyes were wide, flecks of gold among the swirls of green as she examined my chest, tugging her on lower lip with her teeth. "Are you sure? I mean...I could ice it for you, or rub it down?"

Her forehead puckered at the same moment my dick hardened at the thought of her gorgeous, talented hands on me—hands that created masterpieces of abstract art. God, the last thing I needed was having those hands on my skin.

Apparently the run hadn't worked as well as I'd thought.

I needed to fuck her out of my head before I screwed up the one good thing I had going.

"You know, I think I will head out for a little bit. You okay with Lettie?" I asked, looking anywhere but the braless breasts that rose and fell in my face with her breaths.

"Yeah, of course. No rush. Try to relax, okay?"

I nodded, then nearly cursed as a thought came to me. "Shit, sometimes I bring women home..."

She laughed slightly. "I'm well aware of your nocturnal activities. This is your home, Gage. Feel free to..."—she flung her hands out— "do whatever it is you do. Seriously, no judgment."

I nodded again—like an idiot—and retreated up the stairs before I could further make an ass out of myself, or tell her why I really needed to get out.

A shower and a fresh change of clothes later, I was speeding away from my house in the Aston Martin toward my best friends and women who wanted the one thing I was capable of giving: my body.

No judgment, she'd said.

Hell if I wasn't judging myself for this one, though.

CONNECT WITH ME!

Text SAMANTHA to 77222 to be the first to know about new releases, giveaways, & more!

Sign up here for my newsletter for exclusive content and giveaways!

Follow me on Amazon here or BookBub here to stay up to date on all upcoming releases! You can also find me at my website here!

ABOUT THE AUTHOR

Samantha Whiskey is a wife, mom, lover of her dogs and romance novels. No stranger to hockey, hot alpha males, and a high dose of awkwardness, she tucks herself away to write books her PTA will never know about.

ACKNOWLEDGMENTS

Thank you to my incredible husband and my awesome kids without which I would live a super boring life!

Huge thanks must be paid to the amazing authors who have always offered epic advice and constant support! Not to mention creating insanely hot reads to pass the time with!

Big shout out to A.H. for making this shine. And thank you to each and every single one of you AMAZING readers who love the these books as much as I do!